THE MIDNIGHT

Royal Hardback | 9781805222279 | £16.99
Export Trade Paperback | 9781805222286 | £14.99
Ebook | 9781805222293
Audio | 9781805225089

Editor: miranda.jewess@profilebooks.com
Sales: uksales@profilebooks.com
Export: export@profilebooks.com
Publicity: drew.jerrison@profilebooks.com

THE
MIDNIGHT
KING

TARIQ ASHKANANI

 VIPER

First published in Great Britain in 2025 by
VIPER
an imprint of Profile Books Ltd
29 Cloth Fair
London
ECIA 7JQ

www.profilebooks.com

Text design by Crow Books

1 3 5 7 9 10 8 6 4 2

Printed and bound in Great Britain by
CPI Group (UK) Ltd, Croydon, CR0 4YY.

A CIP catalogue record for this book is available from the British Library.

Hardback ISBN 978 1 80522 2279
Trade Paperback ISBN 978 1 80522 2286
eISBN 978 1 80522 2293

FSC
www.fsc.org
MIX
Paper | Supporting
responsible forestry
FSC® C013604

For mum and dad

Author's Note

Many of you will find this book to be in bad taste.

In part, it is due to the violence. Murder is – by its very nature – a violent crime. I believe this to be true no matter how the act is performed. Loud, quiet, bludgeon or lethal injection. A murder is the ending of the most precious thing there is: a life.

In part, it is due to the victims. As with all crimes, there are surely degrees to murder, and so perhaps we should look to the murdered as much as the method. For if a killing is always violent, then it must be at its *most* violent when it is the killing of a child.

In part, it is due to the scale. During the fourteen-year period from August 1994 until May 2008, thirteen children were reported missing from Davidson County and the greater Nashville metropolitan area. Thirteen children who would later be discovered dead. Their bodies wrapped in black garbage bags, bound tightly with nylon rope, tied with the same constrictor knot. Each one of them left by a body of water. Each one of them strangled, their corpses showing clear evidence of having been bathed in bleach post-mortem. Some were found quick, but most were not. Most had rotted away to some degree by the time they were uncovered.

In part, it is due to who I am: Lucas Cole, aka Jack Cross. A man who has written an obscene number of objectively poor novels.

Novels that, to varying degrees, idolise vigilante justice, casual sexism and toxic masculinity. Perhaps it surprises you to know that I am quite familiar with these terms, perhaps it does not. I make no apologies for knowing what sort of novels my audience wants to read, and playing to it for maximum effect. I am a writer, that is my job.

But the main reason that many will struggle with this book is because the crimes are still relatively fresh, their impact still felt in the local community. Here, the name 'Edward Morrison' is akin to that of the bogeyman. It is a name spoken quietly and with some degree of trepidation, when it is spoken at all. Many prefer to use the moniker coined by the media: the 'Music City Monster'. Possibly this dehumanises him, I don't know.

What I do know is that Edward Morrison was convicted of the abduction of a ten-year-old boy and the first-degree murder of the child's parents. While he was never formally prosecuted for killing the thirteen other children (and seven parents, who are often sadly overlooked), this is nothing unusual. To use an unfortunate phrase, it would likely have been overkill: as I type, Morrison now sits on death row, where – legal appeals and congressional interference aside – he awaits his own violent murder, at which point a line might finally be drawn under this unsightly story.

The final point that I wish to make from the outset is that while I have taken these crimes as a starting point, I did not set out to write a factual account of these child murders. There has been plenty written about the so-called Music City Monster already, and it was never my intention to add my work to that collection. My aim is – and always has been – to entertain. If you find this to be distasteful, then I would refer you to the start of my Author's Note.

Accordingly, this book is a work of fiction.

It is not a confession.

Lucas Cole

1

NATHAN

A hanging, in a place like this – it showed dedication.

The ceiling fan was no good. It was clearly broken: a blade missing, the whole thing suspended purely by exposed wiring.

The shower rail above the bath wouldn't work either. Too flimsy. Nathan wrapped his hands around it, and when he pulled gently he felt it flex. Cheap plastic screwed into crumbling drywall.

He spent a couple of minutes surveying the rest of the small, sad room. The results continued to disappoint.

Lightbulb fittings: too neat.

Door handles: too low.

Wardrobe rails: non-existent.

Of course there were other ways to kill yourself. Easier ways. Ways he'd seen on TV or in books. A toaster in the bathtub, a few boxes of pills. A high ledge. A handgun. A sharp knife and some warm water.

The motel was called The View. An ironic name, given where it was. Squeezed tight between an apartment block on one side and a thundering highway on the other. The only view Nathan had from his window was another window, this one with the blinds closed. Permanently, maybe.

The man in the dirty shirt at the front desk had given him a funny look when he'd asked for this room. Tried to palm him off with another. Gotten antsy when Nathan had insisted.

'It's being cleaned,' the man had said.

'I can wait.'

The guy had started to say something, then shrugged and handed over the key. What did it matter, at the end of the day, that one week earlier a man had hanged himself in this room? To the owner behind the desk, the dead man was a stranger. A blot on his bottom line at best. People didn't like staying in motels where guests had died. Didn't like seeing housekeepers crying or squad cars in the parking lot. Suicides were bad for business. So if someone came around and asked to stay in the room for a night, you took their money and you kept quiet.

It was different for Nathan. For Nathan, he wasn't a stranger, this man, this dead man, this hanged man.

It was his father who had made the reservation, who had checked into this motel, who had validated his parking so he wouldn't receive a ticket. It was his father who had systematically checked the room before deciding that the best way to end his life was by looping his belt around the back of the bathroom door, who had decided to wait until he'd showered and dressed in smart jeans and a clean shirt, who had eaten a Snickers and drunk a whiskey and left the wrapper tucked neatly into the empty glass, perhaps all the while sitting at the window, perhaps all the while staring out at that dreadful view.

2

Nathan didn't spend long at the motel. He'd never intended to stay the night, not really. It was just some place he'd needed to see for himself. One last look at the room where it happened.

He spotted it as he left: the bathroom door. The edge of it chipped. Near the floor, the paint scraped away. By his father's shoes, perhaps.

'From one motel to another,' the cab driver said, laughing as he picked him up. 'What's the matter with this place? Bedbugs?'

Sitting quiet in the back, Nathan concentrated on his cell phone. A couple of messages from Verizon welcoming him to Nashville, a text from Kate. *Hope your flight was okay. Dinner at ours tomorrow night when you're rested?*

He thumbed through the remainder of his notifications before circling back, unsure how to respond. His sister clearly wasn't in any great rush to see him.

Flight was fine, he typed. *Dinner tomorrow sounds good.*

It wasn't like he was in much of a rush to see her, either.

It had started to rain. Light, though. Just a spatter of it on the glass. The cab driver was muttering something, gesticulating at another car. A dull ache was building inside Nathan's head. The wrong sounds being amplified. People leaning on their horns, the endless drone of rolling tyres. Exits off the I-40 for Lexington and Atlanta. They entered a tunnel and the sudden change in pressure was like a shotgun blast.

He wondered if it was the same road his father had driven. Out here, to the motel on the edge of the city. Driving slow, maybe. Taking his time. To make sure his mind was made up, to savour the sights.

Or hell, maybe he hadn't planned on killing himself at all. Maybe hanging himself from a bathroom door had been some spur-of-the-moment thing. Truth was, Nathan had never really known what went on in his father's head.

He wondered then if coming here had been a mistake. To his father's house, to Nashville entirely. Acting the dutiful son, like he owed it to the man.

Isaac was waiting for him at his motel. His *actual* motel. A Holiday Inn next to the Opryland Resort. A clean lobby and a vanilla diffuser plugged into the wall. It even had a pool round back.

Nathan was confirming his reservation when he spotted him. The tall, broad-chested man dressed in jeans and a raincoat, rising from a chair in the corner of the room. It took Nathan a moment to place him. To navigate the seventeen years and find the man's face.

'Isaac? What on earth are you doing here?'

'Kate told me where you were staying. Thought you might appreciate a friendly face.' Isaac smiled sadly. 'I'm truly sorry to hear about your dad.'

'That's kind of you to say.'

'Listen, you fancy a drink? Be good to catch up a little. I promise I won't keep you.'

Nathan thought about saying no. Rifled through his reasons, that overwhelming first instinct to retreat. He thought about Kate, too wrapped up in her own bullshit to come visit her brother on his first day back. It had been nice of Isaac to make the effort.

'Sure,' he said. 'I could do with a drink.'

Music City Bar and Grill was a short walk away. They made small talk as they went, the awkwardness of so many years apart settling over them both. Even though it didn't take them long, by the time they arrived Nathan was wondering if he shouldn't have just gone to bed.

Inside, the bar was busy. A three-piece cover band doing the classics for the tourists. Kenny Rogers and Johnny Cash living on as they did every night in nearly every bar across the city.

They got a table near the back. About as far from the rabble as you could get in a place like this. Still, Nathan didn't mind. The background buzz did a half-decent job of dulling the thoughts in his head. A couple of beers would only help it along.

'It's really good to see you again, man,' Isaac said, tilting his glass. 'I just wish, you know . . .'

'Better circumstances?'

'Yeah.'

Nathan nodded and took a long drink. The beer was ice cold. It ran an icy trail down his throat. 'You said you spoke with Kate?'

'Uh huh. I ran into her the other day.'

'How was she?'

Isaac looked at him, his fingers playing with his beer glass. He still hadn't taken a drink. 'You haven't spoken with her?'

'Not for a while now.'

'Oh. I didn't know.'

Nathan shrugged. 'You move three states away, you leave some people behind. It's just how it is.'

'But Kate's family, man. You need to keep those connections alive.'

'It's complicated, Isaac.'

'Every family's complicated.'

'Not like ours.'

Isaac let it go. He finally took a sip and Nathan saw him wince a little as he swallowed. A clamour at the bar pulled his attention as the band started up 'Wagon Wheel'.

'You think they ever get tired of playing the same stuff every night?' Isaac asked.

'Probably,' Nathan said. 'I sure got tired of listening.'

'Tell me, how's Minnesota?'

'I'm in Sioux Falls now.'

'Where's that, North Dakota?'

'South. And it's fine. It's ... cold.' Nathan drifted away for a moment before adding, 'It's cold and it's humid and it's beautiful.'

'You ever think about moving back home?'

'It is home,' Nathan said, and lifted his beer for another drink. 'This is just a vacation.'

The two men fell into another silence, only this time it wasn't too awkward. Maybe it was the beer, or the music. Maybe it was this unexpected burst of normality on a day when Nathan had been bracing himself for the opposite. Sitting here, the past seventeen years seemed to fall away. He was in a bar but he was in a classroom, too. At the back, by the window, his attention drifting. A disconnect that had steadily grown within him all through middle school, fuelled by poisoned knowledge of how the world really was. He'd thrown barriers around himself as a result; Isaac had been one of the few people to try to push through. And no one had been more surprised than Nathan when he let Isaac in, even if only a little.

'Yeah, well, I guess sticking around doesn't always work out for folk,' Isaac said, bringing Nathan back. 'You remember Paul Colston? Had those really bad acne scars down one half of his face?'

'Kid who flooded the toilets outside the cafeteria?'

'The very same. When we finished high school, that guy was working part-time at Best Buy. You know what he's doing now?'

Nathan shook his head.

'He's the fucking *manager* at Best Buy,' Isaac said, grinning. 'You get what I'm saying?'

'That if I'd stayed, I too might have become the manager of an electrical retailer?'

'Of *any* retailer!' Isaac said. 'Target, JCPenney, Sears . . .'

'Bed Bath and Beyond.'

'Oh, you should be so lucky.'

Isaac laughed, and Nathan found himself joining in. He went to take a drink, then stopped and shook his head. Isaac leaned forward, said, 'What is it?'

'I was just thinking earlier about school,' Nathan said. 'About how isolated I made myself. You really helped me get through some rough times. And now here we are, all these years later, and you're doing it again.'

Isaac waved him away. 'All part of the service,' he said, and took another sip of his drink. His face twitched again as it went down.

'You all right?' Nathan asked.

'I'm fine,' Isaac said. 'Heartburn.'

Nathan watched his friend and wondered if it was something more, but he let it be. 'So what are you doing in Nashville these days yourself? I'm guessing you didn't fly all the way out here from Baltimore just for my dad's funeral.'

Isaac grunted. 'I don't work in Baltimore now. Moved back home about six months ago.'

'Well aren't you a regular Paul Colston. You still a detective?'

'No.'

The band hit a key change and the bar went wild. Nathan grimaced and turned his head away slightly. 'What's after detective? Sergeant?'

'I'm a PI,' Isaac said. He gave a lopsided grin and pulled a business card from his wallet. *Isaac Holloway*, it read in sleek, embossed print. *Private Investigator.* 'You need a background check on an unfaithful husband, you let me know.'

'I'll keep that in mind.'

'Actually, I've been doing some work recently for Alison Bennett. Remember her?'

Nathan remembered. The three of them had been close growing up. Spending those long, hot Tennessee summers together. Climbing trees and splashing through rivers. Then, later, graduating to smoking weed and drinking in parks.

'How is she?'

'She's a force of nature, man, same as she ever was. Got herself a law degree, runs her own firm down in Pulaski. Throws me a couple of cases every now and then. I'm still finding my feet a little. Although . . .' Isaac trailed off, moved his barely touched beer to one side. 'You hear about Chloe Xi?'

Nathan shook his head.

'Eight-year-old girl, went missing last week while walking her dog after school.'

'Missing?'

'Yeah. Parents are losing it, as you can imagine. They think the police are dragging their feet, maybe on account of their daughter being a minority, who knows. Anyway, they want an extra pair of eyes on the case.'

Isaac was still talking, his hands gesturing as he described the initial meeting he'd had with the parents. But Nathan barely heard him. He couldn't get past that word.

Missing.

A child was missing.

'You okay?'

Nathan blinked. 'I'm fine. Think the travelling is catching up to me.'

'Course. Listen, I shouldn't have kept you. I'll let you settle in. Keep the card, give me a call. We can catch up later in the week.'

'Sure, thanks.'

And then Nathan was rising, moving away from the table on unsteady legs, pushing his way through the crowd. The band was like a distant memory, its sound muffled and faint. Outside in the cool air, his hands trembled so bad it took three tries to get his cell phone from his pocket.

It was happening again.

No, it was *still* happening.

Chloe Xi. Eight years old.

Missing.

3

By the time the cab had pulled up to his father's old house, Nathan had read a handful of news stories about the missing girl. Chloe Xi had been taken from a public park a half-hour drive from her house in the early afternoon. A crowd of kids and their parents, and not one person had seen her vanish. She had been missing now for nine days.

She was a small, thin girl with jet black hair and a wide smile. The photo most of the outlets had gone with was of her in her school uniform: grey skirt and white shirt, with knee-high white socks and little black shoes. Her hair was tied up in bunches with a pair of red ribbons.

He'd tried not to think about his father's house. The whole way over here, he'd tried.

It was the dinners that really got to him, that had stayed with him all these years. The family gathered around the kitchen table. His father dishing up spaghetti or mashed potatoes to him and Kate, making inane comments about their school or the weather, all the while everyone pretending like this was normal, like the leftovers wouldn't be going into Tupperware boxes and left on the kitchen table, like their father wasn't going to take them down to the base-ment or drive them an hour outside the city to his cabin in the woods, to serve dinner all over again.

And now Nathan was back. Home again, seventeen years later. Through the front door and up the stairs, flicking light switches as he went. Moving fast, too fast to give himself time to think. Across the landing and into his father's bedroom. Throwing open the closet, tossing plain shirts and worn khakis, moving deeper into the musty darkness.

The shoebox was tucked away in the back.

It was called *The Midnight King*.

A collection of words, printed on sheets of crisp, white paper and bound together with screw posts. *A novel*, it read underneath, *by Lucas Cole*.

Of course he knew his father had been a writer. Crime fiction, mainly. Schlocky stuff, lots of big men who solved crimes with their fists and had six-packs despite drinking a half-bottle of whiskey every other night, who always got the girl and never bothered to call her back. Lucas had written dozens of the things. They were piled high on every shelf in the house.

His father had written under a pseudonym – 'Jack Cross'. A name that seemed to conjure up an author almost as strapped as the lead character. In reality, Lucas Cole couldn't have been more different: tall and weedy, with big glasses and a habitual habit of licking his lips when he spoke. But power comes in different forms, in different shapes and sizes, and Nathan's body still bore the scars to prove it.

When Nathan was growing up, his father had spent much of his life tucked away in a grubby little office, typing out his hero fantasy sexist bullshit. The clack of a keyboard running late into the night. Nathan remembered standing on the other side of the door, sometimes with Kate, more often alone, listening to his father type.

Lucas Cole's success – and as much as Nathan hated to admit it, the man *had* found success – came much later. Once Nathan had left home. The book deals and the bestseller lists. Turned out people had an appetite for that stuff after all.

But this . . . this was the first time he'd ever seen a manuscript with his father's real name on it. He wondered if it meant something. It felt like it was important, different from the rest. He flipped open the first page and read the Author's Note. His throat went slick.

As he put it to one side, the shoebox's true contents were revealed: a large collection of small items. Trinkets, mainly. Pieces of junk. Buttons and watch straps. A sock. A pair of glasses. Each of them with a plain, brown name tag, written in his father's neat hand.

Nathan gazed down at them all. They filled the box nearly to the brim. There were more here now, more than there had been when he'd left.

He reached down, his fingertips just about brushing the topmost items. Something screamed in him not to. The same voice that had screamed when Isaac had told him about the missing girl. That had *been* screaming, in fact, ever since. Through his internet searches, as he'd scrolled past that photo of Chloe Xi in her school uniform. Her black hair tied up in bunches, held there by red ribbons.

The same red ribbons that sat proudly on display now, on top of his father's collection.

4

He stuffed the manuscript back into the shoebox and half ran from the room. Taking the stairs two at a time, nearly falling when he reached the bottom, not bothering to lock up as he left. His father's station wagon sat outside, towed there from the motel he'd died in, the keys in a little plastic bag by the front door. Nathan used them now. Tossed the shoebox onto the back seat and tore away from Lucas Cole's house.

Burgess Falls was over an hour away. Less, maybe, this time of night. The manuscript's opening words stayed with him as he drove. Heavy in the car, a passenger riding alongside him. *It is not a confession,* his father had written, and maybe it wasn't but there was truth in there. Enough to keep the tremor running through Nathan's hands as they gripped the wheel, even now. Enough to send him eighty miles east in the dark.

Deep in his heart, he didn't really know what he'd find at the cabin, but he knew he had to look. Chloe Xi had been missing for nine days now – and unless his father's methods had changed in the last seventeen years, then the chances were she was already dead.

He broke the back-door window to get in, his fist balled up in his jacket. He wasn't worried about anyone hearing him. The cabin was tucked away in a small clearing, the closest neighbour a half mile down a dirt track. By now it was late, near midnight and pitch black. The only sound came from the bare forest that surrounded the house. He could hear its thin branches rattling in the wind.

Inside, Nathan flicked on the kitchen light. A bare bulb so bright it made him squint. Like before, he didn't bother to stop and look around. It was just another one of his father's properties, full of nothing but memories he'd rather forget.

He moved quickly through the kitchen, to the door that led down to the cellar. Seventeen years but his arm still remembered, still jerked the handle upwards to dislodge the uneven frame. A rush of cool air and a strange, musky odour. His face felt hot. His back crawled with ants.

A metal chain hung to his left. He pulled it, setting off another bulb, this one in the ceiling below him. It lit up the room all wrong, threw shadows instead of light. The bottom of the stairs stayed in darkness.

'Hello?' he called.

Waited for a response.

Nothing.

Standing there, he was a man but he was also a boy. Ten years old. Knowing his swim shorts were in the dryer. Knowing he would have to go past the girl to get them. The thin girl, the girl with the sad eyes, the girl who mewled like a kitten left out in the cold.

His first step was a shotgun blast in the quiet. The stairs had always creaked but never like this. He paused, listened again for anything, finally getting a grip on himself and turning on his cell's torch. He swept the cellar as he descended. It took him thirty seconds to reach the bottom and by the time he did it was obvious no one was there. No one except the spiders, their webs strung up across the corners of the room.

Nathan trained his torch on the section of wall where his father had installed the anchor points. There was no sign of them now. He stepped close, stood where the thin mattress had once lain but of course that was gone, too. He ran his hand over the surface. It was smooth. Bending forward, he kept his palm flat on the wall until he felt them. The gentle bumps of spackling paste. The only trace of what had once been there.

When he turned to leave he glanced up the stairs to the kitchen above him. The door was ajar, that harsh light slicing through the gap. He imagined what it must have been like to live down here, if living was the right word. Staring up at that door in the darkness, both praying for the light and dreading its arrival. He imagined what he would feel – here, now – if that door was to suddenly close on him, or if it were to swing open wide. He wasn't sure what would be worse.

All he really knew for certain was that Chloe Xi wasn't here. She never had been. No one had, not for a long while.

5

ISAAC

Isaac waited at the bottom of the stairs, a paper folder on his lap half filled with blank pages and bravado.

It was the first time he'd stepped foot in a Nashville police station. Six months since he'd been in a station full stop, but it was like he'd never left. All these places felt the same. All of them filled with the same bullshit, the same little power struggles. The same budget constraints, too. Hermitage Precinct was no different. The only thing cheaper than the plastic seat he was wedged into was his own ill-fitting suit.

He'd lost weight since he'd worn it last. A whole notch on his belt. Even so, the pants didn't sit right. He wanted to squirm but he couldn't – he was on show, sitting under a bright light and a stern gaze; the receptionist had her eye on him. She'd pretty much just left it there ever since he'd sat down, which was – Isaac checked his watch – nearly thirty minutes ago.

He sent her a smile. 'Any update?'

'The detectives know you're here, sir.'

The woman had a nasal tone, like she was pinching her nose as she spoke. She used the word 'sir' as Isaac would an insult. A show of force, a warning shot. He felt it glance off him harmlessly and land somewhere over by the water cooler.

He holstered his smile and flipped open the paper folder. Swapped one gaze for another, this one less severe but with a power of its own. Little Chloe Xi smiled up at him and he felt it in the pit of his stomach.

It was the same photo that had been doing the media circuit. Taken not long after last year's fall vacation was over, a few weeks before Thanksgiving. It wasn't an official school picture, but she was well-turned-out all the same. Her uniform freshly ironed, her white socks pulled up past her knees. Two red ribbons holding her black hair up in bunches, tied in large bows. Isaac looked at the photo and felt like he knew her – hard-working, studious, polite to her family. He also knew better than to trust an opinion based on a single photo, but that was his training. Some of the nastiest folks he'd met took the sweetest pictures.

Still, it had been a smart move by her family. Most people seeing the image – over dinner, maybe, or on the nightly news or on their cell phones before they went to sleep – they'd take one look at her and think exactly what they were supposed to.

Isaac flicked the photo over. Another couple of pictures were stacked behind it, all similar stuff: Chloe sitting at a dinner table, Chloe looking up from watching TV, Chloe with a border terrier at the beach up on Old Hickory. A lot of families took their dogs to Old Hickory. Most of them came back intact.

He moved to the copied police report, scanning it even though he could just about recite it from memory. He was halfway through when he finally heard footsteps coming down those stairs. Slow steps. Plodding. Isaac formed an image of a tired, out-of-shape detective in a crushed suit and looked up to see he wasn't far off the mark.

'Mr Holloway?'

It was said with resignation, like he'd been hoping Isaac might have left. It told Isaac something about the man's character. That he was passive, that he didn't like confrontation. It told him he'd done his homework, too. He knew who Isaac was.

Isaac closed his file and untangled himself from his chair. His stomach started churning. He'd skipped breakfast, and was running on last night's half-eaten dinner. Baby back ribs at the Music City Bar and Grill after Nathan had left. He fought the urge to tug on his tight suit. Dug deep for that winning smile.

'I appreciate you seeing me, Detective . . .?'

'Copeland. Harry Copeland. And listen, just so we're clear here? My partner and I aren't exactly thrilled that the family have engaged a private detective in this case.'

'I know. The parents told me you'd advised against it.'

Copeland raised bushy eyebrows. 'It's nothing personal, Mr Holloway—'

'Please, Isaac.'

'All right. It's nothing personal, Isaac. It's what I always tell anyone who asks whether they should instruct a PI. It muddies the waters, makes me and my partner's job more difficult. I know you were a detective once, so I'm sure you'll understand.'

Isaac had been right about Copeland. The guy *had* done his homework.

He shrugged. 'I get it. And look, you know this family, you know they just want to feel like they're doing everything they can. Me being here is absolutely not a slight on your or your partner's ability to find the girl. I'm sure you both know exactly what you're doing.'

A flicker of hesitation. Copeland trying to work out whether or not he was being insulted. He decided to let it slide.

'Fine, so if we're finished clearing the air, I'm going to have to ask you to leave. We've a lot to get through.'

Isaac raised his folder. 'I've got a theory, if you'd like to hear it.'

Copeland didn't. He was already turning, shaking his big head. 'No offence, but how about you leave the detective work to the detectives?'

'Come on, I'll buy you a coffee. You and your partner. Twenty minutes, that's all.'

'Goodbye, Mr Holloway.'

The detective shuffled back up the stairs to his desk. Isaac waited until he'd gone from view before pulling at his suit jacket. He hadn't really expected much in the way of assistance from anyone here. Hell, was a time he'd treated desperate PIs in much the same way himself.

'Let's hear it, then,' came the nasally voice from behind him. The receptionist was standing with her hands on her hips, her face screwed up like she was sniffing shit.

'What?'

'Your theory. Let's hear it.'

Isaac glanced down at the file he was still clutching. Nothing but blank pages and bravado. He didn't have a theory, he didn't have anything. A last-ditch attempt to get some face time with the detectives. Copeland had seen right through him.

'You want to hear my theory?' Isaac asked. 'You get Detective Copeland to give me a call.'

He dropped a card on her desk. Wasn't fancy, just a name and cell number. No address – last thing he wanted was some prospective client swinging by and finding out that *2306 Brick Church Pike* was actually a Super 8 by Wyndham.

The receptionist grunted as he walked away. He'd been stupid to go to Copeland empty-handed. Stupid maybe to take this case on in the first place. Shit, just being in a police station again was making his guts burn.

Only it was too late to pull out now, wasn't it? And if it was weakness that got him involved in this, then he would need strength to get him out. To choke back the acid that bubbled high in his chest.

He needed to work the case himself, alone, at least for a while. He needed to do it proper. Do it like he used to, like he was still a cop, no matter how his guts protested. He couldn't rightly expect Hermitage Precinct to trade with him on anything less.

The Nashville Public Library sat opposite the station, on the other side of a busy road. Isaac stared at it as he thought about returning to his hotel room. Thought about his back aching as he hunched over the narrow desk, papers spread across the double bed. He crossed the road.

6

Chloe Xi had gone missing on March third. That was ten days ago.

The last reported sighting of her was by a female jogger, but the statement was vague and the details unconfirmed. The woman had told NBC Channel 4 News that she'd seen someone matching Chloe's description wandering into a small patch of woodland by the camping ground. Said the kid had been calling something as she walked.

The family dog was a border terrier called Coco. She hadn't been seen since March third, either.

Isaac set himself up in a quiet corner of the Nashville Public Library. One of those big desks you're meant to share, only it was quiet today and he had the thing to himself. He wasn't leaving until he had enough to take back to Copeland. It was already nearing lunchtime, but that was all right. His day was wide open.

He chewed a Rolaid and read over his interview notes with the family. They'd contacted him when the first week had gone by and the police hadn't made any progress. The Xi's were nice people. Down to earth and genuine. Realistic. They'd have known the same stats that Isaac did: after the first three days, the chances of finding their daughter alive was slim to none. Memories faded, evidence was lost. It had rained once since March third, and it hadn't been a downpour but maybe it had been enough. Enough to degrade whatever trace of

Chloe Xi the police had missed. Soon, all anyone would be looking for would be a body.

Her parents had sat him down in their living room. Offered him tea, fancy stuff. He watched Chloe's mother make it in their little kitchen and it was like a ritual. The father spoke with a quiet voice. Isaac had to lean forward to hear the words. Most of it he already knew, but some he didn't. Like how Chloe had wanted to be a vet when she was older. And that she spent every other Sunday volunteering at a local church.

'So why hire a private investigator?' Isaac asked. 'You not happy with how the police are handling your case?'

'The police won't make Chloe a priority. That's what we want you to do.'

'I mainly work insurance fraud, sometimes a little family stuff.'

'This *is* family stuff.'

Isaac looked into the man's eyes and tried to work out what version of the truth to tell him. That Baltimore had broken him. That he'd gone soft. That he'd made a promise never to work cases like this any more.

In the end, he let his pride take the hit.

'Look, Mr Xi, you both seem real nice, but I just need to make it clear that I'm new to all this. I've just moved back here, and my contacts in the city are a little out of date, you understand? There's other PI firms that might be better suited to helping the police find your daughter.'

The father sank back a little in his chair. Isaac felt his guts twist. Heartburn climbed his throat. He started running through the names of some local people he could recommend.

The mother returned then with the tea. She passed Isaac a cup and he took it, inhaling the scent of wood smoke and pine. They sat in the quiet for a few moments.

'You were a detective, Mr Holloway,' the mother said finally. She stared at Isaac over her untouched tea, the hot cup held firmly between two hands. Her palms must have been burning. 'You've worked these sorts of cases before.'

'I have.'

'But now you are in business for yourself.'

'That's right.'

'It must be difficult, starting over again like this.'

Her eyes had him. Chestnut brown and piercing. They reminded Isaac of another woman. A strung-out junkie who'd been hiding mescaline in a bedroom lampshade. He'd had to smash her fancy flatscreen TV before she'd give it up.

He looked away. 'I suppose it's not a job you work because it's easy.'

'And is it your intention to restrict yourself solely to investigating insurance fraud?'

'Not *solely*—'

'Ah, so how many other missing children are you currently looking for?'

Isaac paused. 'Well . . . none.'

The mother nodded and at last took a sip of her tea. 'Which makes me believe that our Chloe will be more of a priority to you than anyone else.'

'It's not just about priorities, Mrs Xi—'

'No it is not. But I also believe that you will do everything in your power to find my daughter – because you did not become a private investigator to tackle fraudulent whiplash claims and because you are starting over and you have something to prove.' Another sip, another long stare. 'So prove it.'

The father's gaze had drifted as they spoke. Now, his focus was trained on some distant horizon. The man was searching for his daughter in his own living room. Isaac had seen it before – back in

Baltimore, the mother was right about that – and as he pulled out his notebook and started writing, he realised with a sickening certainty that Chloe Xi wasn't the only person who might not come back from this.

7

It was an easy twenty-minute drive from the public library to the beach at Old Hickory. Through Lakewood, past discounted tobacco stores and automotive repair shops, most of them operating out of old, detached houses on the side of the road. It was a practice that kept parts of Nashville feeling quaint, and a nice change from his last posting. It was what he needed.

Isaac hadn't been to the beach since returning to Nashville, but he remembered it well enough. Forming part of the Cumberland river, Old Hickory Lake was man-made – a reservoir built back in the fifties to serve a nearby hydroelectric plant. The beach itself hugged a small stretch of shoreline, connecting up to various campsites, parks and nature trails.

Before he turned off Route 45, he pulled into a Sonic drive-in and ordered a bacon double cheeseburger with fries and a chocolate shake. By the time he reached the beach, his car stank of fast food. It turned his stomach.

There was a sheltered pavilion on the edge of the lake. He took a seat there. Tossed back a couple of Rolaids as he thought things through. Nashville schools started earlier than most parts of the US, but a lot of them finished at around 2.30 p.m. That was nearly an hour ago, but the beach was still quiet. The weather wasn't quite there yet.

Another month, maybe. By the time Good Friday rolled around, this place would be packed. With family barbecues, church outings. With kids crowded around the long, dormitory-style picnic tables and guys out on the water, fishing or falling off paddleboards.

It was a shame Chloe hadn't gone missing next month. There would have been more witnesses.

Ten days had passed now, just about down to the minute. Ten days since she'd been here with her parents, walking the family dog. The jogger's unconfirmed sighting placed her by the edge of the nearby woodland area at 3.35 p.m., alone, just beyond the campground. The woman had said Chloe was calling something. The dog, perhaps. The terrier named Coco.

Isaac ran his gaze over the area now. A man kayaking on the lake and a couple of teenagers draped over a picnic table, smoking weed and laughing. Wasn't surprising that the police had struggled to get many statements.

Chloe's mother had told him how it had happened. She'd described it like she'd gone over it in her head a hundred times since. It made Isaac wary; he knew the more she recited that day, the firmer her recollection became. The easier it was for mistakes to creep in, for uncertainties to become fact.

But he didn't say any of that. He dutifully noted it all down in the same pad that he reached for now. *Jonathan and I . . . we let her wander off. We told her to stay close, but we didn't really think anything would happen. We sat on the picnic bench and drank coffees. Jonathan told me a joke and I remember laughing. I wonder now if I was laughing when she was taken. Do you think that makes me a bad mother, Mr Holloway?*

He looked up from his notebook. The start of the woods was slightly hidden by a row of outdoor restrooms, little wooden hutches that formed a cordon of sorts. The grass around them half-nestled in darkness. Easy enough to lose sight of someone beyond them.

This time of year, the campground was closed to the public. Which meant it was almost exclusively used by those with nowhere else to go. Isaac knew there was a homeless shelter over on Lafayette, but he also knew how quickly it filled up. Most folk who tried the shelter ended up leaving with a mug of thin soup and a bread roll hard enough to break glass. Sometimes they even threw in a promise, too – a bed for tomorrow, if they came back early enough. A promise nearly as weak as the soup. The words going cold before they were finished being said.

Isaac stood and walked over to the restrooms. Tried each of the doors until one swung inwards, its lock broken. Inside he found a man huddled on the floor. A hard face peered up at him from a nest of blankets, white eyes blinking rapidly in the sudden harsh light. Isaac held up the bag of fast food.

'Excuse the intrusion,' he said. 'I'm not with the police, but I do have some questions for you if you're willing to talk to me.' He set the bag down. 'I'll be sitting just outside.'

The homeless man was dressed in a dark sweater and torn jeans. His face was well-worn; Isaac struggled to put an age to him. A half-smoked cigarette dangled from his mouth, and he placed it carefully in a small metal tin before unwrapping the cheeseburger.

'You sure you're not a cop?' the man said, eyeing him warily as he took a bite.

'Used to be,' Isaac said. 'Why, I still look it?'

'No, but you still talk like they do. In your throat.'

'I never noticed.'

'It's a tone, all you boys have it.' He took another bite.

'Well, I'm working for myself now. Name's Isaac.'

The man grunted. 'Matt.'

Isaac let the guy finish eating in peace after that. Once Matt had polished off half the burger, he folded the remainder back into its greasy wrapper and returned it to the bag for later. Made an approving noise when he lifted out the shake.

'Not had one of these in a while,' he said.

'I hope you like chocolate.'

'Oh, chocolate's just fine.' Matt took a long slurp and let out a sigh. There was another long pause, only this one had a strange sort of sadness to it. Isaac watched the man stare out across the water, glassy-eyed.

'You want to know if I was here last week,' Matt said.

Isaac felt his breath catch. 'What makes you say that?'

'Because you were looking for me. Or someone like me.' Matt sniffed and took another drink. 'The food was a nice touch. Most folks, they don't bother to try to butter me up first.'

He didn't need to explain who those other folks were. Isaac knew that vagrancy wasn't technically illegal in Tennessee, just like he also knew that didn't stop local law enforcement from rounding up the homeless and kicking them to another precinct's turf most chances they got. You threw in a couple of outstanding warrants, maybe a few pockets filled with baggies or a small blade for protection, and just like that you had a nice easy stat bump for some lucky officer. The cops called it control of aggressive panhandling. The mayor got to slash the affordable housing target in half, everyone else got to see their hard-earned tax dollars being put to good use. Everyone apart from the homeless, but hey, who really cared about them?

'Her name's Chloe Xi,' Isaac said.

'I know her name.'

'You were here, weren't you? When they showed up?'

Matt went quiet. Studied his chocolate shake like he wanted to stay that way.

Isaac said, 'You know, I really didn't want to take this case. Not at first. Shit like this, it stirs up too much stuff inside me.'

'So why'd you take it?'

'Because I told myself I could work it from a distance. Speak with the detectives, let her parents know they're doing everything they can. Couple of days and then just walk away.'

'You work it for a couple of days, I get the feeling you'll work it to the end.'

'Maybe.' Isaac studied the man sitting next to him. 'Could sure do with your help either way, Matt.'

The homeless man set his drink down on the grass by his knees. Rotated it slowly as he spoke. 'I didn't know what it was about, and when I did, it was too late. I was gone, you understand me?'

'Sure. You saw cops rolling in and took off. I don't blame you.'

'I wanted to say something. Afterwards. But . . .'

He trailed off into silence. Isaac stayed quiet, too scared of losing him to speak.

'She was chasing a dog,' Matt said eventually, almost to himself. 'A small, yappy thing. She was calling its name, Coco, over and over.'

'She run into the forest there?'

'At first. But that damn dog was racing all over the place. Thing was probably after a squirrel.'

'Where did she go, Matt?'

'Right to the water's edge,' he said, his gaze tracking her route all over again. 'She went through that patch of reeds and disappeared. That was all I saw, I swear it.'

Isaac scribbled in his notepad. 'I appreciate that, Matt. Truly.' He got to his feet, his eyes on those distant reeds. 'Enjoy the rest of your meal.'

Matt nodded and looked away. Might have been he was ashamed; for not coming forward sooner, for a lot of reasons.

'You didn't do anything wrong,' Isaac said gently. 'I'd have run too.'

'Maybe. But maybe you'd have come back.'

Isaac didn't quite know how to put into words what he was feeling in his chest, so he didn't say anything at all. He slid his notepad into his pocket and headed off towards the reeds, and when he eventually reached them he glanced back towards the restrooms and saw that the homeless man was gone.

Isaac had been making his way carefully through the tall reeds for nearly twenty minutes when his cell rang. He answered it and kept moving, his gaze sweeping the shoreline.

'Afternoon, Alison. How are things in Pulaski?'

'Oh they're fine. How's Music City?'

'Can't complain,' he said, stooping to inspect the marshy ground for a moment before moving off. 'You calling about the Edgeler file?'

'This a bad time to talk?'

'You kidding? I can't afford not to.'

The woman on the other end of the line let out a laugh. Alison Bennett worked for Bennett and Price, a boutique law firm that operated out of the small town an hour south of Nashville. They'd been close growing up, and when Isaac had returned home he'd put in a call to her law firm to see if there was any work going. She gave him simple jobs mainly. Personal injury, insurance fraud. People who pretended they had limps at the doctor's office and then took the stairs two at a time on their way back to the car.

'I've got a meeting with the other side tomorrow afternoon,' Alison said. 'Sure would be good to have some dirt on this guy.'

Isaac paused and forced his mind to switch tracks. Timothy Edgeler was a hospital porter who was threatening to sue his employers after he cut his index finger on a used scalpel. Six months of blood tests had ruled out HIV and other pathogens, but now the guy was alleging nerve pain in his arm, a healthy dose of PTSD and a crippling fear of leaving his home.

'Let's see,' Isaac said, mentally sorting through his previous week's work. 'I've got him on camera pumping iron at Planet Fitness, a couple of nights out with his drinking buddies and a trip to the Titans game last Friday. How does that sound?'

Alison laughed. 'It sounds perfect. You really film him lifting weights?'

'That's what I said.'

'Honey, what you *actually* said was "pumping iron", which is a phrase I've never heard used seriously for about thirty years. How did you manage to film him?'

'Pretty easily. I've got a camera the size of a button now, so I just joined the gym and did some bicep curls on the bench next to him. Nearly threw my back out trying to keep him in shot.'

'All right, Arnie, good job. When can you send the footage over to me?'

'Still need to finish up my report. Tomorrow morning?'

Alison started to speak but was drowned out by the oppressive drone of a speedboat racing across the nearby water.

'Say again?' Isaac asked.

'I said tomorrow morning's fine. Where are you?'

'Up at the beach on Old Hickory.'

'Oh, please don't tell me you've started paddleboarding. You're too young for a midlife crisis.'

'I'm working a case.'

'And here was me thinking we were exclusive,' she teased.

'You almost sound hurt.'

'I think I might be. What's the case?'

Isaac paused for a moment. Then said, 'That missing girl. Chloe Xi.'

'Ah,' Alison said. Her frown was near audible. 'I didn't think you wanted that sort of work any more.'

'Not sure I do.'

'Uh huh.'

Isaac rolled his eyes as he started moving through the reeds again, his focus back in the present. 'Look, don't worry about it. I'm not planning on getting too involved. Just trying to arrange a sit-down with the detectives, then I'm done.'

He had nearly reached the shoreline. Keeping his cell pressed to his ear with one hand, Isaac pushed aside the last remaining reeds and stepped clear. Ahead of him was a small, rickety-looking pier. It sat low in the water, waves lapping at rotten planks. A coil of rope lay in a tangle by the wooden piling. Isaac stared at it, even as Alison continued speaking, her concerned voice fading out as he turned to look back at the now-distant speedboat.

'How quickly could you cross the lake?' Isaac asked her.

Alison stopped mid-sentence. 'What?'

'Old Hickory Lake,' Isaac repeated slowly. 'In a speedboat. How quickly you think you could cross it?'

'I don't know. Where am I going? Rockland?'

Isaac moved his gaze across the lake, to where he knew the water opened up into the Cumberland river. 'I'm not sure. Further out, maybe.'

'Well there's a bunch of marinas downstream, but I haven't been on the water since I was a kid. Isaac, is this about the missing girl?'

'It's just a thought. Listen, I'll get that report over to you tomorrow morning. Give me a call if there's anything else.'

'All right . . .'

Isaac ended the call and loaded a map of the area. Followed the river, counted a half-dozen marinas within easy reach of Old Hickory beach. He felt his stomach churn as he stepped onto the wooden pier.

The water seemed to swirl around him. The tall reeds closed rank. Acid climbed his throat, his Rolaids lying uselessly in the glove box of his car. For a brief moment he thought he might be sick.

Chloe Xi had been here. Ten days earlier and on this very spot. He could feel the truth of it pulsing through the rotten boards beneath his feet. She had been drawn here – by her dog, or maybe by a man. A man who had waited patiently for her to arrive. Who had sat in a small boat tied to a forgotten pier.

And if he was right – and he knew he was, as much as he wished he wasn't – if he was right then it meant that Chloe hadn't been taken by chance. Because this area wasn't somewhere you stumbled upon by accident. It was silent, it was hidden. It was premeditation.

8

Isaac had been bent over his hotel room double bed for nearly two hours. His back was breaking.

Spread out across the sheets was a large paper map. It showed the intersection of three separate counties along the Cumberland river – Davidson, Wilson and Sumner. A length of water that stretched from Old Hickory just about all the way to Hartsville. It was nearly thirty miles by road, but Isaac knew the distance by boat would be far more.

He'd spent most of his evening poring over the route. Marking marinas, piers, even stretches of shore smooth enough to attempt a landing. It was after 9 p.m. A pizza lay on the bedside table, growing cold. He'd only been able to stomach one slice.

Isaac knew he didn't have enough resources to do this sort of search properly. He needed to know more about the area, he needed to speak to people who regularly used the river. He needed an expert on boats, on their size and type, on how far and how fast they could travel with multiple people on board.

He needed Detective Copeland.

When he was done it was after eleven. The pizza was now two slices down, and his paper folder was a fair bit thicker than it had been this morning.

Isaac stretched his back, twisting until the tight muscles relaxed a little. This was no way to work – he needed more space. He needed a wall board and a reliable internet connection. Hell, he needed out of this hotel. Somewhere without the roaches in the bathroom. Somewhere where he could make a proper dinner. His diet right now consisted of takeout and the occasional home-cooked meal at his parents' house. It was taking its toll. His stomach cramped as if to make a point.

His room was two flights up and overlooked the parking lot. Isaac gazed out the window as he brushed his teeth. He spotted a man lying on a sun lounger, drinking from a brown paper bag and flicking what looked like sunflower seeds into the grubby pool. The guy was lit up from above by the gas station next door. A Shell logo bright enough to see from orbit.

The smell of half-eaten takeout still filled the room. It stank of cold grease. Isaac tied the garbage bag and took it outside into the cool night, down to the trash bins round back. The guy on the lounger was lying on his back, staring up at the night sky, the bottle dangling from one hand.

'Mr Holloway!'

Isaac turned to see the short, squat man from reception waving at him through the glass entrance. He sighed and went inside.

The room was small and painted a sickly yellow. A boxy CRT television was bolted to one wall. Isaac had to duck going in, it was so big. Marc Cohn trudged along Beale Street in black-and-white, the volume turned all the way down. The chatter of a ball game came from a small radio on the counter.

'Evening, Danny. I help you with something?'

Danny grinned. His teeth were amber, his goatee crusted with orange dust; an empty bag of cheese chips sat on the counter. Isaac had been his favourite guest ever since turning up here a couple of months ago and uttering those three magic words: 'long-term stay'. Danny had even promised a discount if Isaac was still here in April.

'How's your evening going, Mr Holloway? Anything I can get you?'

'I think I'm all sorted, Danny. Thanks.'

'How was the pizza?'

'Oh, terrific.'

Danny beamed. 'See! What did I tell you. Best pizza pie in the city. You know I went to Italy once and tried theirs?' He screwed up his mouth at the memory. Cheese dust floated free. 'They got the dough all wrong – I needed a glass of water to finish it, it was so dry.'

Isaac thought again of the layer of grease that had coated the top of his dinner. 'Well, this one certainly wasn't dry.'

'Wonderful. And what about the roaches? They been bothering you again?'

'No, it's been a few days now.'

Danny clapped his hands together. 'That's fantastic. Didn't I say Lenny would take care of it? My cousin, I swear. Best roach exterminator in the city.'

'I bet. Anyway, it's getting late—'

'Listen, while I have you. You got a letter this afternoon.'

'Oh yeah?'

'Yeah, I meant to drop it off today but I never got the chance.'

Even on a good day, Isaac knew the chance of Danny climbing two flights of stairs was slim.

The receptionist bent down and pulled a stack of mail from under the counter. Wiped his mouth as he flipped through them, leaving an orange thumbprint on Isaac's envelope.

'There you go.'

'Thanks . . .'

'You're welcome. Now you have a nice evening, Mr Holloway. And remember: if those roaches come back, you call Lenny.'

'I'll do that.'

'He'll come out *same day*. I swear—'

'Best exterminator in the city,' Isaac said, lifting his envelope in farewell. Danny laughed and rapped his knuckles on the counter. A gesture he'd maybe seen someone do in a movie once.

Outside, Isaac studied the letter. It was addressed to him in name only, no postmark. Thing must have been hand delivered. Trying not to touch the cheese dust, he opened it up as he hurried back to his room.

The afternoon's earlier warmth had faded now. A chill made Isaac shiver. He unfolded the letter, reading by the light of the nearby gas station. Almost immediately his footsteps started to slow, and by the time he was halfway up those stairs he'd come to a dead halt. The wind was gone, the cold forgotten.

'Holy shit,' Isaac said.

9

It was nearing 1 p.m., and Isaac had scored just under two hours' sleep in the last twenty-four. He could feel it, too. A weight behind his eyes, a dryness in the back of his mouth. His head was fog – he'd nearly run a red light on the way back to Hermitage Precinct. The windows stayed down after that.

He'd been sitting in the parking lot for almost forty minutes. Copeland was working today, he'd already checked. Same woman as before on reception. The one with the evil eye. Said the detectives were in a meeting. Said not to bother waiting if he didn't have anything fresh.

Isaac glanced down at the hefty file sitting in his lap. Thing was pine-fresh enough to hang from your rear-view mirror. Copeland wouldn't like it, but he wouldn't be able to ignore it, either. Isaac wouldn't let him.

His cell vibrated in his pocket. A text from Chloe Xi's mother. He read it fast, one eye still on the station doors. It was short and to the point. *A man has been asking about you.*

Isaac didn't have time to process this before the station doors finally swung open and there they were. Detective Copeland and his partner, a guy named Hayes. Both of them pushing fifty and Hayes swinging for a coronary judging by his waistline. Neither cop looked like they'd worked anything harder than their golf game in the last long while. Isaac imagined the Xi family meeting with these two and wasn't surprised they'd sprung for a PI.

One last glance at his tired reflection in the mirror and then he was out of his car, the text message forgotten, the file clutched tight to his chest. He snaked through the half-filled parking lot. Copeland was unlocking a black sedan, laughing. The smile died on his face when he saw Isaac.

'Oh, Christ,' he said. 'What the hell are you doing back here?'

'This the guy from yesterday?' Hayes asked, all beady eyes.

'Yeah, it's me,' Isaac said. He held up the file. 'I need to speak with you both about this case.'

Copeland set his palm on the roof of his car. 'Now look here, I told you already—'

'Leave it to the detectives, I know. But all I'm asking for is twenty minutes. Hell, you give me thirty and lunch is on me.'

'Mr Holloway—'

'I just need to be able to go back to my clients and say I've looked into it. That you boys are doing everything right. I just need to get *paid*.'

Copeland looked across at his partner. Hayes was tapping out a cigarette from a crumpled packet. He bent his head as he lit up.

'I heard about you,' Hayes said, from the corner of his mouth. 'Heard you just about killed someone, heard they had to drag you off him. Must be nice having a boss that takes the flack when you fuck up.'

Isaac gripped that fat file a little tighter. 'I've made peace with what I did,' he said. 'I'm a changed man.'

'You're a burnout. You embarrassed yourself and your station in Baltimore, and you're embarrassing yourself now. Do yourself a favour and go home, Mr Holloway.'

Hayes jerked his head at Copeland and climbed into the car. Copeland almost looked embarrassed. Isaac felt his stomach churn, marched round to Hayes's open window. An urge to grab the cigarette and toss it.

'Now listen here,' he said, leaning in close. 'I don't give a shit what you think about me. All I care about is finding this girl. I've got information here – new information, *pertinent* information – that you're refusing to look at. How about I get on the phone with the TBI, see if they think I'm embarrassing myself?' He paused for effect. 'The District Attorney *has* notified them of this case, I assume?'

Hayes had been tapping out ash from his cigarette. He stopped at Isaac's mention of the Tennessee Bureau of Investigation. Small-minded cop like him, Isaac was hoping he wouldn't want government types sniffing around his files too close.

Copeland angled his head, muttered something to his partner. Hayes took a long drag before aiming those tiny eyes at Isaac. 'You got pertinent information? Fine. Follow us.'

Papa Turney's Old Fashion BBQ was just a couple of minutes' drive from the station. A busy family restaurant where the helpings came in one size only and packed into doggy bags to save time. Baby back ribs the length of your arm. Mac and cheese so yellow you couldn't look directly at it. A band played easy bluegrass on a small stage, under a sign that read *Miss Zeke's Juke Joint*.

Hayes and Copeland were already out back, enjoying a couple of iced teas and the marina view. It was set for two but Isaac pulled up a chair. The file took up most of the table.

'You boys order without me?' Isaac said, trying to catch a waiter's eye. His stomach acid was starting up again but he refused to give Hayes the satisfaction. He'd choke back some brisket with a smile on his face if he had to. Hell, he'd even ask for seconds. 'I heard this place does good catfish.'

Hayes rattled the ice in his drink. 'The catfish is good, the chicken's better. Why don't you come back and try it tomorrow?'

'You're not eating?'

'Not with you. Now I'll give you my full attention, but only until our lunch arrives.' He pointed to a sign on the table that read *15 minutes or your food is free!* and smiled thinly. A pantomime move that nearly made Isaac groan.

Isaac flipped open the file.

'I spoke with a witness who saw Chloe Xi chasing her dog through the reeds at Old Hickory.'

'What witness?'

'A homeless man, sleeping rough at the campsite.'

Copeland shook his head. 'We canvassed that area already.'

'I know, that's what scared him off.'

'And he saw her where?'

Isaac pulled out a map of the area and unfolded it. Slid condiments clear as he did. Hayes muttered and lifted his glass out the way.

'Here,' Isaac said, tapping the map. 'There's a patch of reeds that runs along the shoreline. High enough to just about hide a person completely. And that's not all, there's a—'

Hayes interrupted: 'We spoke to a jogger already. She saw Chloe running into the woods.'

'My guy saw her after that.'

'Your homeless guy.'

'Yeah, my homeless guy. Who *you* missed.'

Hayes narrowed his eyes. Started to speak but Copeland got there first. 'You get his name?'

'Matt.'

'That it?'

'Guy was on edge enough as it was. I didn't want to push him.'

Copeland frowned and shook his head. 'I'm not sure how reliable

Matt's testimony is.'

'Entirely *un*reliable,' Hayes said.

'Search the reeds,' Isaac said. 'She was there, I know it.'

'He knows it,' Hayes said to his partner. 'Well that's good enough for me.'

Copeland pointed to the circled marinas. 'What's all this?'

'There's an old pier just beyond the reeds. Still looks like it's in use, though – I saw fresh rope on the piling. I think whoever took Chloe snatched her there. Used a boat to slip away quick.'

'And these are what, possible landing sites?'

'Exactly. There's probably more, but those were just the ones I could find last night.'

Hayes snorted. 'I thought you looked tired. You should try sleeping.'

Isaac ignored him, kept his eyes on Copeland. The detective was still considering the map.

'All right,' Copeland said. 'We'll look into it. Anything else?' He glanced at the file. 'Hell of a lot more papers in there.'

Isaac paused. *Now or never.* 'I don't think Chloe was his first,' he said.

Hayes had been halfway to taking a drink. Now he set his glass back down. 'Excuse me?'

'Her abductor. He's had practice. Taking a kid from a public beach? Using the pier like that? He knows what he's doing. And besides, she fits a pattern.'

'A *pattern?*'

'Yes, a pattern. Of missing children, all with the same MO.'

Isaac dug into the file proper now. Pulled out police reports and news articles, fanned them out on top of the map. Each one a different kid. Each one a name from the long list that had been left for him at the motel reception.

Twenty children in total. Isaac had looked them up – nineteen of them were dead. Murdered. The twentieth name was the exception: Chloe Xi. And who knew for how long.

Isaac scooped up a batch of police reports and spoke fast. 'These thirteen children were all murdered by the same man. Edward Morrison.'

'Jesus Christ, the Monster? Really?'

'I know, just listen for a moment. Now, Morrison was arrested after ten-year-old Lawrence Hughes escaped and positively ID'd him. Morrison was later convicted for the abduction of Lawrence and the murder of his parents. At that point, the killings stopped. Or at least that's what people thought.' Isaac lifted the second batch of reports. 'But these six children were murdered *after* Morrison's arrest.'

Copeland: 'You said the MO was similar?'

'Not similar, the same.' Isaac started flipping open reports, pointing to photographs. 'Ligature marks on their wrists, you see that? He keeps them somewhere, for a few days at least. And when he finally kills them, it's always by manual strangulation. He damn near crushes their throats.'

'That's it?' The detective frowned. 'I think you're reaching, Isaac.'

'Hold on now, I'm not done yet. These six kids? Once they were dead they were scrubbed clean. With bleach, just like the others. Then they were wrapped in black garbage bags, bound in nylon rope and dumped in or by a body of water, just like the others. And here, the knot on the rope? It's called a constrictor knot.'

'Let me guess. Same one used by Morrison.'

'Not just Morrison. It's a fucking sailor's knot. He knows how to work a boat.'

Hayes leaned across the reports. Isaac didn't think he'd so much as glanced at them. 'Bullshit. I don't remember six more kids turning up like that.'

'Neither do I,' Isaac said. 'But that's because they weren't grouped together in the Nashville metropolitan area any more. They were spread out – most of them are across state lines.' Isaac began tapping newspaper articles. 'There's victims in Phoenix, in Bozeman, in Fort Worth. A little girl over in Tellico Plains, and I've never even *heard* of Tellico Plains.'

'Now listen here—'

'He killed in Washington State and he killed in Rhode Island. A nine-year-old boy found on Halloween just outside Providence. Abducted, tied up, strangled, cleaned, wrapped in black garbage bags, bound in nylon rope tied with a constrictor knot and then dumped by a body of water. All of them. The pattern's the same; you see it?'

'*Isaac*—'

'I know how it sounds, but Morrison was only ever convicted of the abduction of Lawrence Hughes and the murder of his parents. Prosecutors never even *tried* to tie the other murders to him. What if Morrison *wasn't* the Music City Monster? What if—'

'Enough!'

Hayes slammed his hand on the table. His half-empty glass of iced tea jumped clear and shattered on the floor. Everyone at the table went quiet. Everyone at all the tables went quiet. Even the band stopped playing.

'Just *enough*,' the detective repeated quietly. His glare was on the map, then it was on Isaac, then it was out across the marina. He ran a hand through his hair. A calming gesture, maybe. When he finally turned back, his face was composed. He pulled out another cigarette and rolled it between his fingers. 'Edward Morrison is the Music City Monster,' he said, his voice low. 'He murdered seven adults and thirteen children. *Thirteen.* Now he's up at Riverbend sitting on death row where he belongs, and in five weeks' time they'll stick a needle in his arm and that'll be the end of it. As far as I can see, these other deaths are unrelated. Children die every day. It's sad, but it's not a pattern.'

Isaac tried to speak but Hayes didn't let up.

'Now I want you to collect all these bullshit conspiracy papers and fuck off. I don't want to see you hanging around the station any more. I don't want to hear about you talking to witnesses. I don't even want to see you in *church*, you understand me?'

The restaurant was still silent. Isaac's chest was on fire. Flames danced at the base of his throat.

'You don't have to worry about me,' he said, scooping the reports back into his file. 'I stopped going to church a long time ago.'

10

He just about made it to his car before he threw up, his empty stomach cramping hard. Nothing to send back except slivers of thin bile. It came out of him like spit. It came out of him like it was on fire. He wiped his mouth on his shirt sleeve and didn't look back. Moving forward; out of the parking lot, down the I-40. The sunlight flickered above him and the radio was bust. Every station was static in his ears.

Halfway home and his cell buzzed. It was Alison, and he knew why she was calling before he answered.

'Shit, your report,' he said. 'I'm sorry, I completely forgot. I was up all night working this case.'

'Is everything all right?'

'Everything's swell.'

'You want to talk about it?'

'Not particularly. Listen, I'm on my way back to my hotel room. Give me half an hour to email it over. When's your meeting? Damn, it's today, isn't it? All right, give me twenty minutes, I'm almost there.'

'Jesus, Isaac, don't drive off the road for a report. I can push back the meeting. Are you sure you're all right?'

He knew why she was asking. Why she was *really* asking. She thought the Chloe Xi case was too much. After Baltimore, after what he'd done. You burn out one time and people brand it onto your forehead until the end of days.

'Isaac?'

'I'm fine. You don't need to worry about me.'

'You sound stressed. I'm going to cancel the meeting. Do you want me to come and meet you somewhere?'

'Alison, Christ, will you just relax? I'm not fucking stressed. I got indigestion, I don't chew my food. Now I said I'd get your report and I'll get you your damn report. You want it in fifteen minutes? You want it with a handwritten apology?'

'Okay, that's—'

'I am so sick of people not listening to me today. What is the goddamn *point* of any of this if people *will not listen*—'

A car horn blared from somewhere. Some asshole who never learned to drive properly, who didn't know the rules of the road. Isaac had to swerve across two lanes to avoid them, tyres squealing. The file on the passenger seat opened up and papers spilled out. Dead children staring at him from the footwell. Isaac pounded the steering wheel and swore loudly. His stomach was burning so bad it made him sweat. Alison was gone now, hung up maybe, and that made him sweat more.

He shouldn't have shouted at her; Hayes had just gotten him so worked up. The guy was a dinosaur. Stuck in his ways, too stubborn to shift his viewpoint. Too scared to put his neck on the line. The type of cop who used his badge as a discount coupon. Free meals at Papa Turney's and a VIP seat in his local strip joint. The type of cop Isaac had sworn he'd never be. Someone who coasted, who never needed to worry about burning out because they simply didn't give a shit.

Isaac had told everyone he was working this case for just a couple of days. Long enough to check in and report back, like this was something he could walk away from. He'd told that to himself, lied to himself. But maybe the only person he'd fooled was himself. Back at the

Old Hickory campsite, a man he'd never met before had seen right through him. Clear as if he was made of water. *You work it for a couple of days,* Matt had said, *I get the feeling you'll work it to the end.*

Now, pulling into the Super 8 parking lot, the engine spinning into quiet, Isaac dug into the glove box for his Rolaids and came up empty. His stomach was a volcano, spewing hot smoke up his chest. Alison said this case was bad for him and maybe she was right, but his guts had been burning long before Chloe Xi went missing. And now he had a carful of police reports and newspaper clippings. Each of them a different face, a different kid. Each of them a life that had been taken and snuffed out and left in a garbage bag to rot. Each of them a reason why Isaac knew he had to see this through. All the way to the very end, no matter where it took him, no matter what it cost, no matter if it burned him alive.

11

Inside his hotel room now, the curtains drawn. A glass of water from the bathroom sink to dampen the fire in his guts. He dumped the file of papers on his bed and bent over his laptop. Ten minutes to finish compiling Alison's report, ten minutes sitting hunched forward, his body curled inward. It broke his back but it helped with his stomach. Something always had to give.

The report sent, he crouch-walked into the shower and turned it on full. The water was lukewarm and wonderful. He stood under it for an age, washing the morning's sweat and shame away. When he was done he dressed in fresh clothes and drank another glass of water. It was nearly 3 p.m. now, and he'd barely eaten all day. He thought about driving to Pruitt's Discount Pharmacy and picking up some more Rolaids. He thought about giving his parents a call. He gazed down at the murky pool and the now-empty sun lounger and wondered about the man who had been lying there last night. If he was a guest, if he just couldn't take another night in his grubby motel room. A thought that Isaac had often had, lying awake in his bed in the early hours.

'Isaac!'

Someone was hammering on his door. A woman.

Alison.

When he answered she was glaring at him, her hands on her hips. Dressed in a suit, her dark hair tied in a high ponytail. She didn't even ask, she just pushed past and into his room.

'Holy Jesus,' she exclaimed. 'Is *this* where you're staying?'

'Hi, Alison,' Isaac said, closing the door. 'Please, come in.'

She was at the window opening the curtains. The room brightened considerably. 'Actually, I think it was better in the dark,' she murmured.

'I just emailed you the report,' Isaac said. 'I'm sorry it was late. And I'm sorry for earlier. I skipped breakfast, low blood sugar.'

Alison was examining him now. 'You look terrible,' she said. 'You skipped breakfast? How many?'

'Well . . .'

'When was the last time you ate something that wasn't takeout? Look at this place, Isaac. You couldn't at least stay somewhere with a kitchen?'

'Hey, this place is cheap.'

'Unless it's free, you're paying too much. What about your parents?'

'What about them?'

'Can't you stay with them?'

Isaac waved his hand through the air. 'They're old, they've got a routine. Last thing they want is me there.'

Alison shook her head. 'Too much pride. Some things never change.'

'Listen, you eaten yet? There's a half-decent Mexican down the road . . .'

'Have I *eaten*? It's three o'clock in the afternoon. Have you skipped lunch, too?'

'I was busy . . .'

'Well I'm sure as shit not spending my afternoon watching you eat Taco Bell. You know I once asked them what was in their meat taco?'

'Yeah? What'd they say?'

'"*Meat.*"'

She was roaming the room, a predator sniffing out hidden prey. Her eyes fell upon the scattered papers on his bed. 'What's this?'

Isaac sank into a chair by the window. 'It's the case I'm working.'

'Chloe Xi?'

'Yeah.'

'These are . . .' She bent down to inspect them. 'These are missing kids?'

Isaac sighed. 'I've got a theory,' he said. And he told her about what he'd found at the beach, about the letter left for him at reception. About his meeting with Copeland and Hayes earlier that afternoon. Alison, to her credit, sat down on the edge of the bed and listened. She didn't interrupt once.

When Isaac was finished, he shrugged and waved at the reports. 'And that's where I'm at.'

Alison nodded, thinking. As he'd spoken she'd sifted through the papers, scanning them, pulling out ones of interest. 'How did you get these police reports?' she asked.

'I still have some contacts. Wasn't able to get many of them, though. At least, not in the middle of the night.'

'And this letter that someone left for you. With the list of children's names. You have no idea who it's from?'

'None.'

'What about CCTV? This place must have security.'

Isaac rolled his eyes. 'You've not met Danny yet. I asked him already, but he doesn't believe in putting film in the recorder. Says most people that stay here don't want to be caught on tape.'

Alison grunted. She sat hunched forward, her face hard. 'Listen, Isaac . . .'

'I know what you're going to tell me,' Isaac said. 'What happened in Baltimore . . . I lost control, all right? I couldn't see where I was, I got too involved in the case. Too close to it.'

'You don't think this is becoming too close?'

'No, I don't. I think there's a girl out there somewhere and if she's relying on cops like Hayes to find her, then she might as well go ahead and slit her own throat right now.'

'And this, all of this, is the work of Edward Morrison?'

Isaac shook his head. 'Not Edward Morrison, the "Music City Monster".'

'Honey, Edward Morrison *is* the Music City Monster.'

'Is he?' Isaac got to his feet. 'He never admitted it, guy still swears he's innocent.'

'So? Guy's up on death row. Spent the last sixteen years watching the inmates around him disappear, one by one. Why would he change his story now?'

'What if he's telling the truth, Alison? What if the real Monster is still out there? What if he's been taking kids for nearly two decades and no one knew?'

'None of this is your *problem*, Isaac. You're not a cop any more.'

'I know I'm not a cop, but I took on a case, you understand? I met with her parents and I looked her mother in the eye and I said I would do everything I could.'

'And where does this end? When is it enough? When you're beating the shit out of some suspect?'

'Alison—'

'When you're back in the *hospital* again?'

Isaac fell quiet. All of a sudden it had gotten dark outside, and the room was cast in shadow. He took a breath, stepped away to the corner of the room and turned on a lamp. The harsh light made him squint. 'I'm going to death row,' he said finally.

'*What?*

'You want to know where this ends? Well, Riverbend might be the place.'

'You're going to speak with Edward Morrison?'

'They're going to execute him next week, Alison. I don't have time to wait. Chloe Xi doesn't have time.'

'Then don't waste it on someone like him. You think he'll give you the truth?'

'Maybe. Enough to make Hayes and Copeland believe me, anyway. There's more going on here, I know it. I just can't quite . . .'

'Isaac . . .'

'I need to look him in the eye, okay? Just like I did with her mom. I need to know for sure.'

'And when you look into that man's eyes and all you see is nothing? What then?'

Isaac shrugged. 'Then I call it a day. Go back to chasing insurance claims and charging gym membership on my expenses.'

Alison snorted. 'You better have cancelled that membership.'

'I thought you said I was too skinny.'

'I said you looked terrible, which you do by the way. And besides, my firm ain't paying for you to *pump iron* three times a week.'

Isaac smiled. 'That phrase is really growing on you, isn't it?'

'It's really not.' She checked her watch. It was nearing four. 'Listen, there's no way you're getting in to see Morrison tonight, and I'm not heading back to Pulaski before I've seen you eat something that didn't come out a microwave. I know a nice place not too far from here.'

'Is it nicer than Taco Bell?'

'Oh honey, it's nicer than *Pizza Hut*. Come on, my treat.'

'Does this mean we're cool about your late report?'

'We're cool.' Alison was halfway to the door, smiling to herself as she walked. 'I mean, you ain't getting paid for it, but we're cool.'

They walked to the car in silence. Down those two flights of stairs, the peeling metal railings lit up yellow by that twirling Shell logo. Passing the pool, Isaac could see an empty whiskey bottle lying on its side by the lounger.

'You speak to Nathan yet?' he said as they neared Alison's car. It was a two-seater Mazda MX-5, and it came to life as they approached.

'Not yet,' she said. 'I left him a couple voicemails, but he's not called me back. I would like to see him before his daddy's funeral, though. You?'

'Just briefly. I kind of forced it. He's staying at the Holiday Inn over by Opryland.'

'Fancy. How was he?'

Isaac made a non-committal noise. 'Hard to get a read on.'

'I guess some things never change,' Alison said.

It was true that Nathan had always kept people at arm's length. Through most of senior high he'd been known simply as 'that quiet boy', the boy whose locker always jammed, who never had a lab partner, who always brought his lunch from home and ate it sitting alone. But shit, it wasn't like Isaac had ever been that popular himself. For a long while it had just been him and Alison against the world. Then one day Nathan had somehow fallen in with them. Isaac wasn't sure exactly how it had all started.

'You remember he used to wear those long-sleeved sweaters all the time?' Alison said. 'Even in summer. Boy must have been sweating his ass to death.'

Isaac remembered. Remembered why, too. Along his arms, a neat little row of smooth, hairless circles. Isaac had found them confusing; the understanding would come later. Years later, when Nathan had moved away and Isaac had as well, and he saw a young girl with cigarette burns down the tops of her thighs.

'You know he hasn't spoken to Kate since he left?' Isaac said.

'Can't exactly blame him. Girl's a nutjob. You ask me, their daddy did a piss-poor job raising those kids after their mother died.'

'I still remember the way their house used to smell after it rained. Like sour milk.'

'That's mould. My granny had it in her bathroom. She used to get asthma attacks just thinking about going in there.'

Alison started the Mazda up with a roar. Danny stood outside the lobby and watched them leave, a meaty hand buried in an extra-large bag of Doritos.

They'd been driving for nearly ten minutes before either spoke. Wasn't uncomfortable, but even so, Isaac got the feeling that Alison's brain was running hot. He figured after that conversation, how could it not. When she finally turned to him, sitting at a red light by a Dollar General and a couple of kids doing sidewalk doughnuts on electric scooters, he knew what she was going to say before she said a word.

'You really set on going to Riverbend tomorrow to see Edward Morrison?'

'Yeah.'

The light turned green and she stepped on the gas pedal so hard it made Isaac's head rock back.

'Well I'm coming too,' she said.

12

Riverbend was a large collection of beige, squat buildings, packed full of high-risk males and tucked away in the folds of the Cumberland river. Death row on your doorstep; it was barely a twenty-minute drive from downtown Nashville. Close enough to travel there and back before Rocky Bottom had finished their evening set at the Bootlegger's Inn. Close enough to hear them, maybe, if the wind was right.

Alison followed the pike out along the water, staying north of the river most of the way. It was a longer route but it was quieter. Sadder too, somehow. It avoided much of the city, like today wasn't the day to remind yourself of all that living going on just ten miles from a condemned man's window.

They passed semi-trucks carrying medical supplies and SUVs with Jesus stickers on their windscreens. Churches that were damn near like skyscrapers out here, their steeples reaching where even the factory chimneys didn't dare go. Where most of the houses were single storey and set way back from the road. Closer they got to Riverbend, longer they had to drive before they reached another. All of them hidden behind bushy trees that Isaac knew would be bare come wintertime.

The prison road proper was bookended on either side by a pair of fancy brick walls. One read *7475 Cockrill Bend*, and the other read

Riverbend Maximum Security Institution. Both of them had lanterns on top and neat, colourful flower beds underneath.

'Feels like we're about to enter some fancy estate,' Alison muttered as they drove past.

'Must be why they have that sign,' Isaac said, and pointed. *Warning*, it read in large, white writing. *You are now entering the grounds of a correctional facility.*

'At least the view's nice,' Alison said.

As they pulled into the parking lot, Isaac's gaze followed the banks of the river as it rose straight up ahead of them. Dense, green forest fed off the water; bushy treetops packing out the rolling hills for miles around. An image straight out of a postcard. Building a prison so close to this sort of beauty; it almost didn't seem fair.

They were met at the prison entrance by a burly officer with a thick moustache and a crewcut so tight it made his head bulge. He watched them approach, speaking into his radio, his hand resting casually on his holstered Taser. He held open a glass door.

'Welcome to Riverbend,' he said. His voice was a slow, southern drawl. 'You folks here to see Eddie Morrison?'

Alison nodded. 'That's right. I'm Alison Bennett, this is Isaac Holloway. I spoke with the warden yesterday afternoon. Our names should be on Mr Morrison's approved visitors list.'

'Oh they are, they are.' The officer sniffed loudly and backed up a little to let them in. 'Yours about the only ones.'

This close, Isaac could see the man's name badge read *Cranor*. He could also see his bloodshot eyes, a hint of yellow in the whites. A permanent feature, Isaac guessed, from too much drink.

'Now seeing as this is y'all's first time visiting us, I need to go over some *ground rules*,' Cranor said, stressing the words like he was speaking to a couple of unruly schoolkids. 'Don't worry, it won't take long.'

But of course it did. Just about twenty minutes, all in. Body scans and pat-downs, names rechecked on official registers. Another officer silently flipped through their paper files for contraband.

'Now Eddie is currently classified as level B,' Cranor told them. He seemed to like starting his sentences with that word. He spoke over his shoulder, leading them through winding corridors and mag-locked double doors. 'That means contact visitation. No Perspex, you understand? No restraints. Just you and him round a table. You can shake his hand, hell you can even give him a hug if you keep it brief.'

That last part was directed at Alison. She ignored it.

'We need to show him some documents,' Isaac said.

'You go right ahead and show him whatever you want.'

Another set of doors popped open and a siren wailed to go with it. They were back outside. The sudden sunlight made Isaac squint. Cranor kept talking as he walked them down a chainlink passage across the prison yard.

'Now once y'all take your seats, you're only allowed to leave 'em for two reasons: using the restroom or using the vending machine, and you'll need a Debitek card for that. Five dollars upfront but you get three back in credit. You can buy him a snack but that's it. No passing items to him, no taking items from him.'

Isaac could feel the gaze of scattered faces following them as they walked. Prisoners from gen pop, their attention drawn by the door's siren. Bored of lifting weights or running track. Anything to break up the monotony.

'You know Mr Morrison well?' he asked Cranor.

''Bout as well as I'd want to, given the circumstances.'

'And what's he like?'

'Eddie? Oh, he's a pussycat. He ain't no trouble.' Cranor flashed a smile. 'But he ain't got no more hope, you understand? See it's the hope that gets them fired up, makes 'em lash out or talk back. Some folks keep hold of it until the end, and they're the ones you need to watch out for. Stories in their heads of last-minute injunctions, of getting clemency with the damn needle in their arm.'

'But not Mr Morrison?'

'No sir, Eddie ain't got no fancy notions like that. Makes him real easy to manage. You and your lady friend ain't got nothing to worry about.'

Isaac could feel Alison's eyes burning a hole through the side of the officer's head. 'I understand Mr Morrison is due to be executed soon,' he said quickly.

'Yessir, that's right. March twenty-fourth. They're in the chamber right now, prepping the chair.'

Isaac paused. Alison filled the gap. 'The *electric* chair? I didn't think they still used that.'

'They don't, not really. It's mainly a backup, you know, just in case. But folks who've been here as long as Eddie can choose it if they want.' Cranor shrugged. 'Hell of a way to go.'

They walked the rest of the way in silence. Into another building and through more doors, more winding corridors. Cranor pausing every so often to have a word with another guard or to listen to the crackle of his radio. Isaac could smell the sharp tang of disinfectant; rounding a corner, they came across an inmate mopping a large patch of floor. The man paused to stare blankly at them as they passed by. Isaac tried not to think about what might have made the mess.

Eventually they found themselves back outside again. Cranor turned and jerked his head at a low-slung building. 'Here we go, folks,' he said. 'Unit two, death row.'

13

Isaac had seen Edward Morrison before, but only in photographs. Trial photos, printed sixteen years ago. He'd looked them up again last night. Stared at the tall, skinny kid being led into the courtroom. Dressed in a suit that was at least a couple sizes too big. The sleeves bunching up around his handcuffs, the trousers spilling over his shoes. Morrison was pale-skinned, with his blond hair shaved close. Morrison was like a spectre. A ghost of a boy already fading from the world.

And this was where he'd emerged. This small, dimly lit building that stank of bleach and dying rats, that sat on the banks of a wide river only ever seen from afar and only for an hour each day. A life lived alone, in a six-by-nine foot box with no window, where the sole clock that really mattered ran backwards; counting down those precious seconds until someone strapped you to a metal chair and flipped the switch. And shit, maybe that was all right. If Edward Morrison had murdered those children, then maybe that was just fine.

Cranor led Morrison into the room. He entered hunched forward. This ghost of a boy who had become a ghost of a man. Still pale-faced, still dressed in ill-fitting clothes, only this time they weren't a suit. Beige overalls hung off him like he'd recently lost weight. Edward Morrison paused at the doorway and looked at them both, blinking slow, before shuffling across to the metal table and sitting down.

Isaac introduced himself and Alison.

'But I already got a lawyer,' Morrison said. His head was bowed, the words spoken soft and slow and half lost in the folds of his jumpsuit.

'I know,' Alison said. 'We're not wanting to interfere with that. We just want to ask you a couple questions.'

'What about?'

'About the day you were arrested.'

Morrison lifted his head slightly, his gaze sliding over each of them before coming to rest on the vending machine in the corner. Isaac glanced over at it.

'I get you a soda or something?'

'Could I have a Diet Coke? And a Hershey's, if they have any? You'll need a special card, but I can pay you back.'

'That's all right, Edward. My treat.'

Morrison smiled a little. 'The guards here all call me Eddie,' he said. 'Drives me crazy.'

It took a few minutes to sort out the food, but Morrison perked up after. He offered them both a square of his Hershey's bar. Said he didn't use to be a big fan of Cookies 'n' Creme, but all they sold in commissary was milk chocolate with almonds and he sure was sick of that.

'You know what I've not had since I've been inside?' he said.

'What's that?'

'A Big Mac. I swear, sometimes I think I might have dreamt them.'

Isaac's stomach tensed at the mention of fast food. Last night's dinner with Alison – brown rice and broiled chicken – had damped the fire somewhat, but it was still a little on edge. He forced a conciliatory expression, said, 'They're not as good as they used to be. They shrank the patty, threw off the whole meat–bun ratio. Now what you *really* want is the Double Quarter Pounder.'

'But what about the Big Mac sauce?'

'Sometimes they put that on if you ask nice.'

Beside them, Alison rolled her eyes.

Morrison laughed. It was a faint, breathy sound. 'Maybe I'll get both and compare them,' he said, breaking off a neat square of chocolate. 'For my last meal, you know? Get a couple of milkshakes to go with it. They let you spend twenty dollars on whatever you want. I could get a lot for my money there. I could get that apple pie they do, I never tried that.'

'No one has, Edward.'

Alison cleared her throat. She placed the file they'd brought on the table and opened it up, started pulling papers out. 'All right, how about those questions now?'

Morrison nodded and sucked on his Diet Coke. 'Sure.'

'You were arrested at 6.30 a.m. on December twelfth, 2008,' she said, reading from a document. 'Police pulled you from your car outside the home you lived in with your mother.'

'That's right,' Morrison said. 'I'd lost my keys, so I slept in my Toyota overnight.'

'Must have been cold.'

'It was freezing.'

'Your mom not answer the door?'

'She was working double shifts at the Riviera. She said she needed her sleep.'

'Sure was considerate of you, Edward, spending a night like that.'

'Not really. I just didn't want to get yelled at.'

'Uh huh.' Alison flicked through the file. 'Wasn't the first time you'd been arrested, was it?'

'No, ma'am.'

'Shoplifting, assault, drug possession.' She paused to consider the documents. 'Police had their eye on you.'

'Yes, ma'am,' he said. 'It's true I'd been in a couple of fights over the years, but I didn't start them, not one. And that liquor store I robbed? I never used a gun or nothing, I just stuck a bottle of whiskey under my sweater and walked out the door. I don't know why, I know it's stupid. I mean, I don't even *like* whiskey.'

'Fine, let's stick to December twelfth. Shortly before your arrest, a nine-year-old boy named Lawrence Hughes flags down a patrol car. Tells them that he's just escaped from a house where he's been held against his will for the last forty-eight hours. Officers take him to his home address and find his father at the bottom of a set of stairs with a broken neck and his mother bludgeoned to death in her bed.'

'I didn't know anything about that,' Morrison said quietly. 'Like I told you, I was sleeping.'

'But Lawrence gave a description of the man who took him,' Isaac countered, keeping his tone light. 'White male, average height, blond hair.'

'That sounds like it could be a lot of people.'

'Lawrence went on to positively ID you in a photo line-up.'

'Maybe I've just got one of those faces, you know?'

'You were pulled from your car three blocks away from where this kid flagged down the cops,' Alison said.

'How could I keep him in my house? With my mom sleeping upstairs? She's a light sleeper, and we don't even have a basement or anything.'

'Kid never said he was in a basement. Said he never got a look at the house.'

'How'd he never get a look? He was there for forty-eight hours. That's two days. How'd he stay in a house for two days and not know if he's in a basement or not?'

'He said he was blindfolded.'

'Then how'd he know it was me?' Morrison put his chocolate down. He looked upset. 'How'd he know I took him but he can't say what my house looks like? All this stuff, it's just *circumventional*.'

'You mean circumstantial?'

'Yeah, circumstantial. And you two are starting to sound like the cops who questioned me.'

'Same cops you told about climbing through Lawrence Hughes's bathroom window?'

'That's not fair¾'

'Same cops you told "I would use a hammer" when asked about his dead parents?'

Morrison spread his hands out on the metal table. Started rattling his fingertips against the cold surface. 'I didn't kill those people and I didn't take that boy.'

'What about the other kids, Eddie? You take them?'

'I didn't take no one!'

That attracted Cranor's attention. The officer had been standing by the door the whole time, watching. Now he sauntered over. Peered down at them.

'Everything all right here?'

'Everything's fine,' Alison said. 'I've just got a few more questions.'

But Morrison shook his head. 'No. No more questions. I want to go back to my cell.'

Isaac started to speak, but Cranor cut him off. 'You heard him, folks. Interview's over.'

The officer leaned forward and handcuffed Morrison's wrists together again. Once he was secure, Cranor helped him to his feet and led him slowly back towards the door. The half-eaten snacks remained on the table.

Isaac glanced over at Alison, then back at Morrison.

'I ask you one last question?' he said, and when Morrison got half-way out the door without replying, asked it anyway: 'Why the electric chair?'

That got him. The man stopped walking, so suddenly Cranor nearly collided with him. Morrison turned, still hunched forward, his pale eyes finding Isaac's across the room.

'Because for seventeen years they've been telling me how to live,' he said quietly. 'Only seemed fair I get to tell them how I die.' He started to leave, paused, looked back. 'Thank you for the chocolate,' he added.

14

Cranor walked them back to their car afterwards. He didn't bother making small talk and Isaac was grateful. Leaving Riverbend, Alison drove slow. Any other way felt wrong.

The silence continued those first few miles. Past the flower beds, back towards the city. Felt good the closer they got. Felt like colour coming back into the world.

The car bounced as Alison swung onto the on-ramp to the I-40. Isaac looked at her.

'We not taking the pike?'

'I'm heading downtown. I need to be around people right now, shake off that prison vibe.'

They made good time into Lower Broadway and got the last parking space in the Bridge lot. Alison killed the engine and said, 'You think I was too heavy-handed.'

'I didn't say that.'

'You think it, though.'

'Maybe.'

She snorted, climbed out, started walking towards the lunchtime crowds working the honky-tonks. Isaac fell in beside her.

'I needed to test the evidence,' she said, her voice clipped. 'See what he was like when someone got under his skin a little. Your girl can't afford to wait. Hell, the guy's getting fried in a few weeks himself.'

'And?'

'And what?'

'And what did you think about him? When you got under his skin?'

'I think he's a dead end, Isaac.'

They slid through the busy street and into a table at the rear of Acme Feed and Seed. Alison ordered an iced water and a tuna salad, threw Isaac a look until he ordered the same.

'I'm just looking out for your stomach,' she said.

'My stomach thanks you.'

'So what's your take on Morrison?'

Isaac leaned back in his seat. Picked up his water and played with the ice. 'I don't think he did it,' he said finally.

'Really?'

'I think the police needed to catch a killer, and I think Morrison fit the bill. It's confirmation bias, through and through. I saw this sort of thing all the time on the force.'

'What about the evidence?'

'What evidence?'

'What *evidence*?'

Isaac pulled his notebook and started flipping through it. 'The cops never had anything solid on him. Forensics spent a couple of days going over Morrison's house, but failed to find anything that linked to Lawrence Hughes there. Same with Morrison's car. Now, during questioning they lie about this. They tell him they found hair belonging to Hughes in the trunk. They engage him in a hypothetical conversation about it all.'

'A hypothetical conversation?'

'Yeah, you know, "if you did it, where would you have kept him, how would you have killed his parents", that sort of thing. He gives them a bunch of answers that make the jury's heads spin.'

'And Morrison just goes along with this hypothetical conversation? Without a lawyer present?'

Isaac gave her a look. 'You've met him. The guy's not exactly firing on all cylinders.'

'That "circumventional" line? It felt a little forced. Besides, Tennessee doesn't execute prisoners with intellectual disabilities.'

'Come on, Alison. A psychiatrist's report described him as "easily led", and after today I'm inclined to agree. Shit, he didn't care about speaking to us without a lawyer. Didn't even seem to care who we were, so long as I bought him a chocolate bar.'

A waitress dropped off their tuna salads. Alison took a large forkful, chewed it slow.

'I'll give you the house,' she said. 'Hughes was blindfolded most of the time, wasn't able to pick out anything specific. Best he could describe was a funky smell.'

'Maybe your grandma was keeping him in her bathroom.'

'What about the photo ID?' she asked. 'Hughes positively identified Morrison as the man who took him.'

'And if they treated him like they treated Morrison, then I wouldn't be surprised if they only gave the kid one photo to pick from.'

Alison watched him for a moment, then set her fork down. 'Jesus. You like him, don't you.'

'What?'

'Morrison. You like him.'

'I don't like him, I don't know him.'

'But you feel sorry for him.'

Isaac swallowed a mouthful of salad. Lettuce leaves that wedged tight in his throat. He thought about Edward Morrison – the boy in the courtroom and the man in the cell, nearly two decades between them and still so alike. As though the guy had been frozen all those years back. An hour of sunlight a day and a different Hershey bar to brighten up your week. Isaac was amazed the guy could still enjoy anything at this point.

He pushed a green bean around his plate. 'You know they go under twenty-four-hour observation before they're executed?'

'No, I didn't know that. Suicide watch?'

'Yeah. You ever hear anything so ridiculous? Like the state's spent all this money keeping them alive, they don't want to be cheated at the last minute.'

Isaac tried to spear a chunk of tuna but his appetite was gone. He pushed his plate aside. Looked up to see Alison watching him. Her head tilted, her eyes sad.

'You think I'm getting too wrapped up in all this?' he said quietly.

She shrugged. 'I think you weren't hired to defend someone on death row, is all.' She reached over and squeezed his hand. 'Just don't forget there's a little girl still out there.'

Isaac nodded and leaned back in his chair. He gazed down at the bag by his feet, thought of the papers within. 'I got a gut, Alison, same as everyone. It's served me right for years, I can't not listen to it now.'

'Honey, your gut's been churning acid since you took this case. Maybe it's trying to tell you something you don't want to hear.'

He winced. 'That's a little on the nose.'

'Hey, it's your metaphor.'

They smiled. Alison motioned for the check, then said, 'Well if Edward Morrison didn't do it, then that means whoever did is still out there.'

'Worse, it means they never *stopped*. And in a couple of weeks an innocent man is going to be put to death.'

Alison's gaze moved to the stage. A young woman was at the mic, laughing as she pulled a guitar strap over her head. A steady drumbeat started up slow.

'So now what?' she asked.

'Now we go find the Music City Monster. The *real* Monster. Before he murders Chloe Xi.'

'Where'd you want to start?'

Isaac flipped his notepad shut and slid it into his pocket. 'I want to start by having a conversation with Lawrence Hughes. I want to ask him what he really saw when he was being held prisoner, and I want to ask him how the hell he ever managed to escape.'

They were halfway to the car when Isaac's cell went off. He pulled it out, frowning at the number.

Detective Copeland was calling.

15

NATHAN

Nathan closed the door to the cabin's empty cellar but in his mind it would always remain open. Seventeen years it had been open. His whole life it had been open. A constant source of nightmares and abhorrent thoughts. It didn't make a difference how far away he went; no matter where he was living, it was always on the edge of that doorway. Wherever he looked, it was always straight down into the dark.

He moved through into the living room and collapsed onto the couch. He was so tired and yet he'd never been more awake. His father's manuscript lay on the coffee table in front of him. He couldn't remember placing it there.

The Midnight King.
A novel by Lucas Cole.

Nathan picked it up and began to read.

15

NATHAN

THE MIDNIGHT KING

A NOVEL BY LUCAS COLE

Chapter One

Ricky Taylor pauses to remove his glasses and wipe his brow. It's hot, out here in Burgess Falls. A dry heat, like he's in a sauna, and Ricky never did much care for saunas.

Course the altitude isn't helping much either. See he isn't really a hiker, Ricky. And most of his life, that's been just fine. A city boy like him? Biggest hike he's ever done is the twelve steps to his driveway.

It's his wife, Marjory, who's the hiker – coming out here was her idea. A long weekend at her father's old cabin, just the two of them. Away from the kids.

Burgess Falls is only an hour or so outside of Nashville, but with scenery like this, it's easy to forget. They've been walking for nearly two hours now, on a long path that skirts a high cliff edge. Up ahead is a series of waterfalls; apparently Marjory has been wanting Ricky to see them for some time.

For most couples, staying in a cabin outside of town for a few days would be exciting. A chance to reconnect, to perhaps add that spice which fades a little during the course of any marriage, especially once you add a couple of children into the mix.

For Marjory and Ricky, however, it's been anything but.

'Can we at least talk about it?' Ricky says, panting as he tries to catch up to his wife. 'I really feel like this is getting blown out of all proportion.'

Marjory ignores him and keeps walking. She's able to keep up a pretty decent pace, despite the incline. Of course it helps that she's dressed in full hiking gear: Merino top, light leggings and black boots. Ricky, on the other hand, is wearing his favourite pair of jeans and some well-worn sneakers. It isn't so much that he hasn't dressed for the occasion, more that he was hoping the occasion wouldn't happen at all.

He reaches out and grabs his wife's shoulder, spinning her around to face him.

'Dammit, will you slow down a second? You haven't even stopped once to admire the view.'

Marjory finally relents, looking him dead in the eyes. Her face is like granite. 'I'm not sure what else there is to say that wasn't said last night.'

Ricky feels himself sag a little. It isn't like fighting is something new to them, but last night's round was particularly brutal. Sparked – as is so often the case nowadays – by what Ricky had thought was a perfectly innocuous comment: whether Marjory was *sure* she didn't want a third child.

'Look,' she says, twisting her arm back and out of his grasp. 'I've told you my feelings on this already. I've told you a hundred times, Ricky. I really don't like being ambushed every couple of weeks, and I *really* don't like being made to feel guilty just because I don't want to go through another nine months of slow hell—'

'All right—'

'—and honestly, you have no idea what it's like being pregnant. I mean, you *saw* me being sick every morning, didn't you? And the *births*, Jesus, Ricky—'

'*All right*—'

'I can't do it again, I just can't. And I need you to hear me on this. Because I feel like you're not listening . . .'

Ricky nods. What else can he do, really, at this point? He tries to look sympathetic, like he's putting the matter to bed and moving on. He even puts both hands up in a gesture of peace.

Marjory's eyes flash. 'Oh, please don't tell me to calm down. You started this, you can deal with the consequences.'

She turns and marches off. Ricky watches her go. Why can't she see things the way he does? Ricky loves his wife – of course he does, he's been married to her for thirteen years and never once has he even *looked* at another woman, and if that's not love then what *is*? – but she's so fixated on the short term. And sure, he gets it, pregnancy isn't a walk in the park. But it's only nine months.

He knows Marjory loves their kids. Josh and Harriet are young, eight and ten years old, and he knows that starting over from scratch with another child is a difficult thing to do at this point in their lives. And yet, there's times he aches with it. Times he sees a child in the park or walking next to their mother, and they seem to call out to him. Shouting so loud, it's like they sparkle in the sunlight. A secret message, just for him.

Marjory's a fair bit ahead now. Powered by anger and resentment. Her hands swing stiffly by her sides, her fingers still curled into fists. Ricky kicks at a pebble and gazes out at the view. It really is quite spectacular. He can even hear what sounds like the start of the water-falls. Maybe they'll improve his wife's mood.

He hurries after her. As he closes the gap, he finds himself replay-ing last night's argument in his head once more. Picturing the flash of rage in Marjory's eyes, the way she'd tensed up when she real-ised what he was saying – she has this way of shooting her arms out straight and opening her hands, like she's a child's cartoon drawing of a person. A stick figure.

She looks like that now, Ricky thinks. A stick figure, marching for-ward. Already he can see how this day will end: another couple of hours of Marjory leading him round this trail, then sitting in silence as he drives them back to their cabin. They've planned to stay another night – he's booked the days off work and everything – but Ricky isn't sure he can manage it. Another night of dancing around each other, of reading books in silence, or wishing for the hundredth time that Marjory's father had installed cable TV in the place before he died.

Ricky does appreciate, however (despite evidence to the contrary) that his wife is never going to agree with him. He even understands that continually bringing the matter up is only going to make things worse. But what is he supposed to do with how *he* feels?

They're almost at the waterfalls now. Their roar has been growing steadily along this stretch of path, and here it's almost deafening. Ahead of them the route swings a hard left, away from the cliff edge. Ricky takes a breath and forces himself to speed up.

He finally covers the distance between them, and he shouts her name as he reaches for her. She turns, glaring at him, shrugging away his outstretched hand. What was it she said earlier? *You started this, you can deal with the consequences.*

'Marjory,' he says, and grasps for her again, 'I know you're never going to see things the way I do.'

'No, Ricky, I'm not.'

'I don't want to lose you,' he says, and this time he's able to clutch her shoulders. 'I love you.'

Marjory sighs and worms herself backwards, out of his hands. 'I think we—'

The rest of her sentence is lost as she steps off the path. Her voice rises sharply, her arms pinwheeling. They lock eyes, Marjory clutching air. She looks almost confused as she slips off the edge of the cliff.

Ricky listens for a scream – or the sound of her body hitting the rocks below – but whatever noise his wife makes as she falls, it's swallowed up by the roar of the water.

Chapter Two

Things move quickly after that.

It takes Ricky nearly forty minutes to get down to where Marjory has landed. Forty minutes of scrambling down shortcuts, of whispering '*Jesus Jesus Jesus*' under his breath. His damn sneakers slide about so much on the loose gravel, he spends more time on his ass than his feet. By the time he reaches her, his shirt is stuck to him with sweat, his jeans are covered in dirt and he has a nasty gash down his left forearm.

Now forty minutes is a long time. You could cook a nice meal in forty minutes. You could listen to a record. You could watch most of an episode of a network TV show in forty minutes, if you skipped the commercials. And despite Ricky seeing barely anyone else during their hike, in those forty minutes a crowd has gathered around Marjory's body.

He pushes through them, shouting her name. If adrenaline was what got him down here, it's sure starting to fade now. His left arm is throbbing and his legs are beginning to tremble. Nausea rolls and crashes in his stomach, a fluttering that works its way up his throat. For a horrible moment he thinks he might throw up on her. Wouldn't *that* just be the damnedest thing.

Marjory has landed on a slope. Her body is twisted, her face turned the wrong way. Ricky's legs finally start to give in when strong arms grab him: a man on a walkie-talkie, a ranger.

'I need an ETA on that medevac,' the man says into his radio.

In the distance, Ricky can hear sirens.

He spends the next half hour sitting by himself, watching as police arrive and usher people away. Watching as emergency medical technicians examine her – as if there's a chance she's still alive. Watching as his wife is bundled into a body bag and zipped up tight.

'She fell,' he tells the officers when they question him. 'We were talking, and she just fell back. There was nothing I could do.'

I think we—

These were Marjory's final words.

They torment Ricky. He lies in bed at night and repeats that unfinished sentence, over and over. His brain fills in a hundred different endings, as though there's a magic combination that will somehow make things right.

Sometimes he uses them to find comfort.

I think we can discuss this over lunch.

I think we both know I'm overreacting.

I think we should have another child.

That last one is the worst.

Marjory's mother, Rhonda, has been looking after the children. When he finally gets home, she is standing in the upstairs landing, outside their bedroom, clutching one of her daughter's sweaters in her hands. She is tall and thin, and she has obviously been crying.

'She was going to leave you,' Rhonda tells him, her face hard, her voice cruel.

I think we need some time apart.

Ricky dreams in fits and bursts. Waking abruptly with snatches of imagery clutched like water in his hands. Sometimes he catches her before she falls. Other times he pushes her off the cliff himself. He lies awake for hours afterwards, feeling sad, or guilty, or just nothing at all. He feels like a chasm has been opened inside of him. An empty chamber that refuses to be filled.

The coroner returns a verdict of accidental death.

Burgess Falls isn't a difficult trail, he writes in his official report, but often that leads to people becoming complacent. Marjory wasn't the first person to slip from that cliffside, and she would undoubtedly not be the last.

Ricky asks for a copy of the report. He reads it hunched over in his car. It cites a number of contributory causes to Marjory's death; they are called 'vertical deceleration injuries'. Most of them he doesn't understand, and will have to look up later. Some examples include:

Blunt force trauma with sternal fracture.
Bilateral pneumothoraces.
Bilateral pulmonary contusions.
Liver and splenic lacerations.
Devascularised kidneys.
Traumatic brain injury.
The list is extensive. It goes on.

Of the two children, Harriet seems to take the news best.

There are tears, of course, but it doesn't take her long to lock them away. People tell Ricky that she should be expressing her emotions more. A child psychologist says that Harriet is compartmentalising her feelings, like a Gulf War vet after a tour of duty, and that's not healthy in the long run. Ricky agrees, but cannot afford to keep paying the man to fix her.

Josh, on the other hand, is a different story. Two years younger than his sister, Josh has always been the more sensitive child. Quicker to cry, longer to settle. The boy routinely weeps at Disney movies or at the sight of roadkill. He is inconsolable for nearly a month when he discovers what has happened to his mother. Tantrums, refusals to eat or go to school. He even starts wetting the bed again. Like his father and sister, he too has become broken, in his own way.

Life is different for Ricky and the children, but it does go on. After a time, they find a new normal. It is quieter in the house than it was before – at dinners, especially. Ricky starts putting the radio on as they eat just to take the edge off the silence.

Rhonda stays with them for a while (Ricky's own parents having passed away a number of years prior). She helps here and there – making the children their lunches, picking them up from school – but she is old and finds the work tiring. And every time she talks to Ricky, he cannot help but pick up an undertone in her voice. A disdain, like he is a bad smell. Like he is responsible for her daughter's death.

I think we both know who should have really fallen from that cliff, don't we, Ricky?

And then one night, Ricky dreams he is walking down a desolate road in the centre of the city. The buildings around him are empty, the cars absent. The only other sign of life a shimmering shape on the distant horizon.

A child.

Ricky continues to walk, and as he gets closer he realises that it is a young boy, aged no more than ten, dressed in a strange silvery costume, with light brown hair and dark eyes and with his right hand outstretched. He is clutching something – no, he is *giving* something. A white piece of paper.

Reaching for it, Ricky's fingers brush the paper. The moment they do, the boy vanishes.

Ricky stands in the deserted road, truly alone now. He looks down at the paper in his hand. It is a ticket to a school production of *The Wizard of Oz*. Crudely designed and printed on cheap card, it has *St Thomas's* printed on the bottom, underneath a date: *Friday September 16 at 7.30 p.m.*

When Ricky wakes soon after, he realises it is the first time that he has not felt sad, or guilty, or nothing at all. The chamber inside of him is no longer completely empty – there is an ember of something there now. A spark that he must nurture and grow into a flame.

He finds an old envelope in his bedside drawer and scribbles down the information from his dream. The school, the date, the name of the play. He can still picture the boy, with his light brown hair and brown eyes, and he knows what he must do next.

He must find him.

Chapter Three

Ricky doesn't tell anyone about the dream, or about what he's planning. Not that he *knows* what he's planning. Not yet, not truly. His mother used to say that the best way to tackle a problem was to focus on the first step. *Anything beyond that*, she would tell him, *is for another time.*

But really, who would he tell? His children? Rhonda? He can just imagine what *she* would have to say about it. What people would think of him if they found out. Because that was the danger here, of course – being misunderstood. Ricky knew he wasn't a sicko or a pervert. He wasn't what the boys in the schoolyard used to chant about him, what they would write down on scraps of paper and feed into his locker. Scrawled in poor handwriting, the sure-fire sign of a cretin. Bad words, dirty words.

He mulls it all over in the early hours. Unable to sleep, showering at four thirty in the morning. The boiler caught unawares and the water lukewarm. Ricky barely notices it, so caught up in his own head, in his rambling thoughts. Why *does* he want to find the boy? Why has this dream got to him so badly? Something in the boy's expression, perhaps. A sadness – no, a panic. A cry for help. Is there the possibility that the boy, whoever he is, had been pleading for Ricky to come and save him?

Or maybe this is all wrapped up in his last fight with Marjory. Embers of a dying argument sparking connections in his dreams. His ache for a bigger family, her steadfast refusal. His fear that she was going to leave him coming horrifyingly true. Sometimes he is closer to her – in his mind, in his memories. Out there at Burgess Falls, on that cliff edge. Sometimes he is close enough to touch her. To reach out and take hold of her, to stop her mid-sentence.

I

think

we

Ricky shakes his thoughts away. He thinks back over what his mother told him and he focuses on the first step: find the child. *Anything beyond that*, he tells himself as he dresses quietly in the dark, *is for another time*.

The first thing Ricky does is buy himself a notebook. He picks it up from one of those trendy stores in 12 South; an area of Nashville in which someone once threw a brick through the windscreen of Ricky's parents' car when he was a boy, and therefore an area which Ricky will always think of as dangerous, despite the millions of dollars that have clearly been poured into it over the last few years. Now, it seems to be populated mainly by expensive clothing outlets and even more expensive cocktail bars. Ricky pays nearly four dollars for the notebook – a price tag that he becomes physically angry about – but he is already running late for dinner and does not want Rhonda to think anything is amiss.

When he gets home, he goes straight to his bedroom and closes the door. Digging out the envelope from his bedside drawer, he neatly transcribes his late-night scribbles into his new notebook.

St Thomas's.

The Wizard of Oz.

Friday September 16 at 7.30 p.m.

Today is Monday the twelfth. Ricky has four days to find the boy.

Once he's finished, he slides the notebook into his bedside drawer and tears the envelope up into little pieces. These he flushes them down the toilet before he washes up for dinner. He inspects his left arm in the mirror; his forty-minute scramble down to Marjory's body has rewarded him with a long scar, running from his elbow to the top of his wrist. The blemished tissue is a thick, red line. It barely looks like it has healed, in fact it looks like it would reopen again if he scratched it too hard.

He pushes the thought away and goes downstairs. Rhonda has made meatballs for dinner, and Ricky is starving.

Chapter Four

The next morning, Ricky calls his boss at Belmont University, where Ricky spends eight hours a day manning the parking lot, and tells him that he's not feeling too good.

'I think it's food poisoning,' he says down the line. 'Rhonda made meatballs last night and I swear they were barely warmed through.'

He bends forward as he says this last part, adding in a gentle groan – nothing over-the-top, he doesn't want to come on too strong. But if his boss is suspicious, it doesn't show.

'Don't worry about it, take a couple of days. We'll manage without you.'

Ricky's boss is a fat, balding man named Walter. A man so habitually worried about pissing people off – his wife, his employees, the *union* – that he essentially granted Ricky carte blanche when Marjory died. A couple of weeks off (paid, naturally) and an assurance not to worry if he came in late or left early for the next few months. 'Grief is a strange thing,' Walter said, which is sort of funny considering the only thing Walter has ever grieved is a burnt dinner.

Ricky says thanks and hangs up. Downstairs, he can hear Rhonda getting Josh and Harriet ready for school. He checks his watch; the school bus will be at the corner in a couple of minutes. He packs his work overalls and hi-vis jacket into his rucksack and goes to say goodbye.

Josh is standing quietly by the front door, waiting for his sister. Dressed in smart black chinos and a crisp white shirt that is still slightly too big for him despite how long he's owned it. The boy looks swamped, and not just by his clothes. His hair needs a cut – long brown strands that Ricky reaches over to sweep from his eyes. Josh glances at him, and Ricky wishes he could sweep the gaze away, too. It is vacant, his son's thoughts elsewhere. With his mother, perhaps. Josh seems to spend more time with her now than he does in the real world. Ricky pulls the boy into a sudden embrace, hugging him tight.

'I know this has been hard,' he says quietly to him, bending down to kiss the top of his head, 'but I promise, I'm going to make us a family again.'

Rhonda points to the clock on the wall. 'They're going to miss the bus.'

Ricky nods and steps back, watching his children as they file out the front door. 'Have a good day, you two,' he calls after them. 'And Harriet, look after your brother!'

She waves as they trudge down the front path towards the street. Ricky watches them until they vanish from sight. Then he turns and picks up his rucksack.

'I'll be late too if I'm not careful,' he says to Rhonda. 'I'll swing by the store on my way back. Anything you want?'

She looks at him, not bothering to hide her disdain now the children are gone. 'Make sure and pick up some fruit. Josh wants apples – red ones, though, nothing too sour.'

'I know what kind of apples Josh likes.'

'Well, good for you.'

Ricky forces himself to swallow down whatever remark was working its way up. He smiles and heads out the front door.

*

Ricky runs through his mental checklist. He has a lot to do today.

First up – car rental.

'What's your valet service like on these things after people are done?' he asks the guy behind the Avis desk.

The man smiles warmly. 'Don't worry, sir. We deep clean every vehicle as soon as it's returned. I can assure you, there won't be any trace of the previous user.'

Ricky is pleased to hear this.

Afterwards, he drives his rented Honda west across the city to a hardware store in Hillwood where he loads up on the essentials: rope, mainly, along with some thick blankets, a couple of anchor points and some wall screws, a metal door bolt and a roll of heavy-duty duct tape. They have a decent set of binoculars at a good price, and he gets them, too. An electrical outlet a few doors down is advertising a full home-security CCTV system that Ricky knows would come in handy, but he has neither the time nor the money right now to buy and set it all up.

Never mind. It's something he can work on.

Finally, he climbs back into his rental car and heads east, an hour outside the city, back to Burgess Falls. He has to prepare the cabin.

Originally, Ricky had planned to visit a local Walgreens or CVS, somewhere he could pick up a box of pills or a bottle of something. Medication he could grind up and put into a syringe or maybe pour over a cloth. Stuff strong enough to knock the kid out, insurance in case there was a struggle. Part of him had wondered – hoped, even – that the kid had shared his dream and was waiting for Ricky to show up, that he would come with him willingly. But that was only part of him, and the rest didn't agree.

So he'd spent an evening trawling the yellow pages, searching for somewhere that would help, trying to ask confused pharmacists what he was looking for without alerting their suspicions. On his third call, he'd spoken to a man with a deep voice who paused for too long after Ricky finished speaking. Ricky had hung up the phone before the man had even answered, and he hadn't dared try anyone else.

It didn't matter. There were simpler ways to incapacitate someone. All you really had to do was restrict their airflow for a couple of minutes and they'd be out cold. A plastic bag would do the job just fine.

By the time Ricky arrives at the cabin it's nearly noon. He works quickly, stripping one of the beds and moving the mattress and sheets down to the cellar, along with the thick blankets and most of the rope. Above the makeshift bed, he screws the pair of chunky metal anchors into the wall and loops a section of rope through. Ricky's never been great at DIY, but when he pulls on the rope he's pleased to see the anchors don't move.

He screws the new bolt across the cellar door. The humidity has caused the wooden frame to swell and the door to stick – a problem they've lived with every summer – but there's no time to start sanding it down now, and besides, Ricky wouldn't rightly know where to start.

When he finishes at last, his stomach is rumbling. He should have made a packed lunch for himself before he left the house, only that might have prompted Rhonda to ask questions that he really couldn't have faced today.

He checks his watch: 1 p.m. There's still one last thing to take care of, but he decides he's got time to pop into a store and pick up a sandwich. Josh asked for red apples anyway, and Ricky could do with the plastic bag.

St Thomas's is a large middle school out in Inglewood, not far from a small waterway called Cooper Creek. Marjory always thought of this part of Nashville as a low-key mystery; a quiet suburb that was somehow just twenty minutes out from the heart of Music City. It was a place she always wanted to live, but Ricky continually brushed her off. He liked the bustle of downtown, where the tourists swarmed the honky-tonks and crowds of thousands poured into Vanderbilt Stadium every other week to watch the Commodores play.

Marjory, of course, would push back. She would say that he wasn't twenty-one any more. That he didn't even go *out* to the very honky-tonks he insisted on being so close to. Then Ricky would make a point of going down to Broadway for a beer and a bourbon and the argument would go away for another couple of months.

Now, in his rented Honda, Ricky drives slow through the calm streets. The homes here are picturesque – large gardens with double driveways and basketball hoops, front porches and swinging seats and second-storey balconies that wrap themselves all the way around. Now, as he nears the school, he sees a little of what Marjory was maybe talking about.

He parks a street over from St Thomas's, where he can see a tight glimpse of blue in the distance; the Cumberland river, snaking a detour through Tennessee on its long journey west from Harlan County.

The school itself is pretty big. An old redbrick building, it makes Ricky think of something he's seen on one of those History Channel movies about the civil war. Tall pillars by the entrance that run nearly to the roof and a clock tower that looms over the whole area. It's a hell of a lot nicer than the middle school *he* went to, anyway.

Ricky reaches into his inside pocket and pulls out his new notebook. He checks his watch – 2 p.m., plenty of time – and settles down on a patch of grass across from the school. It's a good spot; close enough to see the layout of the place, but far enough away to avoid anyone spotting him (or at least thinking he's suspicious).

He spends nearly an hour sitting there. He sketches the parking lot, marking entrances and exits with large arrows whenever he sees someone using them. He maps out the road he drove in on, and where he should leave his car. He looks at the wide windows that stretch across the front of the building, where distant figures walk back and forth, and he wonders if one of them is the boy from his dream.

Deep in thought, Ricky loses track of the time until the bell in the large clock tower above the school starts ringing. He starts a little, his pen skittering across the page. It's 2.50 p.m. – he should leave before the neighbourhood starts filling with yellow buses and anxious parents in their station wagons. Besides, his trip has served its purpose.

Ricky closes his notebook and slides it back into his inside pocket. Rocking to his feet, he groans a little as he feels his joints pop, but by the time he's reached his car there's a smile on his face and a lightness in his step. He turns back to the school, to those big windows and the shadow-figures that move beyond them.

'See you Friday,' Ricky says quietly.

Chapter Five

The next few days pass slowly. Ricky goes through the motions: making sure the kids get to school on time, giving up his seat on the bus for that old woman with the blue jacket, getting changed in the freezing break room before shuttling cars around a parking lot for seven hours. He is running on autopilot, his mind unable to focus properly on anything but what is going to happen on Friday night.

People notice. His boss, Walter, asks him how he's feeling and Ricky just about blows it.

'The food poisoning,' Walter prompts.

'Oh,' Ricky says, smiling, 'I feel much better now.'

And Walter gives him this look that says he knows. He knows Ricky never had food poisoning, but hey, the guy's wife just died, so if he wants to spend a day crying his eyes out and telling people he ate a bad meatball, then so be it. Walter knows he's lying, but Walter understands – or at least he thinks he does.

At home, time seems to move even slower. Ricky sits at the dinner table, talking to Josh and Harriet but is barely able to hear himself speak. He looks at drawings they bring back from school, listens to stories of their lunch breaks. He eats the food that Rhonda serves them and he eats her disgusting attitude, too. It used to be that she would at least pretend, put on a show for the kids. He wonders if she has stopped pretending, or if she never pretended at all. He wonders if he's starting to see things differently now. The way things have always been, perhaps.

On Thursday morning – the day before the main event – Ricky receives a letter in the post. It is a payout from Marjory's life insurance policy. He had forgotten all about it. Ricky sits on his bed and reads the letter and folds the cheque carefully into his wallet. He knows it's a lot of money, he knows it is easily more than he has ever seen written down on a cheque before. But there is more to it than just the amount.

Life insurance doesn't pay out, he thinks to himself, *if you're a suspect.*

Ricky wonders if this will help with Rhonda. If it will convince her of his innocence.

And then, on Friday morning, on the day of the big show – *St Thomas's High School is proud to present: The Wizard of Oz! Follow the Yellow Brick Road and come on down this Friday. Singing is optional, fun is guaranteed!* – Ricky waves goodbye to Josh and Harriet and returns to his bedroom to collect his rucksack and finds Rhonda there. She is sitting on his bed, on his side of the bed, hunched forward. Reading.

His bedside drawer is open.

She turns at the sound of him. Her face is hard, her features cold and set in place. She stands and lifts the book.

The notebook.

'What is this?' she asks.

Ricky is frozen in the doorway. The sight of his mother-in-law going through his personal possessions is one thing, but the *notebook.*

'Are you going to answer me?' Rhonda says, and starts flicking through pages. 'You've drawn a map of a school, Ricky. With entrances and exits, you understand? You know the sort of people that do this?'

'I know.' He finally finds his voice. 'It's not that.'

'It's not what, Ricky?'

'What you think. It's not what you think.'

'I mean, you do know the sort of people who want to sneak into schools.'

'I know, Rhonda.'

'*Paedophiles*, Ricky. Paedophiles sneak into schools.'

'I *know*, Rhonda.'

'Were you planning on going down there? Is that it? Were you going to go down there tomorrow and watch the children getting changed?'

'Of course not. I'm working tomorrow.'

It's a weird response. Ricky's sweating a little now. His mind frantically trying to work out how he can get out of this, what combination of words he can say to smooth this over. The scar on his left arm tingles, and he scratches it.

Rhonda curls her lip. 'There's something wrong here, Ricky. There's always been something wrong here. With you, with what happened to my daughter.'

'With Marjory?'

Ricky blinks and sees her again. Standing on the edge of the cliff. Sighing, worming herself backwards.

I think we¾

'Marjory was an accident,' he says quickly, and he pulls out his wallet and the life insurance cheque. He holds it up in trembling fingers. 'You see? They paid out, Rhonda. They paid out. They don't *do* that if they think I had some involvement in it.'

Rhonda stares at him. He's still saying all the wrong things, Ricky knows this, can hear himself, can hear the words and he wants to

97

cringe they're so wrong. He's getting boxed in now, his mind moving too slowly to counter Rhonda's attacks. He feels clumsy and light-headed. He feels like she's forcing his hand and she doesn't even know it.

His mother-in-law tosses the notebook onto the bed. 'I think I'm owed some kind of explanation for all this, don't you? Ricky? Ricky, are you even listening to me?'

But Ricky isn't listening to her. All Ricky can hear is the roar of the waterfalls. He is lost in their power, in their primal force, and it builds now in his head, it drowns out everything around it. As loud now as it was on that day up on Burgess Falls. He can still see his wife's face as she pinwheels backwards, can still see her mouth – open and screaming only there's no sound to that, either, because the waterfalls have drowned it, they've drowned it, the waterfalls have drowned *everything*.

I think we have to shut her up, Ricky.

And Ricky nods, grateful to just let the roar take over completely, as he steps into the room and closes the door softly behind him.

Chapter Six

The school parking lot is full.

Ricky surveys it from a block away, his rental tucked down a quiet side street. It is 7.20 p.m., and the dusk air is warm tonight. September in Nashville has always been Ricky's favourite time of year; an all-too-brief few weeks where the summer heat finally loses its edge, where you can work outside all day and not worry about getting burned, then come home and drink a beer in your yard without wearing a sweater. Ricky knows to enjoy this month while it lasts – soon it will be October, and the winter chill will begin to settle itself over the city. He makes a mental note to fix the heating in the cabin before then. The last thing he wants is for anyone to freeze to death in the cellar.

Ricky checks his watch. Just over five minutes to go. He stretches a little, feeling his back pop pleasingly, feeling the reassuring heft of the notebook moving in his jeans pocket. For most of this week, Ricky has been wondering what it would be like – here, now, in these final moments. Whether he would be nervous or excited or scared. He thinks he maybe feels a combination of all three.

He glances at his watch again, his heart rate increasing as the minute hand finally drags itself into place. It is now 7.30 p.m., and when Ricky looks back at the school he sees a sudden glow of light:

the main doors are swinging open and people are spilling out into the balmy evening. He raises his binoculars and trains them on those doors. His hands tremble a little and he braces his elbow on the roof of his car to steady them. A rush of faces passing by – adults, children, people in costume. Ricky tries to focus on their faces but they are moving too quickly. He starts to panic, starts to worry that placing his blind trust in all this might have been a mistake.

The crowd is dispersing rapidly now, everyone moving quickly to their cars. Parents desperate to get home, their backs breaking from sitting in those little plastic chairs for an hour and a half, a wasted evening spent watching their son or daughter stand at the side of the stage dressed as a tree. If they hurry, maybe they can get home in time to catch the end of *SportsCenter* or the latest episode of *NYPD Blue*.

And then, just as Ricky's panic is threatening to overcome him, just as he's ready to toss the binoculars and drive home, dream be damned, something catches his eye. Something that glitters in the sweep of a car's headlights. Something silver – that strange, metallic garb that the boy was wearing in the dream. Ricky's gaze snaps to it, and he almost cries out as he watches the child (*his* child!) being led away from the school by a woman. The mother, presumably. She is gripping his hand tight, pulling him towards their car so hard that her son is practically having to run to keep up.

Ricky feels it stirring in him again. That same sense of purpose, that same lightness in his chest that tells him what he is doing is *right*. He wonders what sort of life the boy has, and finds it scarily easy to imagine. He pictures the mother crouching down, shoving her finger in the child's face. He pictures her slapping him, pictures her passed out on the sofa, pictures her bringing strange men home in the middle of the night, pictures the boy crying himself to sleep listening to sounds coming from the adjacent bedroom that no child should hear; the sound of screams, the sound of furniture being jolted, of front doors slamming and women weeping. Ricky's grip on the binoculars becomes so hard that not even his elbow on the car roof can stop them from shaking.

He climbs in and tosses them onto the front passenger seat. The boy and his mother are in a white Corolla. Ricky tracks it as it leaves the parking lot and joins the steady thrum of traffic on the main road. They pass him as they cross the intersection – close enough for him to see the glower on the mother's face. He waits until two more cars have passed by and then he pulls out behind them.

They drive like this for twenty minutes. Along Kennedy Avenue towards Greenfield, towards the Gallatin Pike. Ricky keeps his distance. His hands are still trembling a little on the steering wheel and when he rolls it to turn the car he can feel how sweaty his palms are, too.

He knows this is no good. If he's too hopped up he's liable to make a mess. It's one thing to be a cog in the machine – it's another to jam the machine up completely.

I think we need to relax a little, Ricky.

Ricky nods and forces himself to breathe steadily. He focuses on the cars in front. On the murals at the side of the road – whales and wolves that watch him pass by. An outstretched hand with a human eye in the centre; a tattoo parlour, maybe. He eases his grip on the steering wheel and by the time he passes under the old CSX railroad trestle his tension has sunk away.

Nearing downtown, the traffic starts to build. Ricky slows, still hanging back a little from the car in front, still keeping the edge of the white Corolla in view. He spends a couple of blocks like this until he notices a car riding on his rear bumper. A large, red-faced man sits behind the wheel who, when Ricky makes eye contact with him in the mirror, starts gesticulating wildly. His meaning is clear: *Close the gap, asshole.*

Ricky feels the panic starting to build again. Too scared to lose sight of the Corolla, he ignores the man and leaves a couple of car lengths in front. He senses motion in his mirror but keeps looking forward.

Suddenly there is the blast of a car horn. The man sounds like he's damn near standing on it.

Noise floods the air, a continuous angry stream. Ricky sees with dismay that the people in the cars ahead of him are starting to turn around. They are going to see him – they are going to *remember* him. Already a little girl is staring. One of the pupils from the school, no doubt.

He makes a split-second decision and rolls his car forward, raising his hand in deference to the driver behind him. The horn finally stops just as the white Corolla slides out of view. Ricky mutters a swear word under his breath.

Then, as they near a junction with a large Kroger supermarket on the corner, Ricky spots the white Corolla break from the line of traffic, swinging left towards Rolling Acres. He indicates quickly and pulls out. Luckily the car behind him stays on the pike. Within a few seconds, he is alone with his target, the pair of them driving deeper and deeper into a tight labyrinth of narrow lanes.

Ricky tries to maintain his distance, but it's getting harder to disguise what he's doing. His clock reads nearly 8 p.m., and in the fading light his headlamps are like beacons.

And then the Corolla abruptly jerks to one side, skidding a little before straightening up. A blow-out in their rear tyre – Ricky can see the car sagging. The woman slows, pulling over to the side of the tight road and turning on her hazards.

Ricky does likewise. This is it.

He exits his car and begins walking towards them. His left arm itches with excitement. It is quiet here, far from the main roads and the busy traffic. The lane itself is hemmed in on both sides by high walls – high enough even to block out any view from the nearest window. It is a perfect spot.

Halfway there, the driver's door swings open and he hears the boy's mother cursing as she climbs out.

'Need a little help?' Ricky calls, his pace steady as he approaches. He can hear the crunch of crisp leaves under his work boots.

She looks over at him. An expression on her face that Ricky knows is relief. It tells him that this woman has never changed a tyre before, but that everything is going to be all right. Someone is here to help her.

'Oh, thank you for stopping,' she says, sweeping her long blond hair back over her head. 'I've got a puncture. I don't suppose you could help me out?'

'Have you got a spare in the trunk?'

'I think so.'

'Well, why don't you pop it open and let's take a look.'

She clasps her hands together and rushes over to the rear of the car. Through the glass, Ricky can see the boy, watching.

The woman is still talking as she digs around in her trunk. 'You know people throw their trash out in these lanes? I bet it was a broken bottle. I swear, I keep saying that the police need to do something about it, but all they ever do is put up more signs. Like that ever makes a difference.'

When Ricky doesn't reply, she turns to look at him. Her gaze goes to the tyre iron he's clutching in his right hand.

'Oh, I see you came prepared,' she says, laughing. A little nervously, maybe.

Ricky smiles. 'I'm learning,' he says.

His first swing manages to snap her head back, sending her eyes rolling as her jaw breaks. She half falls into the trunk but somehow manages to stay upright. The second swing – downward, this time

– crumples her completely. She folds in on herself and Ricky bundles her neatly into the trunk.

He breathes out slowly, letting the adrenaline settle. When he checks her pulse, he's pleased to discover that she's dead. And in only two blows this time.

I think we're improving.

Ricky thinks so, too.

Before he's able to congratulate himself too much, however, the sound of someone scrambling around inside the car draws his attention. Closing the trunk, Ricky sees the boy in the back seat working the door handle, desperately trying to open it. *Thank goodness for child locks,* Ricky muses to himself, as he slides the tyre iron back into his pocket and pulls out the plastic bag.

Chapter Seven

The boy has been awake for a while now.

Ricky can hear him from the kitchen, where he's sat waiting for the pan of chicken soup to finish warming on the stove. It's not the heartiest of meals, he knows that, just as he knows that the cellar is colder than he would have liked, but he only had so much time to work with after the dream. It would have been helpful if his midnight meeting with the kid had been a few weeks earlier – hell, even a couple more days – but you don't always get things handed to you on a plate.

Nothing worthwhile is ever easy, he tells himself. A slogan he had read a few years ago in a self-help book that Marjory had bought him for Christmas. She'd handed it to him along with a pair of socks, a bottle of bourbon, and the words, 'Maybe this will help you be more ambitious,' while simultaneously cradling the silver bracelet he'd burned half a month's salary on.

Most of the book had been pretty worthless (he'd tossed it into the trash halfway through and lied about finishing it) but for some reason that line had always stuck with him. That, and the feeling of complete worthlessness every time he'd seen it sitting on his bedside table.

The boy is quieter now than he was earlier. He started yelling after he woke up, brave words like 'asshole' and 'creep', but Ricky could hear a crack in his voice like the San Andreas fault. That stage had lasted about a half hour, after which the boy had started making these sad, whimpering noises, and Ricky thought he was maybe crying.

The chicken soup is bubbling on the stove now, but Ricky barely notices. His body might be in the cabin but his mind is an hour down the dirt road, in the back of a parked car on the side of a deserted lane. He can't unsee the image of the boy's face inside the bag. The way his little mouth had opened wide, a perfect 'O', and how the plastic had made a tight wall against his lips as he'd sucked in what little air he could.

It's the sound of the soup boiling over the side of the pot that finally brings him back. He takes it off the stove, pours the steaming liquid into two large bowls and places them both onto a tray, along with some thick, crusty bread and a tall glass of milk. The swollen cellar door sticks hard this time, and Ricky has to jerk it upwards to get it to open.

A cool, gentle breeze rushes up to greet him. The hairs on his bare arms rise as he descends. The bowls of soup and the glass of milk rattle a little on the tray, their contents rippling. He can still hear the boy whimpering, but it quietens as Ricky approaches, and by the time he reaches the bottom the room is silent.

The boy is curled up on the mattress, his little arms tied at the wrists to a single length of rope, which Ricky has fed through the metal anchors in the wall. He is still dressed in his silver costume, although there is a pile of fresh clothes next to him. The child's light brown hair is messy and his dark eyes are rimmed with red. There is the faint smell of urine coming from him, or maybe from the bucket by his bed.

Ricky sets the tray down on the floor by the mattress. The boy shrinks back as he does so, and Ricky feels his heart ache.

'It's all right,' he says gently, 'I'm not going to hurt you.'

He isn't sure what else to say. He knows what he *wants* to say, what he would like to get across to the young boy – that all this was preordained, that he knows how bad the boy's life was before, that everything is going to be better now – but he cannot find the right words. Ricky has never been good with words.

So instead he takes his bowl of soup and a little bread, and leaves the rest for the boy. He sits on the lone chair in the centre of the room and starts to eat. The soup is hot, and Ricky winces as he burns the roof of his mouth.

The boy watches him for a long while, until Ricky has nearly finished his bowl. He barely moves the entire time. His costume is thin and the cellar is cold, and Ricky knows how uncomfortable he must be.

'If I untie you,' Ricky says, mopping up the last of his meal with some bread, 'do you promise not to try to run?'

The boy says nothing.

'If you promise,' Ricky continues, 'you could put on some of those warmer clothes. But you'd have to let me tie you up again after. What do you say?'

For a long moment, the boy continues to say nothing. Then, at last, he nods.

Ricky smiles.

Once the boy has pulled a thick woollen sweater and sweatpants over his silver costume, and when his restraints have been locked back in place, Ricky offers him the bowl of soup again. This time the boy takes it.

'What's your name?' Ricky asks, returning to his chair. 'I'm Ricky.'

The boy pauses between mouthfuls. 'Scott,' he says quietly. Then, 'Is my mom all right?'

'Well it's very nice to meet you, Scott. And don't you worry about your mom. She's just fine.'

Ricky wants to ask if the boy had a dream, same as him, but is scared he might laugh at him. He suddenly thinks back to those other boys who laughed at him; the boys who would taunt him, who would write dirty words on pieces of paper and slip them through the gaps into his school locker.

Scott is eating faster now, clearly hungry. Ricky's smile grows wider as he watches the kid dunking his bread into the warm soup.

'There's more in the pot if you want it,' he says.

Scott doesn't say anything, he just keeps eating. His eyes dart around the room, taking everything in. The large washer-dryer against one wall, the camping equipment piled up next to it. The stairs that lead back up to the cosy kitchen and the wide expanse of Burgess Falls.

Every so often, Ricky sees Scott's gaze snap to the back corner. Ricky knows what he's looking at: the skinny object bound in plastic. He doesn't think the boy can really tell what it is – he used nearly an entire roll of plastic sheeting wrapping Rhonda up, and that's almost a hundred feet – but even so, he makes a mental note to take care of her properly in the morning.

'When can I go home?'

Scott is staring at him now, his soup half-finished, the bowl hanging forward. Ricky wants to tell him to be careful or he will spill it over the mattress.

'Soon,' Ricky says, leaning forward to lift the bowl straight. 'Very soon. Now finish your soup. If you don't want any more, I've got hot chocolate and a slice of apple pie I can warm up. I might even have some ice cream in the freezer.'

Of course, Ricky has no intention of letting the boy go home – soon or otherwise. As far as Ricky is concerned, the boy *is* home. He knows it might take a while, but he also knows that he's following the path laid out for him. It is his role now to give Scott a life, a *better* life, and once the boy realises this then he won't *want* to go back. He'll want to stay with Ricky, and – eventually – with Josh and Harriet, too.

I think we're going to make a very happy family together.

But it is a plan filled with problems and pitfalls, so many that even Ricky can see them. Countless ways he could be discovered – a passing hiker, a delivery driver, a loose knot or an unlocked door. He knows it will take time for Scott to accept his new life, just as he knows that the longer it takes, the larger the likelihood of something going wrong.

So it is perhaps not surprising to discover that something *will* go wrong, and far sooner than Ricky fears. Scott was taken from his murdered mother's car on a warm Friday evening in mid-September, but by the dawn of the following Thursday he will be dead.

16

NATHAN

Nathan set the pages down. He couldn't read any further. Not yet.

He was still at the cabin. Still sat on the sofa in the same position he'd been in for over an hour. Cross-legged, hunched forward. He could feel tiredness closing in on him. Stalking him like a predator. He felt like he was going to be sick.

The manuscript was utterly unlike any of Lucas Cole's previous work. There was no sex, for one thing. No lurid paragraphs of female sidekicks admiring themselves in the mirror and describing what they saw. No male hero cracking skulls or unloading automatic machine guns. In their place was an intimacy that Nathan hadn't expected. An openness that his father had never shown in life.

It is not a confession, Lucas Cole had written, and it wasn't. Not really. Not in any way that Nathan remembered. But there *was* truth in it. Broad strokes, perhaps – he didn't believe for one moment that his father had encountered his victims in dreams, nor had his mother fallen to her death from a cliffside – but truth, nonetheless. A fictional story told through the twisted perspective of a real-life serial killer.

The biggest change, of course, was his father himself. Ricky Taylor was written like a meek, timid man. A man forced into becoming a saviour of lost souls. A father who seemed to suffer from a personality disorder, who hid his true self from his family, who was bound by forces beyond his control and craved understanding from a world that would never give it.

Lucas Cole – the real Ricky Taylor – couldn't have been more different. He had never run his hand through his son's hair in that loving fashion, never pulled him into an embrace. Any affection that man had inside him had been directed elsewhere: towards Kate, towards his *other* children. Nathan remembered watching his father stroke the face of a little girl with such tenderness it had almost made him cry. The only times his father had put his hands on *him* was to grip his arms, to lift him up over his shoulder, to carry him to his study where the smell of what was to come next hung thick in the air, the lit cigarette dangling off the edge of the crystal ashtray on the small table by the chair. His father's chair, where his father would sit, and order his son to strip, and order his son to choose where he wanted it. And Nathan would offer his arm, or his leg, or his back, and he would close his eyes and wait and think of blue skies or the way the school bus shook when the doors closed or the sound the taps made as the bath filled or anything other than his father stroking the face of that little girl, because he knew thinking of that would only make him cry, and if he cried then his father would start over, and this time he wouldn't let Nathan choose where.

It was too much. He'd been awake for twenty-four hours straight and his mind was shot. It was sensory overload; his father's death, the missing girl. All those trophies. He laid his head down and surrendered to it.

When he woke it was late morning. His back ached and his stomach growled, but his hands had stopped shaking so maybe that was progress. The battery indicator in his cell phone was lit up red; of course his charger was back at the hotel.

He tried calling his sister. Like him, Kate had been forced to learn the truth about their father at a young age. Like him, she'd seen the headlines and the news reports growing up, had heard the adults murmuring each time a child went missing. Like him, she'd been aware of it and had kept dutifully quiet. If Nathan was complicit in allowing their father to kidnap and murder children, then so was she.

But she was also the only other person in the world that he could talk to about it – which was probably why he hadn't spoken to her in over a decade. It was easier to just pretend that it never happened. Easier to simply ignore the guilt and shame that washed through him on a daily basis, a torrent of it, so much he sometimes thought he might drown in it. And when it got too much, when that deluge rose too high, then he was forced to drive it out: a blade across his forearm, a naked flame against his thigh. Sometimes more, sometimes a lot more. The white-hot pain masking everything, allowing nothing, peeling him open and draining the filth from inside him until he was a hollow shell once more.

And even though it was easier, it wasn't *easy*, living like this. Waking in the night with a scream and not knowing if it had come from you or a young boy twenty years ago, never able to open up to anyone, to share your life with anyone, to truly be yourself with anyone. Never able to settle down or fall in love, and maybe that was a punishment and maybe that was how it should be. Maybe that was what he deserved, this difficult life, because at the end of the day it *was* life, something his father had taken from so many others, something he and Kate had helped him do by keeping quiet.

So he would let the mire grow inside him and then he would empty himself and the cycle would begin again, and it was only easier to live this way because the alternative was not living at all, and as much as

Nathan had been a coward as a boy he was a coward as a man, too, and not living at all was simply too frightening to contemplate.

Did that mean his father was brave? Nathan supposed that it must, because sliding a noose around your neck required courage, and courage was something Nathan had never known.

'*This is Kate. Leave me a message.*'

He did. Garbled sentences, his brain still waking up. 'Call me back,' he finished, ending the call just as his phone died.

Moving into the kitchen, he hunted quickly for anything he could eat for breakfast. Came across a half-eaten packet of soft crackers and some tins of chicken soup, their labels faded and starting to peel. He let them be.

Nathan stared at the shoebox and knew what he had to do next. Someone needed to go through the trophies, someone had to put a face to each of the names. Someone had to piece together what his father had been doing these past seventeen years.

But he couldn't do it here, in Burgess Falls, where the stillness was an audible thrum, where the cellar door lay ajar even though he was sure he'd closed it last night. But of course he couldn't have. Not properly. He was alone in the house, after all.

Nathan made the drive back to Nashville in a little over an hour. In his hotel room he showered for an age, the water as hot as he could stand. He scrubbed himself clean and when he was done his body was red and his skin felt tight. The towel was soft, softer than he was used to. It moved the water around rather than drying him and when he dressed he could feel the dampness on his clothes. In the mirror he caught sight of himself, of the neat rows of circular scars that peppered his arms. He pulled on a long-sleeved sweater and went to find something to eat.

When he finally arrived at Kate's apartment it was nearly 3 p.m. His sister lived in a small, two-bedroom condominium over in Bellevue. The middle floor of a three-storey building, all red brick and white panelling. Rows of balconies just big enough to stand on. Cramped and hemmed in, it made Nathan think of a cheap motel, which made him think of The View, of his father, of the chipped paint on the bathroom door, of how it might feel to slide a rough piece of rope around your neck.

He had to double-check the apartment number. The corridor there was dirty. There was dog shit on the floor by the entrance and a smell like someone had been living there. When he knocked on the door it was answered by a short, balding man dressed in an apron and slippers, who looked at him quizzically before breaking out into a smile.

'You must be Nathan,' he said, his hand outstretched.

'I suppose I must be,' Nathan said, shaking his hand and smiling even though it was the last thing he wanted to do. He wanted to turn and run out of this tight corridor. Past the dog shit and away from the smell, that horrible, cloying smell of human existence that was still so strong in his nose he didn't know how anyone else could stand it, how this man in front of him couldn't smell it, how it didn't make him sick.

'You're early,' the man said. 'We weren't expecting you for another few hours.'

'Yeah, sorry about that. Is Kate in? I need to speak with her.'

'Absolutely, please come in. I'm Bruce, by the way. I've been really looking forward to meeting you.'

'Likewise,' Nathan said.

This was a lie, of course, and part of him wanted to say this, to blurt it out loud. *I'd rather not be here, Bruce.* Or maybe, *I've never given you a single thought.* Or maybe, *So you're the kind of man that marries someone like my sister.*

Because really, what kind of man *did* marry someone like Kate? Kate, who had always looked down her nose at him, who had sneered at him for crying after their mother had passed, who had spent most of her teenage years growing up in her bedroom – alone, like she thought it made her seem tough, always on the phone or sneaking out her window to meet boys. And look at her now. Look who she had ended up with. *Bruce.* A rotund man with thinning hair who was probably half as old as he looked – and maybe he was nice, Nathan didn't necessarily think Bruce was an asshole, but he was clearly a doormat because that was the only type of man that Kate was ever going to end up with. All those boys she hung around with growing up? They weren't the sort to fall under someone's thumb. They were the sort who gave as good as they got. Physically, emotionally. Good for a brief moment but nothing more. They were Kate's equals, and Kate could never settle for someone who might one day get the better of her.

Then Bruce stepped back and Nathan moved inside the apartment. The living room was small and strangely bare. The walls still white like they'd just moved in. It was a show house: no pictures on the walls, no rugs on the wooden floor. No personality.

'Hi, Nate.'

And there she was. His sister, seventeen years older but still unmistakable. The same blond hair bunched up in tight curls, the same deep-set blue eyes, the same serious expression. Her eyebrows peaked as she studied him, assessing whether he was the same snivelling boy she'd last seen boarding a Greyhound in the rain, his dark hair matted to his scalp.

He remembered staring back at her as the bus had pulled away from the station; she'd been sitting in their father's car, their eyes meeting one last time through panes of glass. A look on her face that he'd carried ever since. Sadness for his leaving; envy for his escape. He saw glimpses of it again, now, and for a moment he was back on that bus, clutching his rucksack to his chest, watching a storm tear apart the sky.

'How are you?' she asked.

Nathan held up the shoebox. 'We need to talk,' he said.

17

'Can I get anyone a coffee?' Bruce asked. He looked over at Nathan and beamed. 'I just got a new machine the other week. Grinder, milk frother, the works. I can do you a cappuccino if you'd like?'

Nathan gave a weak smile. 'Regular coffee's fine.'

Bruce clapped his hands together and shuffled out the room, humming to himself.

'He seems nice,' Nathan said.

'He is nice,' Kate said. 'He's good for me.'

'How long have you been together?'

'A long while now.'

'Does he know?'

'About what? Daddy?' She crossed the room and sank into a large armchair. 'What do *you* think, Nate?'

She reached up and flicked at the edges of her blond curls. A nervous tic she'd had as a child. Nathan's eyes went to her wrist; a white bandage sitting under her sleeve.

'How's Sioux Falls?' she asked.

'Sioux Falls is fine,' he said. He sat down opposite her and placed the shoebox and manuscript on the large coffee table between them. 'But I'm not here to talk about Sioux Falls, Kate. I've seen the news. He was still doing it, wasn't he? Right till the end.'

Her gaze stayed level, refusing to dip.

The door swung open and Bruce reappeared. If there was an air of tension, he didn't seem to notice. He was carrying a tray of mugs and he set them down on the table, nodding at the shoebox.

'Old family photos?'

'Something like that,' Nathan said.

'And my goodness, is *The Midnight King* what I think it is?'

Nathan glanced at the manuscript uneasily. Perhaps he shouldn't have left it out.

Bruce was getting excited now. 'You know I've read every one of your dad's books? I have them all in my office upstairs, don't I, Kate?'

'Yes, you do.'

'Some of them are even signed. *Shoot First*, that was a good one. So was *Concealed Carry* and *Nuclear Football*. I even liked *Rust Belt Revenge*, although I thought it was a little preachy at times. What's your favourite, Nathan?'

'I've never read them.'

'You're kidding!'

Kate cleared her throat. Bruce laughed and held his hands up. 'Message received, dear. You two've got catching up to do, and here I am, prattling on as usual. Anyway, I've just put a lovely cut of beef in the oven which I need to keep an eye on. And Nathan, I didn't know how you liked your coffee, but there's some milk and sugar there if you want it.'

'I don't, but thank you.'

Nathan picked up the steaming cup. Bruce, still beaming, wiped his hands down the front of his apron and headed back into the kitchen.

Kate waited until the door had closed again before her gaze dropped towards the shoebox. She stared at it in silence for a moment. Then, 'You've been home,' she said.

'The cabin, too. The missing girl . . . I had to check.'

'You should've called me, I'd have saved you the trip. I can't remember the last time anyone actually went there. You go into the cellar?'

Nathan's throat went dry at the memory. He could still feel the spackling paste on his fingertips. He took a sip of coffee. It wasn't half bad.

'Nothing but plasterboard and fresh paint,' he said.

'You know I've not been able to go back home since they found him,' Kate murmured. 'It's just too much.'

'Please. Dad poisoned that house. As far as I'm concerned, they should burn it to the ground.'

'Nate . . .'

'The cabin, too. Just wipe every trace of him off the face of the earth.'

Kate said nothing, her lips pressed into a tight line. It was now Nathan's turn to study her. He leaned forward.

'You two got close, didn't you? After I left.'

'I don't think Daddy ever let anyone get close,' Kate said, wiping her nose. 'But he liked spending time with me. He liked talking with me.'

'I can't imagine he enjoyed talking with anyone. Not beyond royalty cheques and book launches.'

'That's not fair. You didn't know him like I did. Not at the end.'

'I think I knew enough.'

She paused. 'He didn't blame you, you know.'

'What?'

'For leaving. He never blamed you.'

'Well I sure as hell blamed him.'

Kate sniffed and drew her legs up under her. 'I think he always regretted how things ended.'

'He could have tried to reach out. He had nearly twenty years to reach out. The man didn't care about me.'

'He did, Nate, he told me. He told me how he made you run—'

Nathan shook his head angrily. 'Stop, Kate. Made me run? He didn't have the first clue about why I ran. He thought it was because I was scared of him. *You* thought it was because I was scared of him.'

'You *were* scared of him. We both were. You want to talk about the night you left? It's burned into my brain, I'll never forget.'

She said it like he had. Like it wasn't burned into his brain, too. The spray of blood and the sound of his sister's scream. His father, lit up by lightning, crawling towards them across the kitchen floor.

He snatched up the shoebox. 'Instead of talking about why I left, why don't we talk about why I'm back?'

Kate stared at the cardboard box. 'We should get rid of that.'

'Oh, I'm sure Dad would approve. His kids still keeping his secrets, even after he's gone.'

'It's in the past, Nate. We need to let this go, move on.'

'Move on?' He laughed and shook the box. 'Have you seen inside this lately?'

She looked away. 'Not since I was a kid.'

'Then you might want to take a fresh look.'

He flipped the lid and upended it. Items spilled out onto the coffee table. Glimpses of their father's faded handwriting on the labels. *Holly. Casey. Nadine.*

Thomas.

That last one still stung.

'More than you remember?' he said. 'Because it's certainly more than I do.'

She stared at the pile of trinkets and still – maddeningly still – she barely moved. Nathan watched her frozen expression and wondered what was going through her head. Was she angry at their father for what he'd done? Was she angry with *him* for bringing this into her home? Or was she resigned to it all? Seventeen years was a long time.

Maybe she'd been able to find peace, the sort that he never had.

Finally, she folded her arms and looked straight at him.

'What are you doing, Nate?'

He felt himself sag into his chair as her words landed. He struggled to find a response. 'What am I doing?' he echoed dumbly, and then, as anger flared inside him, he tossed the empty box onto the floor and repeated, 'What am I *doing*?'

'Okay, calm down, I don't want Bruce—'

'*Fuck Bruce.*' Nathan rose to his feet, his fingers curled inwards, held like claws by his side. 'He never stopped, Kate! All these years he kept going, and right under your nose!'

'Don't,' Kate said sharply, standing now too, her thin frame unfolding, her skinny arms shaking. 'Don't lecture me on the past. You have no idea what it's been like. You *left* us, Nate. You left *me*. You left me with him and I had to fend for myself so don't you dare come back here now and tell me that all of this is somehow my fault.'

'But it *is* your fault!' Nathan cried. 'And it's my fault too. What he did? What he made *us* do? Kate, we *allowed* him to do it!'

'Jesus, we were kids—'

'We could have told someone.'

'And then what? Daddy gets himself arrested and we end up in foster care? Or juvie? Christ, you would have been sent straight to a psychiatric ward, you were a *mess* back then . . .'

'Oh, screw you.'

'I can see the scars on your wrist, Nate. Are they serious attempts or were you just looking for some attention?'

'How'd you hurt your arm?'

'I burned it on the stove.'

'You're such an asshole, you know that?'

She glared at him. 'Whatever. You want to blame me for what he's done? Go ahead. Go ahead and then *fuck off.* Take your guilt and your shame and whatever other poison you're carrying around and get it as far away from me as you can.'

'Kate—'

'At least I've accepted my part in all this. You ran away because you were scared. You were a little kid and you were scared and that's fine, but don't come home now and tell me different just because you feel bad for leaving.'

Nathan rubbed his forehead. The argument was spinning away from him, the points that had seemed so clear before were now muddled and confused. He clutched desperately at the first thing he could think of.

'I never meant to leave you behind with him,' he said quietly. 'You were at college, you were gone. You were free.'

'But I came back, Nate. You called me from a payphone with your last quarter and I came back.' She seemed to relax a little, all of a sudden. She wiped her eyes and sank back into her armchair. 'I had to come back so you could leave.'

Nathan sat too. He was so tired. He leaned forward and rifled through the scattered items. Picked out the red ribbons. They didn't have a name tag yet.

'You see these?' he said. 'You know who these belong to?'

Kate's face answered. She knew.

'That girl is out there,' he said, the ribbon trembling a little. 'Dad took her and then he killed himself and if someone doesn't find her soon then she'll die.'

'Oh, Nate, she's already dead.'

'You don't know that.'

'I know she's been gone what, eight days now? Nine? Daddy rarely kept them alive in that cabin longer than five.'

Kate reached up and started playing with the edges of her curls again. Her bandaged wrist moved awkwardly.

'She's been gone too long,' she said softly. 'If Daddy really did take her, then she's dead, Nate. She's been dead for days.'

Nathan started packing the items back into the shoebox. 'You don't know that,' he said again. 'Not for certain.'

Kate didn't respond. She just watched him as he collected everything and placed the lid back on the box.

'What are you going to do with them?' she asked.

'I don't know.' He went to pick up *The Midnight King* and then stopped, slid it towards her. 'You should read this,' he said.

And then he was moving. Back to the front door, the smell of roast beef floating through the air and the sound of Bruce in the kitchen. He was halfway gone when Kate spoke again.

'Dinner's still at seven, if you want it.'

He didn't know if he did. Didn't know if he didn't, either. So he just nodded and left quietly. Down that long corridor, past the dog shit and that awful stench and out into the bright afternoon sun. He collapsed into the driver's seat of the old station wagon, and for the first time since he'd heard about his father's death, he wept.

18

It was late afternoon by the time Nathan finally ate. An overpriced burger and fries, with pickles even though he'd asked for none, served on a metal tray and left outside his hotel room. He ate it at a small table by the window, hunched forward. He'd asked for a room that looked out onto the Cumberland river – there was something about moving water that Nathan had always found calming – but the third floor was too low to see over the trees that ran along the embankment. Instead, he was treated to a pretty decent view of Cooter's, the Dukes of Hazzard museum a couple of blocks away. The famous orange car was parked outside. Nathan didn't know what it was called.

When he was done eating, he took a can of Diet Coke from the minibar and just about drained it in one. Then he plugged in his cell phone, opened his laptop, and set the shoebox down on the bed beside him. He ran his fingers over the worn cardboard before lifting the lid.

At the top were those red ribbons. Chloe Xi's ribbons. He picked them up and placed them to one side. Stared down at what was left. Each item was a trophy, a token of his father's triumph. Taken from children who had been snatched from one family and brought to another. Children who had been kept chained to a wall; most of whom had fought back, who had been quietly strangled on a thin mattress in a dark cellar. Others who had behaved and been brought home to die all the same.

Nathan started with those he was sure of. He pulled up a list of his father's known victims, pored over their details and separated their trophies from the rest. Thirteen children, with names like *Blake* and *Joel* and *Olivia*. Thirteen children with thirteen items. Hair clips and cheap silver rings. A little toy train. A sock.

Some of them he remembered. Some of them weighed more than the rest. Nathan found himself holding onto the toy train, seemingly unable to put it down. It was wooden and cheaply made, its metal wheels loose and hanging at odd angles. He ran his thumb over the crudely carved smokestack and his skin caught on the rough edge as it had done a hundred times before.

The years melted away. He was nine years old and sitting in the middle of his room. Not fully understanding who the other boy was. The boy in the corner, huddled on the spare bed, his knees drawn up, his arms wrapped tight around his legs. Not fully understanding but not fully confused, either. A dim comprehension, like dawn light. They came from the cabin, these parentless children. They were brought by his father. They would share a bedroom, they would share a dinner table. And soon, in perhaps as little as a few days, they would be taken away again.

But before that they would bond, in that singular way only young children can. With barely a word being spoken. With only a look or a smile, or the offer of a toy. The boy's name was Thomas and he'd clutched the train tight in his fist. After a while he'd moved onto the floor to sit next to Nathan. He'd set his train down and silently moved it back and forth. Nathan had rolled a ball into it and knocked it over and Thomas had laughed, and just like that the spell had been broken. They'd spent the rest of the afternoon digging through the toy chest. Through *their* toy chest. Because it was now as much Thomas's as it was Nathan's.

A week later, Nathan would wake to find Thomas was gone.

The wooden train was under the bed, on its side. Nathan had taken it, played with it when he was sure he was alone, run his thumb over the smokestack again and again. He had tried to keep it hidden. Had told himself he was keeping it safe – for Thomas, for when he returned. At some point his father must have reclaimed it. He couldn't remember when.

He would ask his father questions. But later, much later. So much later that he must surely have already known the answers. He would ask where the children went after they left the house. He would ask about the others – the ones who stayed in the cabin, who ate leftovers from dinner packed into Tupperware boxes, who never made it into the house.

His father had gone quiet. Nathan's shoulders had tensed on reflex. Muscle memory, waiting for that iron-like grip to lift him up and carry him to the study. It had been a while since his last punishment, and the longer he went without one the surer he was that one was due.

But his father had instead sat him down and explained about the order of all things. He called it a *hierarchy*. He said that some children were able to climb it, to go from the cabin's cellar to the basement in the family home. He said that some children were special enough to be able to climb it even further – from the basement up to the main house. He said that one day, a child would climb all the way to the very top and stay there, and when that day came their family would finally be complete.

Sitting in his hotel room now, Nathan pushed the memories aside. He placed the wooden train down among the other trinkets, forcing himself not to dwell on them any further. He took a short break. He stretched and drank ice-cold water from the minibar. He knew this next part would be harder.

Six items still remained in the box. Six victims that no one had ever linked together. Six dead children that he had to find. Stacey, Arlo, Jessie, Robin, Harry, Dylan. Their tags written in his father's neat hand. He knew their names but it wasn't enough. It would never be enough.

He broke it down by county. Cross-referencing it with his father's recorded book launches and literary festivals, starting with Davidson and spiralling out. Wilson, Rutherford, Bedford, Marshall. There were so many. He pulled up lists of murdered children aged between nine and thirteen, discovered after December 2008. There were so many more.

He travelled outside Tennessee. Moving across state lines, following his father's digital footprints. West into Texas, into Arizona. Northwards to Montana and Washington State.

It took him nearly three hours to find who each remaining item belonged to. Pulling out a sheet of paper from his bag, he scribbled down the list of names. Nineteen in total. Thirteen his father had taken from the greater Nashville metropolitan area, six more he'd pursued across the country. Chloe Xi's name went at the end; an even twenty.

None of them were linked in any way beyond their age. Nathan had read the theories over the years; the newspaper stories and armchair psychiatrists positing that the Music City Monster targeted children because it was the only way he could become aroused. That he was a paedophile, even if he never sexually assaulted them.

But as far as Nathan knew, this wasn't the case. His father had only ever wanted another son or daughter to fold into his family. *The Midnight King* might have been about a man named Ricky Taylor, but that part at least was lifted straight from reality.

The list complete, Nathan folded it neatly in half. He stared at it, unsure about the next step. The more information he shared about his past – about his father – the more difficult things would get for him.

And not just for him, but for Kate, too. There would be questions, there would almost certainly be charges. As much as Kate believed it hadn't been their fault, Nathan wasn't so sure others would agree.

But there was an opportunity here to do the right thing. To do what he'd spent most of his life avoiding. Justice for all those dead children, justice for their murdered parents, justice for the man sitting on death row in his father's place. It had always been easier to just light a match and hold it close until the pain pushed everything else aside. And when that hadn't worked, when the deluge inside him rose so high it bubbled from his throat, then there'd been other methods to drain it. Methods he always swore he would never repeat. A promise to himself he would keep only until it happened again.

And sure, perhaps Lucas Cole was responsible for all that. Kate certainly believed it; in her eyes, they were both victims of their father. Another two names to add to the list. She would for ever see Nathan not as he was now, but as a frightened little boy, the same boy who had called her from a payphone in the rain, crying, begging her to come home and save him.

I didn't run because I was scared of you.

It was the mantra that had fuelled his anger towards his father these last few years. And it was true, at least on some level, but it was complicated too, and getting answers involved looking deep inside himself, and that was one place Nathan had no interest in going.

Packing the items back into the shoe box, he paused when he got to the ribbons. Chloe Xi was a local girl, which meant his father had returned to his original hunting ground. Maybe there was a reason for that, a connection he couldn't see. Maybe his father thought it was safe, that enough time had passed and enough people had forgotten about Edward Morrison. Or maybe Lucas Cole had simply gotten tired of driving halfway across the country each time he wanted to kill a child.

The clock on the wall said it was after 6 p.m. It wasn't late, but his body was tired. From sleeping on that old sofa, maybe. He just didn't have the energy to see Kate again tonight.

He went to slide the list of names into his pocket and found Isaac's card already there. He'd forgotten Isaac had ever handed it to him; their brief drink seemed like a lifetime ago now. After a moment he stuffed it back, along with the list, before picking up the keys to his father's station wagon and heading for the door.

He phoned his sister as he drove.

'Hi, Nate,' she said. Her voice was low; she sounded about as tired as him. He briefly wondered if Bruce was in the room with her. 'I know this afternoon was . . . Well, it was a lot.'

'Yeah, it was.'

'I never wanted to drag you through everything all over again. I'm sorry I lost my temper a little.'

'Me too,' he said, hearing the words and realising how much he meant them.

It was getting dark out, and he flicked his headlights on. The road was near empty ahead of him but he took it slow anyway. His window cracked, the warm air rushing over him. He'd forgotten how quiet the suburbs could get in this city, people pulled towards the neon glow of Broadway and 12 South. When they went, they took the very light with them.

'Listen, I'm not going to make dinner tonight,' he said.

Kate paused, then said, 'That's fine. I understand.'

'It's just . . .'

'A little too much right now?'

'Yeah, maybe.'

Nathan switched his cell to his other ear, bending his neck to pin it in place. His headlights lit up a gentle curve and the large houses that lined both sides of the road, most of them with their curtains drawn. He suddenly felt a little woozy.

'Hey, where's Dad being kept?' he asked.

'What?'

'Like, the funeral home, or whatever.'

'You want to go see him?'

Nathan rubbed his temple. He glanced down at the passenger seat, at the shoebox, thought about the folded list of names in his pocket. 'Yeah, I got stuff I need to say to him.'

Kate sighed and he thought he could hear her nodding. 'Sure, of course. He's at Gracehill, over in Blair Heights. It's late though, I'm not sure if they're open.'

'That's all right, I'll give them a call and check. Thanks.'

'Let me know if you want to talk more tomorrow, or in the morning before the funeral. But if you don't, it's all right. I get it.'

Nathan felt his throat tighten. He moved the cell away and swallowed noiselessly. 'I'll let you know,' he said. 'I've got to phone that funeral home.'

'Okay.'

He hung up and rolled his neck, wincing a little. He could feel the tension in his shoulders. Knots of the stuff, sitting just beneath his skin. He needed a proper night's sleep. He needed a proper night's sleep in a *bed*.

Waiting at traffic lights, he quickly looked up Gracehill. They were open until seven. He had time.

An older man with thin, greying hair answered the door at Gracehill Funeral Home. He gave a sad smile – one that he had undoubtedly perfected over the years – and ushered Nathan inside. He introduced himself as George; a first-name-only tactic that some people might have found endearing.

Like a lot of Nashville businesses, Gracehill operated out of a converted two-storey house in an area of the city that felt more like a suburb than anything else. It was nestled between an appliance repair shop and an advertising agency, and in what could only be described as an unfortunate irony, sat three doors down from a senior living complex.

At least they don't have far to go, Nathan had thought to himself as he drove past.

Now, inside the warm and inviting entrance hall of Gracehill, he refused the offer of coffee and asked if Lucas Cole was being kept here.

'Mr Cole?' George said. 'Yes, he is. Are you family?'

'I'm his son,' Nathan said.

The words were wrapped in razor wire; they cut his throat on the way out. If George had noticed, however, he gave no sign. George was a professional. Nathan was sure he'd heard worse.

'I'm terribly sorry for your loss, Mr Cole,' he said. 'Please, have a seat and give me a moment to prepare the visiting room.'

Nathan waited in a large leather armchair. There were potted plants in each corner and a counter along one wall, a coffee machine and some flyers stacked neatly on top. He glanced at the flyer closest to him. A cross dominated the front cover. Underneath it in giant, looped text, it read: *JESUS ACCEPTS YOU.*

George returned and showed off that sad smile once more. 'Please,' he said, 'this way.'

The visiting room was down a short corridor.

'I understand your father was a popular man,' George said as they walked. 'There should be quite the turnout for the ceremony.'

'Is that right?'

'Oh, yes. And I must say, I was quite a fan of his work.' The funeral director smiled warmly. 'It must be nice to have something of his to hold onto. Something physical.'

'Sure, it's great.'

'Your sister was telling me that your father was a keen boater, too. Have you given any thought to where you'll spread his ashes? My brother liked to sail, and we took a trip out to—'

'I'd rather not talk about this right now.'

George – still always the professional – bowed his head in understanding. They walked in silence the rest of the way.

The visiting room was a simple space. Bright flowers lined the walls and burning candles sat under each window. George must have just lit them; the smell of freshly struck matches was in the air. At the far end of the room was his father. He lay in a black coffin with the top half of the lid open. Nathan stood and stared at it.

'I'll give you some privacy,' George said, before retreating.

Nathan waited by the door. Until the sound of George's footsteps had faded, until the world had gone quiet. It might have been only a few minutes but it felt like more. Some part of him, he was sure, would have been happy standing by that door for hours. Longer, perhaps, if it meant not having to make the short trip across the room.

Eventually, however, he took that first step, the floorboards creaking under his shoes, the open casket growing slowly larger as he moved towards it.

His father's face played on his mind as he drew near. Anguished and in pain, frightened. The same expression he'd worn the last time Nathan had seen him; crawling on his belly, half out the front door, half in the rain, his thin arm outstretched, his clothes soaked with blood.

His father had been taken by surprise that day. A broken thighbone and the shock of his children turning on him. Of *Kate* turning on him.

Kate. The daughter that Lucas Cole had seen himself in. Her smarts, her strength – especially after their mother passed. Kate had been the favourite and she had known it, had flaunted it, had used it to push back against the boundaries their father had set down. It was just another reason for Nathan to hate him. For choosing her, for making him feel weak, for forcing him to carry the secret of what went on all these years.

Closer. The lining of the coffin coming into view. White satin. Then the shadow of something more: his father's arm. He was dressed in a black suit with a dark blue shirt and matching tie. His collar was buttoned up and there was make-up around his neck to cover the bruising. Nathan could see fingerprints in it.

His father's eyes were closed, his hair cut short, his face neatly shaved. It might have been the embalming process, or it might simply have been the passage of time, but Nathan had never seen his father looking so thin and frail. Staring at him now, the notion that this man had ever held any power over him was hard to believe.

He suddenly wished he could go back and tell his younger self about this moment. That through all the difficult years, through the abandonment, the shame, the fear, through all of it he would emerge here, now, bent over the coffin of this man, this dead man, this whisper of a man, this man who had been more interested in children who weren't his own, who did not deserve the title father, who had never *been* a father, who had made his son feel insignificant and incapable and who would go into the ground leaving the world a better place for it.

'*I didn't run because I was scared of you,*' Nathan said quietly, and in one quick motion he spat in his father's face, a thin splatter of saliva on his cheek. Then he reached up and pulled the casket closed.

19

Nathan crashed out as soon as he got back to his hotel room. Too tired even to shower, his aching body melting into the mattress. He slept until late the next day, waking in the exact same position he'd started, the afternoon sun streaming through his window.

And now he was on Broadway, lost in the noise. Waiting for his sister in a honky-tonk he didn't know the name of, only that it was loud and packed and he'd been lucky to find a couple of seats at the bar. His visit to the funeral home the day before had stayed with him. He caught sight of himself in a mirror and it was his father's pale face that stared back.

Kate was running late. He ordered a beer. One beer to try to release some of the tension that lived inside his bones. But as the clock hands spun, one beer turned into three, into five, into that strange sensation where you feel just fine only you know as soon as you stop the room will start swaying.

A band played easy listening on a small stage. The singer was a middle-aged woman, doing 'I Will Always Love You' – the Dolly Parton version, the version he'd always liked best – and she was good. Nice and slow, a relaxed tempo, no grandstanding. She even got the talking part right.

Around him, the evening crowd ate burgers and ribs and laughed and sang along. A man in the corner was going for the high notes, channelling his inner Whitney Houston to the rest of his friends. They clapped and cheered and Nathan drained his beer and ordered another and a plate of wings to go with it.

He played with his empty glass as the band started up their next track. A single keyboard note, over and over, and when the drumbeat kicked in he recognised it just as the rest of the bar did. '9 to 5'. These guys sure did like their Dolly.

He tuned out the cheers and the foot-stamping and his eyes fell upon the television above the bar. A news report, muted but with subtitles. A story about Chloe Xi. The barman slid a fresh beer across and Nathan took it without a word, his eyes on the set.

'*There was a break in the case of missing Nashville girl Chloe Xi today,*' the reporter said. '*The sad discovery of a body – not Chloe's, but the family dog's. A terrier named Coco.*'

Photographs of Chloe Xi faded in: playing sports, sitting on the sofa with a white terrier, dressed in her school uniform, those red ribbons still in her hair.

'*The discovery was made in the early hours of this morning*', the reporter continued, '*by detectives following a tip from a local private investigator hired by the Xi family to assist the investigation.*'

Stock footage of Old Hickory beach. Shots of the water, people on jet skis and tossing frisbees in the surf.

A local PI, Nathan thought to himself, and he pictured Isaac's card and wondered.

The focus shifted. An older couple, holding hands in a small living room. Chloe's parents. They talked about the day their daughter vanished.

Nathan took a long drink. The beer was cold, it made him shiver. The man in the corner was on his chair now, chanting, his voice a needle skipping across Nathan's brain. The barman returned with chicken wings and a portion of fries, placing the plate down and saying something, his mouth moving but the words lost.

'What?' Nathan said.

'I asked if you wanted any condiments.'

'No, I'm fine. Thank you.'

The barman gave him a look before turning away to serve someone else. Nathan knew he'd be telling the rest of the staff to keep an eye on him, that he'd probably had enough, but it wasn't the drink, of course it wasn't the drink. It was Chloe Xi, it was his father, it was the man in the corner of the room shouting the lyrics, not even bothering to try to sing the tune, stamping his feet like he was some sort of fucking tribal king.

'The dog was found here, in the rushes you can see behind me.' The reporter was at Old Hickory beach now, his face solemn, gesturing to the crime scene officers in white jumpsuits who milled around the area. *'Early reports indicate that the animal was stabbed a number of times, presumably by the person or persons who took young Chloe. But the family dog didn't go down without a fight; the presence of blood in the animal's mouth appears to indicate that Coco fought to protect her owner, and may even have left her abductor with an injury. Detectives are currently speaking with local hospitals to see if anyone has been treated for a dog bite in the last week.'*

Nathan stared at his plate of food. The glaze on the wings shimmered in the dim light. It looked plastic, like a child's toy. He pushed it away and got to his feet. Drained his beer, spilling some of it down his front, his eyes on the man across the room, and when the glass was empty he weighed it in his hand like a pitcher winding up a throw. From the corner of his eye he could see the barman shift his head.

'Sorry I'm late.'

He turned. Kate was standing behind him. Their eyes met briefly, hers moving to the glass in his hand. He set it down on the bar.

'I ordered already,' he said.

She gave a tight smile and slid onto the barstool next to his. 'That's fine,' she said. 'I'm not actually that hungry, anyhow.'

When the barman returned, Kate ordered a club soda.

'Make it two,' Nathan said. He pushed the plate of food between them and picked at a French fry.

'Did you go and see him?' Kate asked.

He nodded.

'How was he?'

Nathan shrugged. 'Still dead.'

She frowned and looked at the television set, watching in silence for a moment. 'I caught some of it on the radio on the way in. Do you think they'll find her?'

'He always seemed to want them to be found,' Nathan said. 'I never really understood why.'

'They were innocent children. He thought they deserved to have a proper funeral.'

'Well, you did know him better than me.'

'I didn't get it from him,' she said, and reached into her handbag. 'I got it from this.' And she set *The Midnight King* down next to the chicken wings.

Nathan tossed his French fry back onto the plate, untouched. 'Any good?'

'I thought you'd read it.'

'I read some. Hit a little too close to home.'

Their club sodas arrived. Kate took a long drink. She wiped her mouth and said, 'Actually, I thought it was pretty far from the truth, to be honest. Felt like a vanity project, and a poor one at that. All that nonsense about his dreams. And this Vincent character, who just comes out of nowhere and—'

Nathan held up a hand. 'Stop. I don't want to hear it.'

'Then why'd you give it to me?'

'I don't know. I was going to throw it away.'

'Scared you might learn something about Daddy you didn't like?'

'I'm not sure there's anything that could make me like him less.'

'Then why'd you come home at all?'

'I don't know that either, Kate. Because it felt like the right thing to do. Only now I'm here all I want to do is leave but I can't, can I?'

'Why not? Because of him?'

'Because of *her*,' he hissed, and jerked his head at the television. 'And because I've spent seventeen years in hiding, ashamed of who I was, of who I *am*, and I guess I always figured I'd confront him one day and find some resolution or whatever, find some peace. You know for a while I actually thought he might make the first move, might reach out to *me*, but instead he fucking *hangs himself* and I swear, Kate, I swear sometimes I think he did it on purpose, just to spite me.'

He was breathing heavily. It took a few moments to settle down. When he had, he looked around the bar, but nobody seemed to be paying him any attention. Not even Kate, who was staring at her soda, turning the glass around and around, the base leaving a circle of condensation on the wood.

'He had dementia,' she said quietly.

'What?'

'Daddy. It was bad, by the end. He'd forget things, then remember them wrong. One time I found him crying. Hunched over on his living-room floor, sobbing like a baby. Sobbing so hard he threw up.'

'Jesus. I . . . I can't imagine him like that.'

'I think he maybe remembered what he'd done.' Kate finally looked at him and gave a sad smile. 'I think that's why he killed himself.'

She started to gather her things. Nathan watched her get to her feet and said, 'I've been thinking a lot recently about the day I left.'

'Anything in particular?'

The feeling of Dad's hand on my chest, he thought. The way it had pinned him to the wall, a skinny arm with a strength that went beyond the physical. Or the sight of Kate, bursting into the room like a spectre, lit up from behind in a flash of lightning, her face bruised and crazed and swinging a golf club into their father's thigh. Swinging it hard enough to make him bleed, make him scream and fall to the floor and Nathan hadn't even thought, he'd just turned and *run*. Out into the storm, his backpack clutched tight in one hand. Out to Kate's waiting car and to the bus station and away from Tennessee.

Nathan's eyes found hers and he said, 'I think he was going to kill me that night.'

'I think he was too.'

'I'm not sure I ever thanked you for what you did.'

'Pay for my club soda and we'll call it quits.'

'I'm being serious. You stayed with him. Why?'

'I broke his leg, Nate. He couldn't walk for weeks. Couldn't drive, could barely use the toilet without holding onto my arm.' Her face flushed at the memories. 'Have you any idea what that's like? Seeing someone like that? Someone like *him*?'

'But you never left, even after he was better you never left. I kept thinking I'd hear from you.'

'Funny. I kept thinking I'd hear from *you*.'

Nathan nodded, his eyes dropping back to the bar. She was right, of course. He'd asked for her help and she'd turned up like a force of nature to set him free. And what had he done in return? He'd kept his head down, he'd kept moving. Never looking back. Never checking to see if Kate needed him the way that he'd needed her. He'd told himself that she was strong, that she could survive without him – could *leave* without him – and he'd abandoned her.

She was turning to go when he spoke. His voice was barely audible above the din of the bar. 'Did you blame me?'

'What?'

'You came back to help me leave and you ended up trapped there. Did you blame me?'

He could feel his sister pause, her body twisting as she glanced back at him. 'I blamed you,' she said, her voice nearly as low as his. 'At first, sure, I blamed you.'

'Only at first? What made you change your mind?'

Kate was quiet for so long that Nathan thought she might have left. He turned and found her gazing at the rows of coloured bottles behind the bar. Finally she looked at him and gave a small shrug. 'I stopped feeling angry at you,' she said sadly. 'I just stopped feeling anything at all.'

She left then, slipping through the crowd towards the door. Nathan watched her go, his chest sore, his throat tight. Above him, the news reporter was wrapping up his story. He was still standing on the beach at Old Hickory.

'*The working theory,*' the subtitles read, '*is that Chloe Xi was taken from this spot and forced into a waiting boat, moored at this out-of-the-way pier.*'

Nathan frowned.

'*Where she went from there? Well, that's a harder question to answer. As local residents will attest, there's over a dozen marinas, piers and boathouses that her abductor could have taken her to. Combing each of them for further clues is going to take detectives some time. Time that Chloe Xi may be running out of.*'

He closed his eyes. Images rushed in. His father, crouched in the tall grass at Old Hickory, waiting, a blade in a closed fist. Had he called for her as she passed by? Had he pretended to be hurt? Had he used her name? One hand to grab the dog's collar and pin it down, another to drive the knife into its side. Three, four, five times. A frenzied kill.

Nathan snatched up the manuscript and slid off the stool onto unsteady feet. He pulled money from his wallet, clumsily, his fingers working like they were underwater. He suddenly wished he hadn't had so much to drink. Pushing through the crowd, he moved for the exit. For Kate.

My brother liked to sail, George had said at the funeral home. Christ, he'd practically spelled it out. *Your father was a keen boater.*

Maybe he was, what did Nathan know. If it helped him snatch kids, his father would have learned to fly. But if he *had* taken Chloe in those rushes, if he'd dragged her onto a waiting boat then he had to have a place he could take her to. Somewhere safe, somewhere quiet. Somewhere he could keep her, maybe somewhere she was still at.

He burst onto the street. This late, Broadway was filled with people jostling from bar to bar. There was no sign of his sister. Nathan pulled out his cell phone and headed for his station wagon.

She answered on the second ring. 'Nate, is everything—'

'Did Dad have a boat?'

'What?'

'The guy at the funeral home yesterday, he said Dad had a boat. Is that true?'

'Yeah. I mean, he liked to go out on the river. Blew an entire advance on a decent-sized one.'

'Kate, where did he keep it?'

His sister fell quiet. 'Why?'

'Jesus, because they think whoever took Chloe used a boat to get away. A fucking *boat*. Now where is it?'

He could hear her moving around. A car engine starting. 'Are you still at the bar? I'll come pick you up.'

'I'll meet you there, where is it?'

A pause. 'He stored it at a marina over at Blue Turtle Bay. It's probably still there.'

'No, a marina's too public. There must have been somewhere else.

Somewhere quieter.'

'I don't know what to tell you, Nate. I only ever saw it at the marina.'

'All right, thanks.'

He ended the call and kept moving. Back to the station wagon, back to his father's house. If there was another location then there had to be a paper trail. He squeezed the car keys and felt his heart race. He was over the limit, he knew that, and yet somehow he'd never felt more sober.

20

Nathan pulled up sharply outside his father's house, bouncing the front wheel of the station wagon onto the sidewalk. Inside, he headed straight to the study. Trying not to think about what used to happen in there. His body turning on him; the scent of cigarette smoke in the air. He grasped the handle, his grip faltering for only a moment, before he threw open the door.

The room was incredibly tidy. A large desk against one wall, shelves lined with novels, a couple of filing cabinets tucked away in the corner. He spotted the crystal ashtray and forced his gaze upwards, to the books, to the name *Jack Cross* in large, glossy type across most of the spines.

He pulled open the first filing cabinet. It was filled with folders, all of them neatly named: *Insurance, Pension, Savings*. He thumbed through them all, moved onto the next drawer, then the drawer below that.

Madison storage.

Nathan paused, then pulled the folder. Flipping it open, he scanned the contents. He got halfway down the first page before he started running for the door.

He rang Kate as he floored the car, a passing SUV leaning on their horn as he tore by them.

'Dad bought a storage unit a few years back,' he said when she answered. He spoke fast, before she had a chance to say anything. 'It's over in Madison. One-four-one Canton Pass.'

'All right, hang on, Nate, I can meet you somewhere.'

'No time, I'm on my way there now.'

'Nate, be *careful*—'

He ended the call and pressed his foot down to the floor.

It took him just a half hour to reach the storage unit. As soon as he did – brakes squealing, tyres skidding a good few feet on the rough track – he knew he was in the right place. The building was perfect: tucked away down a quiet dirt track, trees on three sides and the water's edge on the fourth. A short slope connected the unit's large sliding doors with the Cumberland River. It wasn't exactly in the middle of nowhere, but for his father's uses it was hidden well enough.

He just about fell out of the car, dust still in the air as he stumbled towards those doors. It was early evening and the sun was sliding out of the sky. He was cold but his jacket was on the passenger seat, forgotten.

The doors were bolted shut. The padlock looked brand new but the metal plate it was secured to was starting to rust. Nathan looked around for something to break it with, a rock, anything, finally running back to the station wagon – the engine still running – and popping the trunk. He grabbed a tyre iron and returned to the door. Taking a breath, he swung it as hard as he could at the lock.

The iron shook and the padlock bounced. He swung it again, and again, and again. Each time he somehow found more strength than the time before, his hair falling about his eyes, the back of his head breaking out in sweat.

Finally the rusted plate fell. Dropping the tyre iron, Nathan scrabbled at the padlock and pulled the whole thing off. Grabbing the chunky handle, he slid the huge door along its track, grunting with the effort.

The day's dying light flooded the unit. Most of the space was taken up by a large blue-and-white boat; Nathan didn't know what type, something with a motor and a little cabin to sit in as you steered. He had to turn sideways to get past it. Once inside, the unit opened up a little. Another door was set against one wall. This one swung open easily.

Nathan stepped through to a second, much smaller room. It was dark in here, and he fumbled for a light switch, running his fingers along the wall until he gave up and used his cell phone. He switched on the flash and swung it around.

The room was near bare. A couple of worktables with tools against one wall, a collection of rope and sailing equipment hanging on another.

And in the centre, a metal trapdoor.

Nathan fell upon it. The panel was clearly newer than the rest of the building; he wasn't going to be able to break open this lock. He hammered on the thing, yelling, but heard nothing back.

Scrambling to his feet, he moved to the worktables and started opening drawers. More tools, more boating equipment. Finally he tried a cupboard and there, hanging on a small nail, was a set of silver keys.

Snatching them up, Nathan ran back to the trapdoor and grasped the padlock. The first key he tried fitted perfectly, and with a sharp turn the bolt popped free. He started shouting again, his hands trembling as he wrestled the padlock off and tossed it, the keys still inside. When he pulled on the door it swung upwards on a well-oiled hinge. An overpowering stench filled the air, and Nathan pressed his nose into the crook of his arm. It was a hot, fetid odour. It was excrement and sweat and the rot of slow death. A short set of steps led downwards, into a small, hollowed-out space. Nathan fumbled for his cell before noticing a switch recessed into the frame. He flicked it.

The space below him lit up. Nathan squinted at the sudden brightness, but even before he closed his eyes, he saw.

Chloe Xi was inside, dressed in grey sweatpants and a dark top, sitting, her back flat against the wall, her legs drawn up to her chest, her head bowed, her arms in her lap and shackled on a long chain to anchor points bolted above her.

Nathan's heart lurched. He launched himself down the steps, calling her name. Third time he said it she finally responded, her head stirring, her drowsy eyes opening, and then he was beside her and he was pulling on the chains but of course they held fast, they looked brand new, looped through another damn padlock.

He turned to climb the steps and retrieve the keys and Chloe mumbled something, her voice barely more than a rasp, her chains clinking as she tried to move. He motioned for her to stay calm and scrambled up, kicking over a pair of now-empty soup bowls in his haste.

The room was faintly lit from the space below, but it was still mainly shadows. He couldn't see the padlock on the ground. Where had he dropped it? He pulled his cell again, turned on the flash, moved it around until he saw it lying in the dirt and grabbed it, pulling the keys free.

Back down the steps now, back into the hollowed space. Chloe was moving more. She was pulling against her chains, crying, her breathing coming in weak rasps. Nathan tried the second key in the padlock and it worked, it popped open and the chains fell away and with a moan Chloe rocked forward and into his arms.

She was shaking, clutching at him, her thin frame trying to move past him, towards the steps, towards the upstairs room and the boat and the freedom of the cool evening air and it broke Nathan's heart, it really did, but he hadn't come all this way just to falter now, not after everything he'd been through, not after all those years living with a murderer for a father; watching from the kitchen as he tried to force soup into the mouths of scared little children, watching as he lost his temper, as he hurled the bowl against the basement wall, as he paced and shouted and swore and finally wrapped his hands around their throats and squeezed; watching it all and wondering what it was like to snuff out a life, to feel a person shudder and go still, to feel them take a breath and never let it out, wondering how for all these years his father had never truly understood him, had thought he was weak, had thought he ran away because he was scared – and he *was* scared, he was terrified, but not of his father, not really, not in the way people thought, not in the way Kate thought, because if he was scared of anything then he was scared of the ideas and urges that would pulse through him as he sat in that kitchen and watched, because he was scared of *himself* and *that* was why he ran, *that* was why he begged his sister to help him escape, hoping that distance would cure him and for a while it did, for a while he was free from it but the urges would return, they always returned and he would choke stray cats to satisfy it, hunched over in alleyways, hidden behind wire fences and piles of rubbish, and when that wasn't enough he took people's pets, their dogs and their rabbits, took them from their homes or their cars, and there was a thrill there just in taking them but it wasn't enough, it was never enough, the urges still returned and living alone these past seventeen years, living with all that shit inside made him realise that it wasn't about distance, it wasn't about time or inner strength or any of that bullshit, it was about *who you were*, and maybe his father had made him this way or maybe he'd always been like this, but now he was here, in his father's prison cell with his father's prisoner, and he would finally be able to show his father who he was, would finally be able to prove that he was never scared of him because *he* was the strong child, *he* was the strong child, *he* was the strong child, and so he peeled Chloe's little body away from his and slid his hands around her throat and squeezed it tight until she went limp, until she shuddered and went still, until she took that last breath and never let it out.

21

ISAAC

Cruiser lights. Out past the Hickory Bay apartment blocks. Three cars at least. Down by the water, their overheads pulsing hues the colour of old bruises. A dark omen in the falling dusk.

Police tape stretched from a dying maple to a faded sign that read *Mallard Point Park*. Alison brought her Mazda to a stop, not bothering to pull completely off the road.

'Ma'am, you can't park here.'

A young officer. Nervous, clipboard clutched in an outstretched hand.

Isaac said, 'Tell Detective Copeland that Isaac Holloway is here to see him.'

The boy paused – unused to being spoken to in that way by a civilian, maybe – but then leaned his head to his shoulder-mounted radio and made the call. A few moments later there was the crackle of a response.

'Wait here,' the officer told them.

They stood off to one side, where the trees were thinner, where there was a better view of the small crowd at the water's edge. As they did so, a figure turned towards them.

It had been twenty-seven minutes since Copeland called. Now, they tracked the man's slow, steady trudge towards them. It was the walk of a man who was not quite broken, but who was perhaps not that far off. Cases like these had a weight to them. Isaac knew it, remembered it, felt it still. Some days it was lighter – some days it was almost gone – but today the weight was especially heavy. So heavy it bent the trees and bowed the sky.

Isaac watched the stooped detective approach and felt like crying.

'Mr Holloway,' Copeland said. His voice was quiet. Respectful in a way a voice should never have to be.

'Thank you for the phone call,' Isaac said. 'I appreciate that.'

Copeland nodded. His gaze went to Alison. 'Are you working with Mr Holloway?'

'I suppose I am, yes. My name's Alison Bennett. I'm an attorney.'

'What can you tell us?' Isaac asked.

'Not much. A dog walker came across her earlier today, wrapped in a couple of black garbage bags and tied with rope. Looks like she floated downstream a ways before being caught up in the brush.'

'Any obvious cause of death?'

'Off the record? Strangulation, judging from the bruising. But we'll need to wait for the coroner's report to be sure.'

'When should we expect that?'

Copeland paused. He looked away, scratched his neck.

'Look, Mr Holloway, you really helped us out with the tip about the family dog, and I can see how much this case means to you. But this is as far as I can take you.'

'You're cutting me out?'

'You were hired by the family to find Chloe Xi, not her killer. I shouldn't even be having this conversation, but I didn't want you finding out on the evening news.'

'Your partner feel the same way?'

The three of them turned to look across the park. Hayes was motionless, watching.

'Don't worry about my partner, he's got a lot on his plate.' The tired detective took a step closer and held out his hand. 'Thank you for your assistance, Mr Holloway.'

Isaac stared at Copeland's outstretched palm for a moment, then shook it.

'You said she was inside a couple of black garbage bags that were bound with rope?'

'That's right.'

'That rope tied with a constrictor knot, Detective?'

Copeland gave a faint smile. Then he turned and trudged slowly back across the park, his head bent forward once more.

The story had broken by the time Isaac got back to his motel room. He sat and watched news footage; anchors with sad faces and zoom shots of white tents in Mallard Point Park. Hayes gave a brief statement. They ran his clip three times. Isaac watched each one with a bottle of water, his stomach burning.

Then it was 10 p.m. and the news cycle moved on. Reality TV and comedy reruns. A family grieved their dead child while Jim and Pam made eyes across the office. Isaac felt the gentle pull of society shifting focus, like the gravity of a new world. The promise of something else, something better, if they could just forget about what had come before.

22

They brought Edward Morrison into the room shackled, shuffling, hunched forward. Isaac watched from the visitor's table with a can of Diet Coke and a Hershey's already set out.

It felt strange. The theatrics of it all. The way he gave a man's name and took a seat and they brought him out for display. Like they were dealing with livestock. Like the man wasn't a man at all.

Morrison took a seat and waited until Officer Cranor had removed his restraints before speaking.

'Didn't I talk to you yesterday?'

'You did.'

'Where's your lady friend?'

'It's just me, I'm afraid.'

'That's all right.' Morrison's pale blue eyes slid to the items on the table. 'Are these for me?'

'Sure are, Edward. I was hoping we could have another talk.'

Morrison nodded but his gaze was on the soda. He reached for it, cracked it open and took a long sip. Isaac waited patiently.

'You know I don't normally drink Diet Coke first thing in the morning,' Morrison said, his Southern accent syrup-thick. 'Makes my teeth feel funny.'

Isaac forced a smile. Just the thought of drinking that soda on an empty stomach made him sweat.

'You get to watch the news in here, Edward?' he asked. 'You get to read the paper?'

Morrison nodded, setting the drink down and grinning. 'Oh yeah, I get to watch TV. I got my own set and everything. No cable, though. You believe that?'

'I do. You see the news last night?'

'Yup.' Morrison peeled the wrapper off the chocolate and started breaking squares. 'You're talking about that girl they found, aren't you?'

Isaac shifted in his seat. 'What do you know about her?'

'Same as anyone else, I suppose. My lawyer sure got excited about it though.'

'You talked to your lawyer already?'

'He phoned me this morning. I just got done speaking with him before you came.'

'Uh huh. And what did he say?'

'He called it an *opportunity*.' Morrison was setting out the little squares of chocolate in neat rows on the table now. 'He said they found her just like the others, bleached clean and everything. He said if whoever really killed those kids is still out there I might get a retrial. Said he was going to write to the governor, ask for clemency. You want some of my Hershey's?'

'I'm all right, Edward. Did you tell your lawyer about me and my friend coming to visit you yesterday?'

Morrison started to eat the chocolate, a square at a time. 'Yeah.'

'What did he say?'

'That I'm not supposed to talk to you without him.'

'You want me to go?'

'No, it's okay.'

Isaac studied the man across from him. He watched Morrison

work his way along the row of chocolate squares, popping each piece into his mouth in a child-like manner. He knew Alison was right; Tennessee law prohibited the execution of anyone with intellectual disabilities. But he also knew the realities of the system.

'How come you're here, anyhow?' Morrison asked, pausing to look up at him. 'Why're you wanting to talk to me about all this?'

'Because I believe you,' Isaac said. 'I don't think you're the Music City Monster. I think he's still out there, whoever he is.'

'Are you trying to catch him?'

'That's not my job any more.'

'But you're trying anyway, aren't you?'

The comment caught Isaac off guard. He took a moment before responding. 'Yeah, I guess I am.'

'Why?'

It was a fair question. The same one Isaac saw in Alison's eyes every time she looked at him. Same one he'd been avoiding ever since Chloe Xi's parents had made that first phone call. Or maybe before that, maybe ever since he'd returned home. Six months he'd been back in Nashville. Six months of scrabbling around in the streets for cases, for adulterers and abusers. Six months of wading through filth and washing it off in a dirty motel best he could.

Then Alison had come along and offered him a lifeline. Insurance claims; nothing fancy but at least it was clean. More than that, it was a chance to start over. To atone for what he'd done back in Baltimore.

He still thought about it. Sometimes still had nightmares about it. Working a case like Chloe's, how could he not. The man had cried as Isaac gripped his throat, as he'd rooted out his windpipe, his fingers sinking into soft flesh. This piece of shit. This empty shell. This husk, this paper-thin composite of a human being.

So of course he still thought about it. And people looked at him; people who knew, they looked at him and they asked themselves why he'd take on a case like this, and he'd avoid answering and that was fine, but now it was Edward Morrison asking the question, and for some reason Isaac felt like he owed the man a straight answer.

Her name had been Safia Hashim. Ten years old and dressed in a Hello Kitty outfit. A garbage truck had dropped her off at the local dump. Rigour had come and gone, her body starting to putrefy.

Isaac had traced the truck's route. Visited every stop along the way. Finally found one of her shoes behind a dumpster in Grove Park, spent three days knocking on doors and flashing her photo until he ended up at a dilapidated apartment block with pushers for doormen. Six floors up and the skinhead who answered the door just about jumped out his window when he saw Safia's picture. Her other shoe was lying on the floor by the TV.

It wasn't like Isaac had children of his own. Safia wasn't even the first dead kid he'd investigated. Maybe it all just reached a tipping point. Maybe there's only so much horrible shit you can process before your brain begins to crack.

Whatever it was, it changed him. It he hadn't already called it in, he probably would've beaten that rapist to death. Managed to get him halfway there before his colleagues dragged him off. Isaac didn't remember the next part too well, but apparently he broke another officer's jaw before they managed to wrestle him to the floor.

They put it down to exhaustion. Couple days spent banged up in a hospital bed with his stomach on fire and when he finally got out, he wasn't a detective any more.

And he knew that everyone around him – his parents, Alison, hell even Copeland and Hayes – everyone saw him chasing after Chloe Xi and wondered how long it would be before his brain cracked again, before he wound up lying face down in a ditch by the side of the road, or worse: strangling some sorry piece-of-shit child murderer to death with his bare hands, like that was some bad thing.

Isaac knew he'd pinned too much on finding her alive. Now she was dead, he had to switch focus. Copeland said the family didn't hire him to catch a killer, and maybe that was true. So maybe he wouldn't do it for them. Maybe he'd catch this psycho for himself.

Morrison listened to his story without saying a word. When Isaac was done, it was like something had changed between them. He left shortly afterwards. It was nearly 11 a.m., and Isaac had a funeral after lunch. He just had one stop to make first.

23

Lawrence Hughes lived in a one-bedroom studio apartment over in Donelson. Guy's front door was so flimsy, Isaac nearly caved it in just by knocking. The airport was a couple miles down the road. Sooner or later a jet engine was going to blow the thing off its hinges.

'Mr Hughes?' he called, peering through a grease-stained window. Stacks of takeout cartons and pizza boxes littered the single room. There was no sign of anyone inside.

Behind him, Alison leaned against his battered Ford and watched. She was dressed in a smart black suit with a crisp, well-ironed blouse. A sharp contrast to Isaac's outfit, even if he had managed to clean the worst of the coffee stains from his jacket. His shirt was crushed – a conscious decision to avoid asking Danny at the front desk for an iron.

He went to knock one last time, then let his knuckles fall. Either Hughes wasn't home or he was hiding in his bathroom. They didn't have time to find out which. In thirty minutes, Nathan's father was being put into the ground.

'We're going to be late,' Alison warned as he neared the car.

'We'll be fine,' he said, glancing down at his shirt and running a palm over a visible crease. 'These things never start on time.'

'Did you think about ironing that before you left this morning?'

He glanced at her across the roof as he climbed in. She was smiling at him.

'It's a new shirt,' he said defensively. 'Label said it was non-iron.'

'Oh, I just presumed you'd pulled it out the bottom of a suitcase.'

'What if I'd told you my iron is broken? Is that more believable?'

Alison laughed. 'Is this where you tell me your mom still does your laundry?'

'She's retired, she needs something to do. It's either that or join the neighbourhood watch.' Isaac started up the car and pulled away from the kerb. 'I'm actually going round for dinner tonight if you fancy it.'

'Your parents won't mind?'

'Please, my mom's desperate to see you again. And besides, she's making chicken-fried steak with okra, and you should see the size of her skillet. You'll be saving my dad from a fortnight of leftovers.'

'Then sure, that'll be nice.'

'Great.' Isaac glanced at his watch and gently sped up. 'Just don't ask her to do your laundry, I've got dibs on that machine.'

The service for Lucas Cole was held at a small church in Belle Meade, not far from the iconic Bluebird Cafe. Isaac glanced at the tiny venue as they drove past. He'd been there once, years earlier and before he'd left the city. A date with a girl who'd been more interested in the man on stage than the one she was sitting opposite. Isaac hadn't heard from her again.

The church was full when they arrived. Alison raised an eyebrow at him as they slipped in and stood at the back.

Isaac ran his gaze over the crowd. There were a lot of people here. He often forgot that Lucas Cole wasn't just his schoolfriend's father; he was a local author, a minor celebrity.

Despite the volume of books Lucas had written, Isaac had never actually read any of them. Not all the way through, anyway. He'd tried to – more from a sense of duty towards Nathan than anything else, he'd never been much of a reader – but had failed to get beyond the first fifty pages. They were schlocky, filled with crude character-isations and tired storytelling. He vaguely remembered a swimwear model pulling a Walther PPK from the waistband of her bikini. The whole thing was faintly embarrassing.

But shit, who was he to judge? Lucas Cole knew his market; these things sold by the truckload.

A large photograph of Lucas sat at the front of the church. Same picture that adorned the programmes on every seat. It showed him outdoors, leaning against a fencepost. Blond hair swept back and with a faraway look in his blue eyes. It was a horrible pose. The type of All-American-Hero shot that Isaac hated. Like the guy was on his Texas ranch surveying cattle and not standing in a city park staring at the bachelor party on a beer bus across the street.

Alison nudged him and nodded across the room. He followed her gaze and saw Nathan, standing in the front row.

'I thought he'd be with the coffin,' she whispered.

Isaac shrugged. 'Those two were complicated,' he said. 'I don't think we know the half of it.'

'Well he looks awful.'

She was right. His face was pale, his hair a mess. He stood like gravity was pressing him into the floor. Stooped forward, his clothes hanging off him.

'Poor guy,' Alison said quietly. 'He's dressed worse than you are.'

Isaac started to protest when an older man standing beside him said, 'This is a lovely church, isn't it?'

Isaac turned and smiled politely. 'It's very nice.'

'How did you two know Lucas?'

'We're friends of the family.'

The man nodded. Isaac switched his attention back to the front row. Nathan was staring at them now. Through the crowd, his white face an unmoving mask. Alison raised her hand in greeting but got no response. When Nathan finally turned away, Isaac realised he'd been holding his breath.

'I used to fish with Lucas,' the old man said. 'I could tell you some stories.'

'I'm sure,' Isaac murmured, still watching his friend. Uncomfortable but unable to fully explain why.

'He used to go fishing in Santeetlah. Said one time he caught the biggest wild rainbow trout in the state of North Carolina. Said it was so big, when he drove back into Tennessee, it was the biggest wild rainbow trout in *that* state, too.'

The old man laughed quietly to himself. Isaac forced another smile just as the church doors swung open. Lucas Cole at last made his grand entrance, carried aloft inside a black coffin.

Isaac glanced back at Nathan, and was surprised to see his friend was transformed. No longer hunched forward but standing tall, the clothes that had once seemed to swamp him now filled out completely. And more than that, his pale face was flushed, his features twisted into a hard look, an expression of pure fury, an anger that was directed completely at his dead father.

The service was brief. A minister who spoke in platitudes, rattling off phrases that could have applied to anyone. Isaac got the impression he'd been drafted in at the last minute. Dusted off an old speech and swapped the names out. Lucas Cole's family weren't much better – neither Nathan nor Kate contributed anything. Isaac wondered whether their silence said more.

The atmosphere followed them outside. He waited with Alison, chewing a Rolaid and watching as people filed out. People with their heads bowed, with their gazes at the ground or on their cell phones. When Nathan and Kate didn't show, they ducked back in but found the church empty.

The day was turning muggy. A heat that seemed to cook you from the inside. Isaac drove with the windows down, pressure thudding like drumbeat. Local news was now reporting that Chloe Xi had officially died of strangulation.

'Same method as the others,' Isaac said quietly.

Alison reached over and changed the station.

It took them the best part of thirty minutes to reach his parents' house in La Vergne, and neither of them said much more the whole way. Pulling up outside a small, detached property in a quiet suburb, Alison asked him if he was feeling all right.

'I'm fine,' Isaac said, killing the engine and climbing out. 'Just something about that service that didn't sit right.'

'It's a funeral,' she said, following him. 'It's not supposed to sit right.'

Isaac wasn't sure he agreed. But he wasn't sure about a lot of things right now, so he kept his mouth shut and grunted as he swung open the front door.

The sudden smell of his mother's home-made Cajun seasoning made his mouth water and his stomach cramp. They walked through the bright hallway to the kitchen at the back of the house. His mother was at the stove, rattling pots, dressed in a plain frock with an apron wrapped around her waist. She was humming as she worked.

Isaac watched her for a moment. Already he could feel the malaise lifting. 'Hey, Ma.'

She turned, blinking as she smiled. 'Isaac! You're early. I wasn't expecting you for another hour or so.'

'Service wrapped up quick, I guess.'

She crossed the room with a slight limp, her arms open wide, and embraced them both. One after the other, just as tight. 'Alison, it's so good to see you again. How are you, girl? How's your mom doing?'

'We're both doing great, Mrs Holloway. And thanks for the invite, it smells incredible.'

'Oh please, call me Grace. And thank *you* for forcing my son here to finally come home for dinner.'

'Ma,' Isaac said, dragging the word out as he shrugged off his coat. 'I'm busy with work, I told you.'

'Too busy to eat a proper meal?' Grace asked.

'I eat proper.'

'You eat *Rolaids*, boy. Like candy, I've seen you.' She looked pointedly at Alison. 'Tell me he doesn't look sickly to you.'

'He's looked better.'

'There, you hear that?' Grace shook her head as she returned to the stove. 'I bet you been eating nothing but fast food in that motel room of yours.'

Alison grinned. 'I had to take him out to dinner yesterday just to stop him eating Taco Bell.'

Grace paused and glanced back. 'You took him out to dinner?'

'Not like that, Ma,' Isaac said. 'We're working a case together.'

'What case? That little girl that went missing? Because they found her now.'

'I know.'

'You don't need to keep looking for her.'

'I *know*, Ma.'

Grace gave him a narrowed look. 'Well I just hope you paid for dinner. I know I raised you right.'

'Don't worry, I expensed it,' Isaac said, smiling. 'Where's Dad?'

'Oh, he's in his workshop again. I knocked over a lamp and he's mending it for me.'

Isaac went over and put his hand on his mother's shoulder. 'You doing okay?'

'I'm *fine*. Go say hello to your father then set the table.'

He leaned in and gave her a kiss on the cheek. She batted him away, laughing, her eyes crinkling. Isaac led Alison through the utility room towards the garden. He asked if she wanted a beer.

'Sure,' she said. Then, when he'd passed her a cool bottle from the large fridge, added, 'Is everything all right with your mom?'

'Arthritis in her knees, flares up now and again.'

'She on any medication?'

'Tablets, but they make her feel sick. I keep telling her to go back to the doctors.'

'I see where you get your stubbornness from.'

They stepped out into the back garden. A patio which led onto a long stretch of well-maintained lawn. At the end, tucked against a fence, was a small wooden hut. They headed over towards it.

Alison motioned with her beer. 'That your daddy's workshop?'

'Yeah. He'd live there if he could, I reckon.'

'He still doing those animal wood carvings?'

'Nah, he gave up on them a while back. Too fiddly. He likes making more practical stuff now. Stools, little cabinets, that sort of thing.'

'Sounds impressive.'

'You want to get on his good side, ask him what type of oil he uses to treat the wood. He'll talk your ear off all night.'

Isaac knocked on the door before ducking inside. His father was sitting hunched over a workbench, surrounded by various tools and pieces of oddly shaped wood. He was dressed in typical Tennessee garb: bootcut jeans and a plaid shirt. The walls of the hut were lined with fishing tackle and colourful bait, and there was an earthy, smoky smell in the air.

'Hi, Dad.'

His father grunted, still focused on his workbench. A number of small brushes dangled from his mouth. Isaac went over and placed a fresh beer down beside him.

'That the lamp Mom knocked over?'

A nod from his father. Then, finally setting the ceramic base carefully to one side, he removed the brushes from his mouth and dropped them into a glass jar. He licked his dry lips and reached for the beer. 'It's a cheap thing, I told her we should just buy a new one.'

'But then it'll feel like the lamp won.'

His father grunted again as he took a long drink. 'You staying for dinner? Your mother's making enough food to feed a stadium.'

'How long were you eating it for last time?'

'About six weeks. There's still some okra in the freezer.'

'Don't worry, I'll give you a hand. I brought Alison along too.'

'Hi, Mr Holloway.'

At the sound of her voice, Isaac's father lowered his bottle and craned his head round. His bushy eyebrows rose. 'Alison! My goodness, it's been a while. How are you?'

'I'm good. How are you?'

'Can't complain. You still running that law practice down in Pulaski?'

'Yessir, nearly five years now.'

'Good for you.'

'Isaac was telling me about your work in here.' She pointed to a small stool in the corner of the room. 'Did you make this? It's beautiful.'

The older man waved a hand through the air. 'It's a mess. One of the damn legs keeps wobbling.'

'Well, if you ever decide to sell anything, let me know. I'd love something for the office.'

Isaac smiled at the sight of his father unsuccessfully trying to mask his pride. 'How's Mom doing?' he asked.

'Oh, she's fine. Some bad days now and then, but not too often. Less, if she took her damn pills.'

'You ever tried to crush them up in her food?'

His father snorted. 'The day she catches me doing that is the day I end up in the ground.' His face softened suddenly. 'Speaking of which, how was the funeral?'

'It was fine. A little impersonal, maybe.'

'That's just how it is now. No one takes the time to get to know the person before they bury them. It's just another job to these people.'

'Not like the good old days, huh?'

'No it is not.' His father smiled and hauled himself to his feet. 'Come on, let's get inside and set the table before your mother tries to hobble out here to find us. Last thing I want is another lamp to mend.'

24

Alison pushed her plate away. 'Oh my goodness, Mrs Holloway, that was delicious.'

Grace beamed at her from across the table. 'Thank you, honey. Can I get you some more?'

'Ma, she's had two plates already. Don't make her eat a third just to be polite.'

'I know she's had two plates, I'm just asking.'

'Mrs Holloway, if I have any more of that gravy, I will not be fitting in my suit tomorrow,' Alison said, laughing.

'Well that's fine, I'll give you some sides to take away. You can have them for lunch.'

'Give some to Isaac too,' his father said from across the table. 'Give him a couple days' worth.'

Isaac was sure he saw a hint of a smile play at the corners of his father's mouth.

'Oh, don't you worry,' Grace said, reaching around to stack up the dinner plates. 'There ain't no way my boy is leaving here without a week's worth of proper meals.'

'I don't have a fridge, Ma. It's a motel room.'

'You got a minibar, don't you? You just clear out those little bottles of scotch and you'll have space. That stuff 'll just rot your stomach as it is. Now, who's for coffee and sweet potato pie?'

Grace started to rise, but Isaac got there first. He placed his hand gently on her shoulder. 'I'll get it, Ma. You just stay there and rest your knee.'

'Oh, my knee's fine.'

'Yeah, well, rest it anyway.'

Isaac picked up the pile of empty plates and carried them through to the small kitchen. He listened to the chatter, smiling as he placed the kettle on the stove to boil. He leaned against the counter. Stretched his back a little, felt it give pleasingly.

'Say, you like fishing, Mr Holloway?' Alison asked. 'I saw all that gear in your workshop.'

'Sure, I like fishing,' his father said. 'I was out trying to catch trout over at Caney Fork just last week.'

'Did you get anything?'

'Nah. I've not caught anything worth keeping for a while now. Maybe I've just lost the knack.'

Isaac went to the fridge and took out a bottle of milk. Cracked the lid and recoiled at the smell. Stuff was as sour as Alison's grandmother's bathroom. The kettle began to whistle on the stove.

'You should try fishing over at Santeetlah,' Alison said. 'Lucas Cole caught a trout there the size of his damn head or something.'

'Is that right?'

'Biggest one in two states, is what he was saying.'

His father snorted. 'Well, I'm getting too old to reel in anything bigger than my fist these days. And besides, Santeetlah? That's way out past Tellico Plains. I ain't got the time to drive two hundred miles just to catch trout.'

Isaac paused. The conversation faded out. Lost to the kettle's howl and his own pounding head. Lawrence Hughes had told detectives about a smell when he was captive. Same smell Isaac had just gotten from the bottle of milk. Same smell he'd encountered before, as a young boy, playing at a friend's house.

The kettle's scream cut through his thoughts. He lifted it and the silence was somehow even louder.

He crossed back to the dining room again. Alison was speaking, but he interrupted her. 'What did you say?' he asked his father.

'Huh?'

'About where Lucas Cole caught that fish.'

'Said I'm getting too old to catch—'

'No, where did you say it was?'

'Santeetlah? It's across the state border, out past Tellico Plains. Hell of a ways to go for some fishing.'

Isaac closed his eyes. *Tellico Plains.* He thought back to his lunchtime meeting with Detectives Hayes and Copeland. Catfish and iced tea on the marina at Papa Turney's.

A little girl over in Tellico Plains, and I've never even heard of Tellico Plains.

'Isaac?' Alison asked quietly. 'You good?'

He wasn't good. Deep in the darkest part of his mind, he was very fucking far from good.

Opening his eyes, he went to his jacket hanging on the door. Checked the pockets, pulled out the programme from the funeral. The one with the big photo of Lucas Cole on the front. He stared at it and he thought about the description that Lawrence Hughes had given the cops seventeen years ago.

'Hey Ma? You go ahead and box me up some of that pie. I'll come back for it later.'

His mother craned her neck to stare at him. 'Why? Where on earth you going?'

'I need to pay someone a visit.'

*

168

Back across the city. Back to Donelson. Isaac drove fast, too fast, enough that even Alison told him to cut it out.

'I'm going to need you to walk me through this,' she said. 'You think it's Nathan's *daddy*?'

'He fits, Alison. Jesus Christ, he fucking *fits*.'

'Because he travelled the country doing book tours?'

'Because he was there! Tellico Plains. He snatched a little girl and he bragged about how big a fish he caught. He *bragged* about it.'

'You're reaching, Isaac.'

'What about the smell? The mould in the house? Lawrence Hughes said the place he was kept stank like sour milk. Alison, I've been *in* that house! I know that smell!'

'I bet half the houses in the city have that smell. I'm telling you, you're reaching.'

'You want to know why Nathan wore those sweaters?' Isaac took his eyes off the road long enough to glance over at her. 'In school, all summer long. You want to know why?'

'Why?'

'Because Lucas Cole fucking *burned* him, Alison. Kid had cigarette burns all over his arms, and God knows what else.'

'Nathan had *cigarette* burns? From his *daddy*?'

'That's what I'm saying.'

'How'd you know that? I never knew that.'

'I caught a glimpse of them one time. He was changing his sweater or something, I don't really remember. Honestly, I didn't think anything of them myself until years later. But shit, maybe you're right. Maybe I am reaching.' He pulled up to the kerb with a squeal of brakes. 'Let's go find out, shall we?'

He leapt from his car. Took the steps to the front door three at a time. An airplane screamed overhead, coming in low on approach.

Isaac hammered on the door. 'Lawrence Hughes,' he shouted.

When he peered through the window, it didn't look like much had changed from this morning. He glanced back at his car. Alison was standing there again, only this time she wasn't checking her watch.

'Come on, now,' he yelled, pounding on the door. 'Don't make me stand here all night.'

Finally, there was the sound of the lock sliding back. The door opened a touch. A cheap metal chain hung across the gap and behind it was the face of a thin, nervous-looking man.

'Who are you?' Lawrence asked. His voice sounded weak and tinny, his sunken eyes doing the jitters.

'My name's Isaac Holloway. I'm helping investigate the murder of Chloe Xi, the young girl that's been on the news the past few days.'

'I've seen her. What's that got to do with me?'

Isaac waited a moment as another plane howled above them. He reached into his pocket for the funeral programme.

'Seventeen years ago, you were taken and held captive by – hold on, easy there.' Isaac jammed his shoe into the sliver of space as Lawrence tried to close the door. 'I just want to ask you one question, all right? One question and then I'll leave you be.'

The pressure on his foot eased a little. Isaac took a breath and spoke quick. 'Now seventeen years ago you were taken and held captive by the Music City Monster. Only person to see his face and live.'

'So?' Lawrence was trembling now, his fingers twitching at the chain. 'Hurry up and ask your damn question.'

Isaac held up the programme and pointed to Lucas Cole. 'Was this him?'

25

NATHAN

Nathan considered that he was fortunate, in a way, to have murdered a child. Manoeuvring a fully grown adult into the trunk of his car would have been far more difficult.

He'd gone through the motions almost on reflex. His conscious mind retreating, his body moving on its own. It knew what to do and he let it take over. He watched from afar as he unwrapped his hands from around her small throat, as he draped her carefully over one shoulder, as he carried her body out into the cool night.

The trunk was just closed when he heard it: the sound of tyres rolling over the dirt track behind him. He felt himself slide back into control as headlights washed over the storage unit. When he turned they were dazzling, so bright he couldn't make out who was driving. He raised his hand over his eyes as the lights finally cut out. Coloured spots across his vision that faded as the car door opened and his sister emerged.

'Nate?'

Her voice was quiet. It was barely audible over the sound of the river. She looked over at the unit, as if seeing it for the first time. He'd forgotten that he ever told her the address.

He tried to find the right words. 'This is where . . .'

I strangled someone.

I strangled a little girl.

'This is where Daddy kept his boat?' Kate said. 'He always told me it was down at the marina. I never even knew this place existed.'

She sounded sad when she said it. Like their father had never lied to them before.

Nathan slid his hands into his pockets to hide their trembling. He was sure it must be obvious to her what he'd done. His posture, his sweat, his pale skin like a beacon in the dark. There was a dead girl not three yards from where Kate stood and yet all she could see was the storage unit. He had a mad idea of throwing open the trunk, of dragging Chloe's body out. A crazed vision of his sister taking him in her arms and consoling him, forgiving him, letting him cry on her shoulder and telling him that everything was going to be all right, that she was going to help him, that they were family and they'd get through this together.

But that was the selfish side of him. The side of him that would drag someone into his own personal hell just so he didn't have to experience it alone.

He was so very, very tired of being alone.

She said, 'Have you been inside?'

'Yes.'

'What did you find?'

Nathan could feel bile in the back of his throat. He swallowed it down. Knew if he was sick in front of Kate then it was all over. 'Nothing,' he said. 'I found nothing.'

His sister finally looked away from the storage unit and stared at him. In the dim light, her face was unreadable. For a long, tortuous moment, he was sure she was going to call bullshit. That she was going to go take a look inside herself. Nathan realised that if she did, he wasn't sure what he would do. He wasn't sure if he would stop her, wasn't sure if he *could* stop her. And yet, that part of his brain kept screaming to tell her the truth, to let her in.

But as hard as it was being alone, it was harder still to change, and so he said nothing and finally Kate nodded and turned to leave.

'I can see how much this means to you,' she said. 'I promise we'll try to find her, all right? Together.'

'Sure.'

She opened her door, went to get in and then paused. Looked back. 'You need to stop blaming yourself for what happened,' she said gently. 'We were victims too, Nate. We were just like all the other kids.'

'We're still living, aren't we?'

She cocked her head. 'Sometimes I'm not so sure about that,' she said.

Later, when he was finally driving home – the lone car on a dark road – he felt the night's events catching up with him. He slowed and pulled over, the station wagon rolling to a rough stop as his tyres left the blacktop. Falling out onto the verge, he dropped to his hands and knees and finally threw up bile in long, thin streams. When he was done, the dirt stank of it.

Nearly thirty minutes had passed since he'd arrived at the Madison storage unit. It was incredible, really, how little time it took for a life to change so completely. No – for *two* lives.

He sat back against the cool metal of the station wagon. Listening to the hush of the nearby river, Nathan felt the familiar tingle as his body started to relax. The adrenaline fading, the nerves plateauing. A strange craving for salt. It made his brain feel like it was floating inside his skull. He'd experienced it before – with animals, mainly, although he'd also tried various pharmaceuticals – but nothing compared to this. Previous times had been rough. An undercurrent that had left him shaking.

But the stronger the rush, the longer the urges stayed quiet. At first he'd been able to stretch it out; to keep the compulsions at bay for a long while. One time he'd snapped a dog's neck and that had felt pretty good. He'd gotten nearly a whole year out of that.

He climbed back into the car and slid it into drive, rejoining the road. After a half mile of quiet he reached over and flicked on the radio. Bluegrass, his father's favourite. It was probably the station he'd been listening to on his way to that hotel room. On his way to that bathroom door.

Lucas Cole had always seen his son as a scared, snivelling boy. Only now there was a dead girl in the trunk that said otherwise. A girl that his father had left behind. A girl that Nathan had been forced to take care of. He wondered what his father would say, if he could see him now.

When he arrived back at his father's house, he decided to leave Chloe Xi in the trunk until he knew what to do with her. He showered and cleaned his teeth and changed into fresh clothes. Then he made himself a large mug of warm milk. He drank it while sitting at the kitchen table, his father's manuscript lying in front of him.

The Midnight King.

A novel by Lucas Cole.

He remembered what Kate had thought about it. He thumbed through the pages, the manuscript feeling lighter than he remembered. Perhaps he left some pages behind when he snatched it up off the bar. He skimmed the opening chapters again. Ricky Taylor and his descent into madness. His wife's accident at Burgess Falls, his dreams about the small child, his brutal roadside murder of the child's mother.

Moving beyond that, he read snatches of text. Paragraphs of Ricky and his children – his *biological* children. Thin portraits of Kate and himself, sketched with all the surface characterisation that he'd expect from his father's writing. He saw scenes of them around the dinner table, Ricky laying out replacement anchor points and warming tins of chicken soup. That horrifying clash of family life and serial murder. The most impressive part of the novel wasn't in the novel at all – it was his father's innate ability to compartmentalise his life. Balancing his urges with normality was something Nathan had always struggled with.

Halfway through, he stopped. Folded back whatever page he was on and re-read it. Ricky had a young boy in a bath, was talking to him amiably as he poured boiling water over his legs. The boy was dead, of course. Strangled like all the others. As he read on, Ricky picked up a large bottle of bleach and a fresh, unopened sponge.

Nathan carefully pushed the milk to one side. Hunching forward over the table, he began to read the page properly – paying careful attention to how Ricky Taylor disposed of his bodies.

THE MIDNIGHT KING

A NOVEL BY LUCAS COLE

Chapter Nine

I think we should straight up stab you in the fucking cunt and leave you to bleed to death.

Ricky flinches. He doesn't much care for bad language. His mother always said that someone who resorts to swearing is someone of low intelligence. She'd often say it while looking at his father, who would do that funny sort of stare, like he was caught up in whatever he was reading in the paper, like he hadn't heard the words even though he clearly had, he was sitting just across the room, and now his cheeks were reddening and the newspaper was getting crushed at the edges from gripping onto it so tight.

I think we need to stop being so fucking precious about words, Ricky. There are more important things going on right now.

Ricky knows this is probably true. Really, so what if the girl who served him at the gas station was a little rude? It wasn't *his* fault the bottles of bleach didn't have their tops screwed on properly. And what did they *think* was going to happen if they stacked them like that? Like a pyramid right by the door?

So, yes, he agrees that there *are* more important things going on right now, and that while he *personally* wouldn't stab anyone in the you-know-what – rude gas station attendant or otherwise – he does appreciate someone getting worked up on his behalf for once. With Scott gone, it's nice to know he's not totally alone.

He spends another couple of minutes getting everything ready as he waits for the kettle to boil.

Sponges.

Bleach.

Black garbage bags.

Rope.

It's a short list, which pleases Ricky. He knows it would be longer if he was trying to actually hide the body. It would include things like *shovel* or *quicklime* or *bone saw* and, look, he can dig a grave or whatever, he's pretty sure about that, but sawing up a dead child is a step beyond. It requires a different strength, a mental strength, and Ricky isn't so sure he's ready for that yet.

Besides, it's not just the act. It's what it signifies. Scott was an innocent boy who lived a brutal life with an abusive mother, and she really did a number on him because all that kid did was cry for her. For six days he cried for her, for six days he pulled at his chain and threw his chicken soup across the room and wet the bed and *Ricky's* mom, Ricky's mom she would say *you can lead a horse to water* and that's what he'd done, he'd led that kid all the way to the damn ocean but he couldn't make him drink a single drop.

Only, like he said, none of that is Scott's fault. The boy is blameless. He deserves to be found, to be given a proper funeral. He deserves to go with some dignity. And lying naked in a bathtub waiting to be scrubbed clean isn't much, Ricky knows that, but it's more than he'd get if his limbs were being sawn off and packed into trash bags and tossed into the Cumberland river. It's a lot more.

The kettle begins to howl, the water boiled. Ricky stares at it.

I think we should make a move, hmm?

Ricky nods. Yes, they should. He bundles the nylon rope, sponges and bottles of bleach into the black garbage bags and hoists them over one shoulder, before picking up the kettle and heading upstairs.

Chapter Ten

It takes Ricky nearly an hour to finish cleaning. He wears thick rubber gloves and pours bleach and boiling water over Scott's skin, scrubbing every inch of him. He makes sure to go over the fingernails and between the toes. He makes sure to scrub the gums. With each pass of the sponge he can almost see the dirt and the grime and the trace evidence wash away.

Afterwards, he drains the pale white water and lifts the glowing boy up in his arms. He folds him over and slides him into a black garbage bag.

I think we should use a second bag, Ricky, to avoid any leakage.

Ricky nods and double-bags the small boy. He binds the whole package up with the nylon rope and then, after a moment's thought, ties the rope tightly using a constrictor knot. It was one of the first he learned as a boy when his father took him sailing. His father made him learn a whole bunch of them, but he can only really remember the constrictor knot and the clove hitch now.

When he's done, he sits back and peels the gloves off. He has a thin sheen of sweat on his forehead. He stares at the dark package on his bathroom floor.

I think we did a good job.

Ricky thinks so too.

I think we should go drop him off now.

Ricky thinks so too.

I think we shouldn't blame ourselves for what happened. The boy didn't give you a choice.

This, Ricky struggles with. He thinks back to Scott's mother. Hears the whistle of the tyre iron, the crack of her jaw. It was different with the boy; his death was quieter, more intimate. It was less violent. It was almost peaceful. Ricky imagines that suffocating to death must be like falling asleep.

If Ricky is honest with himself, it isn't how the boy died that bothers him. It's the fact that the boy died at all. Ricky had tried to rescue Scott, had tried to set him free, and he'd failed.

I think we will get another chance, Ricky.

Ricky hopes so.

He collects up the boy-package and carries him downstairs and out of the cabin into the cold night. It's a twelve-mile drive to the sewer pipe and he wants to get there and back before sunrise. He still has more cleaning to do – the trunk, the bath, the basement, and that one will take some time.

Driving slow, Ricky turns on the radio and¾

Chapter Fifteen

The third dream finally arrives on a freezing night in late August. Nearly five months have passed since they dredged little Jessica from the flooded underpass. Five months that Ricky has spent fraying at the edges. Snapping at his kids, turning up late to work. Walter has been patient with him – patient in the way that only a man scared of confrontation can be – but Ricky knows that even his boss has limits.

The biggest struggle, Ricky has found, is with something he has *always* struggled with: talking. Marjory used to complain that he never listened to her when she got back from work, and it was true, he didn't. He tried, though. Tried to follow her office stories and keep track of who-said-what in the staff room, but Jesus they had been boring.

Besides, it wasn't like he unloaded much onto her when *he* got home. His silence had been a two-way street. Marjory would ask him about his day, of course, like her own dull stint wasn't enough for her, like she had to have his, too. And Ricky would try, he'd try in the way he always tried. A couple of words, a stock phrase. His mind utterly unable to conjure up anything that had happened at work worthy enough to bring home with him.

Only now, lying awake in the quiet night with his bedside clock reading 12.04 a.m., Ricky turns his head and stares at the empty space in the bed beside him and more than anything he wishes Marjory was here to tell him about her day.

So he focuses on the dream, instead. It is much like the first two: a quiet road, a lone child on the horizon. Another boy this time. He has short blond hair and a slight gap between his two front teeth. Like with Scott and Jessica, he exudes a dreadful sadness. An unspoken plea for help, a longing for a normal family life. And like before he hands Ricky an item: a business card for a man named Clive Fields, an accountant who works in the financial district. His father, perhaps. On the back, handwritten in scrawling black ink, is a date and time just over a week in the future.

Sitting up, Ricky scribbles the details in his notebook. It has a permanent place now on his bedside table. Once he's finished, he glances back over the early pages, the planning he carried out to rescue Scott and Jessica. He remembers the nerves he felt beforehand, how he sat and waited, trying not to stare at the clock, trying to keep his mind open for the opportunity that would reveal itself. He remembers the adrenaline as he took them, the rush of anticipation, of possibility. The feeling that what he was doing was *right*.

Why else would they come to him like this? These poor souls, these lost children. Reaching out across space and time through their dreams to find him. Him, their dark protector, their night-time companion, their midnight king.

And, of course, he remembers how each previous story has ended. Bent over a bathtub with boiling water and black garbage bags across the bathroom floor.

Maybe this time it will be different.

As he settles back down again, he wonders about Clive Fields. He wonders what he does to his son to make him so sad. Today is Thursday; tomorrow he will phone Walter and tell him he isn't coming in to work – perhaps Josh isn't feeling well – and instead he'll get the bus across town to the financial district and find a spot where he can watch Fields. Maybe he'll even follow him a little. Get a feel for the man, find out where he lives.

Tired now, his eyes heavy with sleep, Ricky turns his head and stares at the empty space beside him and realises that perhaps it's not so bad being alone. That in fact he may not even be as alone as he once thought.

I think we're going to be just fine, Ricky.

Ricky thinks so too.

26

NATHAN

Nathan stopped flicking through the manuscript. There was still more but his head was pounding, the words on the page starting to quiver. He'd read enough, anyway – to get an idea of what went on inside his father's head, to crawl inside his own and stay there. He sat at the kitchen table for some time after he was done reading, his warm milk growing cool.

He thought back to his conversation with Kate earlier in the day. Hunched over a bar in some dusty honky-tonk. She'd called *The Midnight King* a vanity project and a poor one at that. Maybe she was right and maybe she was missing the point all at the same time.

Lucas Cole hadn't left a note before he hanged himself. He'd written a novel instead. What if he couldn't put into words what he really thought about himself? What if he'd had to take a step back, let someone else play his role? Someone like Ricky Taylor?

Nathan wasn't naive enough to think that his father wrote a book in order to apologise or set any sort of record straight. If that was the case, he'd have mailed a signed confession to Riverbend already and Edward Morrison would be halfway to Fiji on the state's dime. No, Lucas Cole wasn't interested in anyone else's story but his own.

And besides, how much of it was even true? Those schizo conversations he was having? Marjqry falling from a cliffside? Nathan's mother had died of *cancer*, and she'd taken her time doing it, too. Fading away in some piece-of-shit hospice. The sort of place that made you look forward to checking out. Not to mention those dream-children, pleading for

I think we—

help, his father the hero of his own tale, of course. The valiant protector, beating mothers with tyre irons and pulling plastic bags over their kids' heads. Nathan stands up and scratches his left arm. He wanders over to the fridge. His back is aching all of a sudden, a roaring in his ears and he's starving, too, his stomach cramping. He should have eaten those

I think we¾

chicken wings from that bar earlier tonight. There's nothing in his father's fridge but some watery vegetables and a furry block of cheese. He needs to pick up some groceries. He briefly wonders why Rhonda let the fridge get this empty, then remembers that Rhonda is wrapped up in plastic sheets in the cabin cellar, then remembers that Rhonda isn't real.

God he's hungry. He doesn't know if it's too late to order takeout, in fact he doesn't know what time it actually *is*. The clock on the cooker says it's 4 a.m. but that can't be right. That would mean he'd been sitting in the kitchen for hours. He looks back at the table. The mug of milk has a hard skin.

I think we need to get rid of her body.

Nathan nods. The longer Chloe Xi lies in his trunk, the more evidence she'll leave behind. He doesn't like it but he needs to take some of his father's advice: sponge, bleach, black garbage bags, rope. Clean her down and then leave her somewhere she'll be found in a day or so. The park by the Hickory Bay apartment blocks might work. The river flows close to it. So close that she'd probably drift right onto the swing set. The thought of it all makes him want to puke.

I think we can manage this together, Nathan.

Nathan hopes so.

27

ISAAC

Isaac paced his motel room, crunching Rolaids. One eye on the muted television set in the corner, a steady drip of late-night news. Nothing on Chloe Xi beyond what he already knew. He thought back to what Copeland had told him at the park. *This is as far as I can take you.* Like he couldn't get there on his own. Like he was a child.

The room was a mess. The bed unmade, strewn with folders and loose sheets of paper. Scribbled notes, names, half-formed thoughts. A row of glass bottles on the chest of drawers; the minibar packed full of his mother's okra and black-eyed peas.

He'd spent the last six hours trawling through Lucas Cole's life. Hunched over his desk, his muscles howling. By the time he was done he'd managed to place Cole at four abduction sites within the Nashville metropolitan area: a writer's retreat just outside Hartsville, a holiday in Murfreesboro, and book tours in Franklin and Smyrna. Four trips to within twenty miles of a child vanishing, later turning up dead.

And Tellico Plains made five.

Only it wasn't enough. It was circumstantial, it was coincidence. He took this to Hayes and Copeland now and he'd be laughed out the station. The thought of it made his stomach cramp.

So he paced his motel room and he crunched Rolaids, and he drank ice-cold water from the bathroom sink and he ran background checks and dug through property assets, and he hoped that something would jump out but nothing did. If Cole owned a boat or a storage unit, then it was off the books.

By the time he gave in for the night it wasn't just his stomach that ached. His chest did too. A shallowness to his breathing, a pulse like a hummingbird's wings. Isaac wasn't stupid. He recognised the signs. The same symptoms he'd felt in Baltimore, searching for Safia Hashim.

He was glad Alison wasn't here. She wouldn't approve. She'd tell him his body was sending him a warning. She'd tell him that he wasn't sure it was Cole, that he *couldn't* be sure. She'd tell him that he was fixating on Cole just like the cops had done with Edward Morrison all those years ago. She'd tell him that he *knew* Cole, had spent time with him as a young boy, had been in his house with Nathan and she was right, but just because the man had never tried anything on *him* didn't mean he was innocent. As far as Isaac was concerned, Lucas Cole had already admitted his guilt. A confession penned with a lit cigarette and burned into his son's flesh.

Besides, the truth was that Isaac was quicker on his own. He was smarter. It had taken him three days to find Safia's killer. Three days of not eating, of not sleeping. Three days of staring at her photo on the nightly news and knowing that he'd go three weeks if he had to.

Isaac lay face down on a bed covered with the scribbled names of dead children. The last twenty-four hours washed over him. Cruiser lights at Mallard Point Park. Edward Morrison lining up Hershey squares. Lawrence Hughes slamming a door in his face.

Lawrence had seemed scared, a look of panic at the photo of Lucas Cole. Not enough for anything official, but still. Enough for Isaac.

'What do you want from me?' Lawrence had asked.

'I want you to come down to the station, tell the detectives the wrong man is sitting on death row.'

'The wrong man?'

'Yeah, the wrong man. AKA Edward Morrison. The guy *you* accused of kidnapping you seventeen years ago.'

'Edward Morrison *did* kidnap me—'

'Sure he did. Then he decided to have a nap in his car after you escaped. Did you even manage to get a look at the guy who snatched you?'

''Course I got a look at him. The fucker kept me there for two days. I picked his photo out for the cops.'

'Oh yeah? They tell you which one they liked best?'

'I don't have to listen to this—'

'No you don't, but if you keep your mouth shut an innocent man's going to the electric chair—'

Hughes finally got his door shut at that. Isaac had balled up his fists, pounded on the thing long enough for a neighbour to tell him to beat it. Alison had put her hand on his shoulder.

'Easy there, Rampart,' she'd said quietly. 'Let's not do something we later regret.'

Now, in his motel room, Isaac finally drifted off to sleep. His curtains open, his body lit up yellow by the gas station glow, his whole life one big regret.

28

He felt better in the morning.

Coffee, black, from the maker in the kitchen. He drank it in three shots sitting on the small walkway outside his room. Gazed down at the deserted pool and that twirling Shell. It was early still, not yet seven, and Nashville was waking up around him. Traffic on the I-65. Cars queuing for Egg McMuffins at the drive-thru. Chloe's murder had been knocked from the top spot on the breakfast news; a brawl at the Bridgestone Arena during last night's Predators game. Isaac had never been much of an ice hockey fan.

He showered, dressed in a clean suit and made himself another cup of coffee. Took it back outside and tried to enjoy it this time. At half seven he saw Danny stumble into work. The guy parked across three spaces and was wearing a stained T-shirt. He glanced up at Isaac as he unlocked the office. Gave him a wave. Isaac smiled and raised his mug.

At quarter to eight he was descending the stairs to the parking lot, carrying a bottle of water and his mother's fried okra in a Tupperware box. He was running on caffeine and adrenaline, enough to get him through to lunchtime. The okra would take him the rest of the way.

He knew what he had wasn't enough. Not to prove Lucas Cole's involvement. But Chloe Xi's dog had been found with blood in her mouth and Isaac would bet his entire supply of Rolaids whose blood it was. Better yet, whose corpse had the bite mark to prove it.

His Ford started up, loud in the quiet, and maybe that flutter in his chest was a little bit stronger already. His dashboard clicked 7.47. The county medical examiner's office opened at eight, and Isaac would be there when it did.

Her name was Nicola Greene. He'd checked her out online. Low-res government photo of a stern-looking woman, her dark hair tied up so tight it probably took years off. She glared at him now across her desk.

'You're asking for a copy of *what?*'

It was after ten. Isaac had waited over two hours for her to show up. Sat in a hard plastic seat, wilting under the aggressive air con, his early-morning buzz a distant memory. When she'd finally blown in she'd barely seen him. Half running to her office clutching a stack of folders to her chest.

'Ms Greene, I'm asking for a copy of—'

'It's *Doctor* Greene. And who did you say you are again?'

Isaac put on his best shit-eating smile and said, 'Ma'am, my name is Isaac Holloway. I'm a private investigator. I've been hired by the immediate family of Lucas Cole, and I'm looking for a copy of Mr Cole's autopsy report.'

'His autopsy report.'

'That's right. I understand they're available to members of the public here in Tennessee.'

Dr Greene sighed. She went to sit down, found her chair covered by cardboard boxes. Isaac watched awkwardly as she moved them onto the floor and dug out her keyboard from underneath a sea of papers.

'Looks like they keep you busy,' he said.

'Well, people do insist on dying.'

'Even on weekends?'

'Especially on weekends.' She swapped her pumps for heels as she waited for her computer to log in. Finally she began tapping keys. 'Have you filled in an autopsy request form?'

'No, I—'

'Just thought you'd skip the queue.'

'Well, you see—'

'What did you say his name was?'

'Cole. Lucas Cole.'

She grunted as she peered at her screen. Isaac waited, forced himself to keep his mouth shut. After a few moments she glanced back at him.

'Lucas Cole. Date of birth April twelfth, 1958.'

Isaac had no idea when the man's birthday was, but he beamed regardless. 'That's him.'

'Yes, I remember. Found deceased in a motel room. You said you've been hired by Mr Cole's family?'

'That's right.'

'And what's their angle? I'm not going to get some Ivy League prick coming down to refute my findings, am I?'

'No ma'am, no Ivy League pricks.' Isaac stepped closer. Leaned in like he was sharing a secret. 'Honestly? His relatives aren't exactly taking the news well. Half of them aren't talking to the other half – I think there might be a question over his life insurance policy. I'm sure you can imagine.'

Dr Greene grunted like she was sure she couldn't care less.

'Anyway, they're just looking for some closure. Asked me to pull everything together and present it to them, real simple like. All I need is the autopsy report and I think I can bring these people some peace.' He smiled and stood up straight. 'Obviously I'm also happy to pay whatever fee your office requires.'

'Isn't that kind of you.'

'Well, it's all on expenses anyhow.'

A creak as she leaned back in her chair. 'Unfortunately, Mr Holloway, as much as I'd like to help you bring Mr Cole's family some closure, I'm not able to provide you with his autopsy report. At least not today.'

Isaac sagged slightly. 'Can I ask why?'

'Tissue samples were retained from the deceased for the purpose of a toxicology report, the results of which I'm still waiting on. It's really a formality, but I can't sign off on the report or the death certificate until I have them.'

'Even though you released the body for a funeral? Is that standard practice in Tennessee?'

'It's not uncommon for a death certificate to be issued after burial.'

'And how long is that likely to be?'

'Weeks, maybe months.'

'*Months?*'

Dr Greene shrugged. 'Like I said, people keep dying.'

'Don't I know it, doc. You're killing me here.'

'I'm sorry I can't be of more help. Tell the family my office can notify them once the report is ready if they'd like a copy.'

Isaac nodded. He ran his hand over his mouth, thinking. Truth was, he didn't really need the autopsy report. Not all of it, anyway. But he would have to tip his hand if he wanted more.

Dr Greene was staring at him. 'Unless there's something else . . .'

'Are you able to tell me the state of the body when you examined it?'

'The state of the body?'

'In particular, any evidence of an animal attack . . .'

'Now Mr Holloway, I just told you that I'm not able to provide you with the report—'

'I know, and I'm not asking for it. I'm just asking for this one thing.'

'Why? Are the family worried that he was killed by a bear rather than a noose?' She pushed her chair back and stood up. 'I'm sorry Mr Holloway, but I'm late for a call with the Mayor's office, so I'm going to have to ask you to leave.'

The air inside his Ford was hot and thick with the smell of fried okra. A corner of the Tupperware box was open.

'Jesus,' he muttered, starting up the engine and opening the windows.

His cell beeped. A text from Alison. *How are you getting on? Please don't overdo it.* Isaac didn't bother replying. He drained half his water bottle instead, held two fingers against his windpipe and after a couple minutes felt his heart rate slow. He'd forgotten how stuck up these medical folk got about their reports. But Nicola Greene was a setback, that was all. She wasn't the only person who could tell him about the state of Lucas Cole's corpse.

Halfway there and the morning news came on. The headlines were almost the same as before. The Bridgestone Arena fight. Chloe's discovery. And then, at the end, a smudge of a story that caught Isaac's attention. It wasn't even a full report, it was a line. A piece of information not important enough to hold up the local football results.

The Governor had refused Edward Morrison's request for executive clemency. In one week's time, he went to the electric chair.

29

A boy let him into Gracehill Funeral Home. Kid couldn't have been older than sixteen. Dressed in a white shirt two sizes too big and a black tie that hung halfway to his knees. Isaac started to get a bad feeling.

'How can I help you, sir?' the kid asked.

'My name's Isaac Holloway. I'm an investigator looking into the death of someone who you recently handled.'

'Oh . . .'

'The deceased's name was Lucas Cole. I wonder if I could speak to whoever prepared his body.'

'I, uh, I can have a look for you?'

'If you could.'

The boy went behind the front desk and opened a thick ledger. Started flicking through it, running a skinny finger down the pages.

'You said his name was Lucas Cole?'

'That's right.'

'Yeah, here he is. Looks like George . . . I mean Mr Darnielle handled everything.'

'Is Mr Darnielle around?'

'I'm afraid he's not here right now. I don't know when he's due back. Maybe if you leave your number I can get him to give you a call?'

Isaac handed over his card. Pointed to the cell number on the back. 'I'm going across the street to get a coffee,' he said. 'You tell him to phone me as soon as he gets in.'

Isaac sat on the hood of his car and drank three coffees before George Darnielle showed. By then it was mid-afternoon. His heart rate was pushing 110, his stomach bloated. Gas from the lukewarm okra. He'd managed to eat a third of it before his gag reflex kicked in.

Alison had sent another text, the message much the same as before: *Any update? Give me a ring when you get the chance.* He'd ignored this one too. Not because he was busy, but because with each passing minute he could feel control slipping further away. He was jittery, nervous. An atrium in his chest. No way he could speak to Alison now without it showing. She'd be halfway to Nashville before the call was done.

A brown Subaru pulled into the funeral home parking lot. Isaac watched an older man with grey hair climb slowly out and enter the building. Through the glass, he could see the skinny kid behind the desk holding up Isaac's business card.

Sliding down from the hood, Isaac tossed the leftover coffee. He was pushing open the front doors before the boy finished making the call. His cell buzzed in his pocket as he approached the front desk.

'That him?' Isaac asked.

'Yessir,' the kid said, hanging up.

The grey-haired man was standing off to one side. He looked up, sad smile already in place. 'Ah, you must be the gentleman who was asking about Mr Cole,' he said.

'And you must be Mr Darnielle.'

'Please, call me George. How may I help you today?'

'Well, George, your boy here probably told you that I've been hired by Mr Cole's family to look into his passing.'

'His passing?'

'Say, you think we could talk privately?'

It was hot in here. Either the air con wasn't working or his mother's cooking was doing a number on him. He wiped his brow, saw George's eyes drift; first to his trembling fingers, then to the boy on reception.

'Give us a minute, Lyle.'

The kid nodded and slunk away into an office.

George smiled again. That same smile, the one full of sadness. Guy probably used it twenty hours of the day, but somehow it still seemed genuine. 'Now, perhaps you could tell me what this is all about?'

Isaac cleared his throat and moved closer to the counter. 'I'm looking to find out if Mr Cole had suffered any physical injuries prior to his death.'

'Any physical injuries . . .'

'Aside from the obvious ligature marks, of course.'

'Yes, of course. And what sort of *injuries* did you have in mind, exactly?'

'Animal bites, George. Big, angry animal bites.'

George took a deep breath and glanced away. When he looked back his smile was gone. 'I'm sorry, I just can't give out that sort of personal information.'

'I understand this is perhaps an unusual request, but—'

'You say you've been hired by Mr Cole's family?'

'That's right.'

'Then perhaps it would be best if we could speak with them directly. I believe I have his son's number on file here.'

Isaac tried not to let his face show at the mention of Nathan. A stupid move, lying about his client. He took another step forward. Leaned on the counter.

'Listen. This is a sensitive matter. Not all the family are aware of my involvement. I just need a couple of my questions answered and

I'll be on my way.'

George shook his head. His hand kept reaching for the phone. 'I'm afraid Gracehill policy is clear on this, sir. I can't share that information with you.'

He picked up the handset. Isaac pressed a finger down on the receiver. 'Relax, George, you've made your point. I'm leaving.'

'I'm sorry I can't help you any further.'

'Yeah, I'll just bet,' Isaac muttered as he pushed open the glass doors.

His anger grew as he crossed the parking lot. At George, at himself. He couldn't seem to find the right headspace today. Couldn't seem to focus. Already it was after 4 p.m. and he'd spent too long sitting in chairs waiting for people like George Darnielle to show up and tell him to get lost. By the time he reached his Ford, his stomach was aching. He climbed in and the immediate stench of that hot, fetid okra reached down his throat and made him gag.

'Fuck!' he shouted.

Starting her up, Isaac tossed the half-empty Tupperware box from the window as he tore out the lot. He shook pins and needles from his hands. There was one last person he could try and it wouldn't be easy but he didn't have much of a choice.

It took him forty minutes to get there. A call to the Holiday Inn by Opryland and a stop at a liquor store to pick up a six-pack of light beer. He held them up as Nathan answered the front door. The man's eyes widened for a moment in surprise.

'Hey, pal,' Isaac said. 'Sorry to drop in on you like this, but I wondered if you had any plans for tonight.'

For a moment, Nathan didn't respond. Isaac got the sudden impression that he had someone with him. A girl, maybe. Then he smiled and stepped back, like a switch had gone off in his head.

'Please,' Nathan said, 'come in.'

30

Isaac had thought about it on the drive over. This house. This semi-detached with a smell like stale milk when it rained heavy, with a view of the river if you stood on the dresser in the box room. He'd never spent much time here – a handful of afternoons at best – and he found it strange, the jumble of half-memories this place threw up.

'Must be a little surreal,' he said as he stepped inside, 'living here again after all this time.'

'It is,' Nathan said. He closed the door and turned the deadbolt and the faint noise of passing cars faded away. 'In some ways, it feels as though I never really left.'

His mouth made a thin line. It might have been a smile. The most he would allow himself, perhaps. In the dimly lit entrance hall the man looked half vanished. His blond hair thin and near white, his eyes sunken, his skin pale. He stood with a hunch and his fingers trembled as he gestured towards the kitchen.

'I'm sorry we never talked at your dad's funeral,' Isaac said. 'Alison and I tried to find you afterwards, but you'd left already.'

'Yes,' Nathan said. 'Yes, I really wasn't up to talking that day.'

'No, of course.'

Into the kitchen now. So cold Isaac felt the skin on his arms prickle. Nathan turned on the overhead light. The harsh glare dropped the temperature even further. Isaac squinted, set the beers down, pulled one, passed it across. Saw the tremble again in his friend's hand as he took it.

The room was a freezer. As sparse as an interrogator's den. A single plate and glass by the sink, a neat pile of mail and an old-fashioned letter opener with an ivory handle. A manuscript lay on the counter.

'*The Midnight King*,' Isaac said, reading the title aloud. 'This your dad's?'

'Yes. Some unfinished work I found in his study.'

'I imagine that's nice, having something that he didn't share with the world.'

'I suppose.'

'May I?' Isaac half reached for it questioningly.

'I'd rather you didn't.'

Nathan picked it up and dropped it onto the pile of mail. Isaac smiled and nodded. 'Sorry, didn't mean to pry.'

'It's fine.' Nathan cracked his beer. 'How did you know I was here, by the way?'

'I didn't, not for sure. I actually tried your hotel again first. Guy on the front desk told me you'd checked out already. I just figured you'd be staying here. Why pay for a hotel when you've got a perfectly good house, right?'

Nathan smiled and rubbed his left forearm. 'Right.' He nodded at the beers. 'Are you joining me? Or is your stomach still giving you trouble?'

Isaac pulled a can and held it up. 'Cheers,' he said. He sipped it, the ice-cold liquid like gasoline in his guts.

'Shall we move into the living room?' Nathan said. 'I've got the fire on.'

'Sounds good.'

'It's just through the—'

'Through the archway. I remember.'

It wasn't just the house that was cold. An uncomfortable feeling that Isaac had been working the wrong angle all this time. So focused on the father he hadn't left any room for the son. It was one thing to be a monster, it was surely something else to be raised by one.

The sitting room was much like the kitchen. Neat, clean. Cushions plumped on the sofa, a glass of water on the large coffee table. A log fire burned quietly in the corner. Isaac watched the flames dance behind blackened glass. Odd, how little heat they seemed to give out.

The floorboards creaked as Nathan entered the room behind him. Isaac turned sharp. Too sharp. He felt a cold trickle of beer run down his hand.

'What did you think of the funeral service?' Nathan asked. His voice was low and raspy, nearly lost to the tall ceilings.

'It was good,' Isaac said. 'It was a great turnout.'

'Hmm,' Nathan said. 'I thought it was rather impersonal, myself. But then, I suppose that's how he would have wanted it.'

'Did you see him much? Your father? After you, uh—'

'After I left him to fend for himself with a broken leg?'

Isaac paused. Sat on the sofa and wiped his damp hand on his thigh. 'I was going to say after you moved.'

Nathan gave that thin smile again. He was in the doorway still, at the edge of the large room. He was still scratching his left arm, over and over.

'You hurt yourself or something?' Isaac asked.

'What? No, I . . .' Nathan let his hand fall away. 'Yes, yes actually I think maybe I did. I think it was a hiking accident.'

The man looked like he was about to burst into tears. Isaac gestured to a chair. 'Take a seat, pal. You're making me nervous.'

'I'm sorry.'

'Look, if you'd rather I left, just say. I don't want to impose.'

'Actually, I—'

A muffled *thump* from above cut him short. Both men's eyes snapped to the ceiling.

'You got company, Nate?'

The house was so quiet all Isaac could hear was his pulse. It roared in his ears. He dropped his gaze and Nathan was staring at him.

'Rats,' he said. 'In the roof space.'

'Some rats.'

'Yes.'

Isaac shifted on the sofa. His gut was screaming at him now and it wasn't the beer. 'You know you really did a vanishing act when you moved. I tried calling you.'

'I know.'

'Left you a bunch of messages. Alison, too.'

'I know, Isaac. I . . . I wasn't in a very good place back then.'

'We figured.'

'Did people talk about me?'

'You dropped out of school in your final year, Nathan. Your sister turned up pushing your dad around in a wheelchair. Sure, people talked.'

Nathan finally moved into the room. He stood at the opposite end of the couch. 'What did they say?' he asked.

Isaac shrugged. 'Who can remember? What's important is you, pal. You said you weren't in a good place when you left. You somewhere better now?'

Nathan's face was unreadable. He played with the tab on his can. It made a faint ringing sound. 'Define "better",' he said.

'What happened with your dad? Why'd you leave?'

'Did you never ask Kate?'

Isaac shook his head. 'I tried to, man. Alison and me both did. But she didn't seem too interested in talking. Told us you'd gone to stay with family somewhere, but we never really bought it.'

Nathan nodded and said nothing. He stared into the fire.

'I always wondered if it was because of your dad,' Isaac said, setting his beer down on the coffee table. 'If that was why you left.'

'Why would you think that?'

'Because I know what he did, Nathan. When you were growing up. I know he¾'

'You know he what?' Nathan turned back towards him. Isaac could see flames in his eyes. 'What do you know he did, Isaac?'

'I know he hurt you.'

The words fell between them, growing in the silence until they just about filled the room. A physicality that Isaac had felt before. Standing in a child molester's living room he'd felt it. Pressing his fingers into the man's throat he'd felt it more. Sometimes it was as light as air and sometimes it was heavy enough to crush steel, but the truth always had a weight to it.

Nathan seemed to feel it too. He stepped back, sagging onto the arm of a chair.

Isaac leaned closer. 'I saw them. The marks he left on you. The burn marks.'

'When?'

'Here, I think. You took off your sweater. Maybe you forgot I was there.'

'Maybe I was hoping you'd see.' Nathan was speaking so softly now that Isaac had to strain to hear him. 'Maybe I was hoping you'd help.'

Isaac flinched at that. The weight bearing down on him suddenly a little heavier. 'I didn't understand,' he murmured. 'I didn't understand what they were, what they meant. What he was doing to you . . .'

It struck him then. A flash of insight. Like a frame from a different movie spliced into the roll. Nathan, sitting there, flickering out of existence and Edward Morrison taking his place. The same sad look, the same resignation. The same sunken eyes and blond hair. The same men for ever trapped by their past, by the decision of others, by the actions of Lucas Cole.

'It doesn't matter,' Nathan said finally. He took a long drink of his beer. 'It would probably only have made things worse for me, you speaking up.'

'Nathan¾'

'Did you know he had dementia?'

'No, I didn't.'

Nathan nodded, swirling his can around in a lazy circle. 'I wonder what he was like, towards the end. If losing his mind softened him in some way.'

Isaac shifted uncomfortably in his seat. He forced himself to focus on why he'd come here in the first place. 'Did you get a chance to go and see him? Before the funeral, I mean.'

'At Gracehill? Yes, I did. It was . . . cathartic.'

'How did he look?'

Nathan took another long, slow drink. He finished his beer and set the can down on the table. Rising to his feet, he said, 'Like a corpse, Isaac. He looked like a corpse. And no, I didn't see any – how did you describe them? – *animal bites*, if that's what you're asking.'

Isaac froze.

Nathan drifted closer. 'George Darnielle phoned me after you'd left. Said he'd had a very interesting conversation with a private investigator. Said he'd been asking the strangest questions.'

'Nathan, listen¾'

'You're still working her case, aren't you? The missing girl.'

Isaac recalled the text from Chloe Xi's mother. *A man has been asking about you.* 'Yeah, I'm still working her case. Only she's a dead girl now.'

'And you think my father had something to do with it.'

Nathan, still moving ever nearer, slid his hand into his pocket. Isaac suddenly remembered there had been a letter opener in the kitchen. It had an ivory handle. His own hand twitched to his side, a detective's reflex.

'Wait,' he said.

Another loud *thump* from above. Nathan's head turned towards it. Isaac rose, stepping neatly away from the sofa and around the coffee table.

'Stay back,' he said.

'Isaac—'

He moved quickly from the room and into the kitchen. Before Nathan caught up, he snatched the top items of mail and headed for the front door. One last glance at the kitchen counter as he left. The letter opener was still there.

31

Isaac drove for three blocks before he had to pull over. His chest was hurting. He went to press two fingers against his throat then figured what was the point. It was fast, it was too fast. His eyes on the rearview mirror, like he might see Nathan walking down the darkened street towards him.

He forced himself to focus. On his breathing, on what he'd managed to steal from Nathan's kitchen. Two pieces of mail addressed to Lucas Cole and that damned manuscript, *The Midnight King*. Isaac stared at it for a moment then tossed it onto the passenger seat.

The first item was a circular. Some charity bullshit. The second was more interesting.

A bank statement.

Excited now, he flicked on the overhead light. The world outside vanished in the glare. Smoothing out the document, he pored over it, unsure what he was looking for. Payments for a berth at a local marina, perhaps. A purchase made near Old Hickory on the day of Chloe's disappearance. *Something.*

But reading through the list of payments, there was nothing. No suspicious transaction, no obvious trail. Nothing he could take to Copeland and Hayes.

Isaac switched off the light and sat back. He gazed down at the papers in his lap, at the manuscript on the seat beside him. Traffic thundered past. His car rocked with it. Glimmers of clarity punching through the churn: Lucas Cole raising a family in that house, raising Nathan in that house. In that cold house. The house that stank of stale milk when it rained, where you could see the river if you stood on the dresser. Lucas Cole, stealing children, strangling children, dumping children across the state for years, then coming home to his family, coming home to Nathan, Nathan who had left, who had run, who had only returned when his father had booked a hotel on the edge of the city and hanged himself off a bathroom door.

A dump truck roared by. It brought Isaac back.

He still felt like he was missing pieces. Still felt like his perspective was all wrong. Someone had left him that list a few nights earlier. Someone who knew the names of Lucas Cole's victims. Could it have been Nathan?

His cell buzzed. Isaac glanced at the screen, his thumb hovering for a moment before he ended the call. He needed more time to let his brain work it through. He almost had it.

He dropped his phone onto the passenger seat. It landed on top of the manuscript.

The Midnight King.

A novel by Lucas Cole.

Isaac picked it up and began to read.

THE MIDNIGHT KING

A NOVEL BY LUCAS COLE

Chapter Twenty-nine

Brooke has spent nearly eight days in the sewer system, and when the storm drains behind the condos on Long Boulevard finally overflow, her little body floats out onto the street. Half-naked and still tied in black garbage bags, she manages to make it to the end of the block before someone spots her.

Five inches in over twenty-four hours, according to the local weatherman. Biblical, according to everyone else. Dark clouds that sweep back and forth across the city like search beams. Like they are rooting her out.

Of course Ricky doesn't pay any of this much attention. The only higher power he believes in now is his own. The only voice he listens to is one no one else can hear.

I think we'll do better next time.

Ricky nods as he eats Froot Loops and watches the story develop on the morning news. They're showing helicopter footage of Long Boulevard. White tents and sombre tones and blood-red text that reads *NASHVILLE SERIAL KILLER STRIKES AGAIN*. That strange intersection between respect and sensationalism. Factual reporting with a Hollywood twist. They even have a name for him: the Music City Monster. It's more original than he was expecting.

It also isn't that accurate, either. Ricky isn't a monster – not really.

Sure, he strangles kids, but he isn't some sicko. He doesn't get turned on by it, there's no thrill in it for him. He's read about those types of people in books. People like John Wayne Gacy and Ted Bundy. It turns his stomach, the sort of things they did. Mutilations, sexual acts. Physical violence on a terrifying scale. The Midnight King doesn't kill children. The Midnight King tries to save them.

I think we shouldn't let it bother us.

Ricky knows this, but it is difficult. He changes the channel and finds an episode of *Cheers* that he hasn't seen before. He laughs as he finishes his Fruit Loops. Norm is arguing about his bar tab again.

Brooke is the thirteenth child that Ricky has tried to save. Thirteen dreams, thirteen abductions, thirteen trips to the local hardware store for bleach and rope and black garbage bags. It would be simpler to buy them in bulk – cheaper, too – but that would mean planning for failure, and Ricky doesn't think that's the right mindset to have.

It's all about positivity. He tells himself this as he rinses his breakfast bowl and refills the coffee machine. As he updates the shopping list and rubs moisturiser onto his still-aching left arm. He tells himself that nothing worthwhile is ever easy. It is the same line he has told himself repeatedly these past few years. Every time he heats a tin of chicken soup on the cabin stove. Every time he tightens the bolts on the basement wall. Every time he looks into a child's eyes and sees that they cannot be saved. Worse, that it is *him* who cannot save them.

They have been a difficult few years for Ricky. The weight of his mission aside, every child that he has packaged up and left outside is another opportunity for local law enforcement to track him down. He has been vigilant in his aftercare, of course – the bleaching, the scrubbing – but it is not the trace evidence on the body that worries him. His biggest vulnerability, Ricky knows, comes earlier in the process.

Most of the children he has rescued have come quietly. His dreams have helped with that. He has been able to catch many of them alone, in a playpark or walking home after school. There have even been occasions when he's been able to simply collect them from their beds as they sleep. He's always wondered what the next morning must be like for those parents; entering their child's room to discover them gone, seeing that empty bed. Do they feel scared? They must know they've brought this upon themselves, that they've failed as parents. Perhaps they feel guilty. Or perhaps the realisation that they no longer need to take care of a child – a child they never loved in the first place – is a relief.

Regardless, it is this stage of his mission that has always been the hardest for Ricky. Because while most of the children have come quietly, others have not. Others have fought him, have shouted for help or tried to run. They have forced his hand. Forced him to hurt them in order to keep them quiet, to put bags over their heads or gags in their mouths. Sometimes, if he has been too slow, they have managed to get the attention of one of their parents, and then Ricky's hand has been forced even further. And it's not like Ricky has a problem with beating a woman to death, far from it, but it's the chain of events that follows. The longer he stays in the child's house, the more he swings his tyre iron, or his hammer, or his carving knife, the more blood and brain matter is sprayed around, the more of a trail he leaves for the police to follow.

And he is careful, of course he is careful. A lot more than he was that first time when he rescued little Scott. He wears gloves now. He wipes down surfaces. He still trusts in the dream but he prepares for the worst all the same. There is a reassurance, Ricky has discovered, in preparing like this. In some way it signifies the importance of his mission.

Nothing worthwhile is ever easy.

The line helps, if only a little. It gives him permission to find his work difficult, to get angry, to cry. Ricky still cries sometimes – in the moment, mainly, pressing his thumbs into a shallow windpipe or rinsing bleach from the crook of a small arm. He doesn't try to stop any more. One time he sobbed for nearly an hour and afterwards he was so tired he had to wait until the next day to move the body. Poor Sally had to spend the night in the bathtub.

Thirteen dreams, thirteen souls, thirteen missions. Ricky is consumed by it. Growing ever closer to his midnight children and ever further apart from his true family. Josh and Harriet are older now, but they are still children themselves, and the burden of what they have seen and heard these past few years weighs heavily on their little shoulders.

Even now, as Ricky eats Froot Loops and watches the morning news, Josh sits upstairs in his room. On the edge of his bed, his hands clasped together on his lap. He stares at the wall. At the cracked, yellowed paint. He has been sitting like this for hours now; too scared to go to sleep, too tired to do anything else. Wedged tight between his palms is a small, wooden train. He finds himself holding it more and more these days. It is a reminder, both of the young boy who once briefly shared his room and of what his father is truly capable of.

Like his father, he too is plagued by dreams. They fester inside him, these blackened worlds. Incoherent and unrelenting. At night he sees only the great maw, and at first it was distant but it drifts ever closer. Now it is nearly upon him. Now it is close enough to hear and it is close enough to smell, and when he wakes in his bed its scent is in the room and on the sheets. It stalks him, this nightmare creature. It wishes to be made real. Fed by murder, by the dark deeds of his father, the barrier of the dreamscape weakening as it grows strong, and it is surely only a matter of time before it comes through completely.

And so Josh knows what he must do if he is to survive. He has perhaps known it for a while now, only it is one thing to know the truth and quite another to act on it.

If Josh is to live then he must stop his father and starve the monster.

He must save a child.

Chapter Thirty

Two months pass. They are uneventful months, they are the end of winter. The mornings become warm, and light, and there is white blossom on the dogwood trees and birdsong, too, so loud that sometimes Josh cannot sleep, so loud that sometimes Josh cannot dream. Those mornings are the best mornings. He does not mind waking early. He does not mind being awake while his father and sister sleep. It gives him time to think, to mentally prepare himself for the day ahead. And, if it has been a particularly bad night – of which there seem to be a growing number – it gives him time to strip his bedsheets and change out of his cold, damp pyjamas and shower away the pungent smell.

It does not help, of course, that the washing machine is in the basement.

The interlude ends one morning in late April, when Josh returns to his room to find his father standing by his unmade bed. Ricky is bent over the bare mattress, peering at it, his nose wrinkling, and when he turns he regards his son with a look of dismay and disgust.

'I hoped you might have grown out of this by now,' Ricky says.

Josh stares at the floor. His cheeks burn. He sweats into his clean shirt.

'Come with me,' Ricky says.

And Josh follows his father out into the hallway and for a moment he thinks he sees Harriet's door closing, and he wonders if his sister has been listening, and he wonders for how long.

When Ricky nears his study, Josh tenses, but his father continues past. He goes downstairs without slowing, pausing only at the front door to pull on a pair of shoes and a warm coat, and Josh does the same. When they step outside Josh realises how early it is; there is no sign of the dawn light, and the sky is black. He can still hear the sounds of the birds somewhere above them, only what was once a sweet, harping tune has become something altogether more ugly. As Josh climbs into the front passenger seat of his father's station wagon, he thinks it sounds more like a baying laugh.

Ricky does not speak to him as they drive. Josh stares out his window, his eyes streaming a little from lack of sleep. Before too long he has lost track of where they are; his father manoeuvring through side streets and narrow lanes. Quickly and confidently, as though it is a route he has driven many times before.

When they finally park it is outside a modest house in a quiet suburb. Josh gazes at it; up the steps and past the little front porch, and he tries to see through the drawn curtains and the screen door, as if he might picture the family sleeping inside. As if he might warn them of what is about to happen.

'Follow me,' Ricky says, turning off the engine, 'and do exactly as I say.'

'Dad?'

Ricky pauses. His door is half open, his face turned away. 'What?'

'Where are we? Why am I here?'

'Because I was told to bring you,' Ricky says, and he climbs out and glances back at his son before closing his door. 'I suppose we'll find out why soon enough.'

Josh watches him walk around the front of the car. His eyes fall on the silver set of keys hanging from the ignition, still swinging slightly. He briefly entertains the idea of starting the engine and running his father over. Of driving to a police station, or a hospital, or another city or as far as he can get before he either crashes or runs out of gas.

But of course he does none of these things. He was never going to do any of these things. Nor, he realises in that moment, is he ever going to do any of the *other* things that he has thought about, lying on his bed in the early hours, fresh from the shower and filled with heroic notions. He never was, and deep inside he has always known this. Pretending otherwise simply gave him something to live for.

So Josh slides out into the cold night, and he gently closes his door with a soft *click*, and he stays close to his father as they move around the side of the house to the wooden gate, where Ricky pulls a thin strip of metal from his pocket and feeds it through the slats. He gives it a sharp jerk upwards and the latch rises, the gate swinging inwards.

'Watch the gravel,' his father whispers, nodding at the ground. 'Stay on the paving.'

They make their way around the side of the house. All the while, Josh listens for the sound of traffic, or for someone moving around inside. He watches for a light to turn on or for a neighbour to appear at a window. He hopes for all of this and also he hopes for none of it, and he is scared and ashamed and for one brief, horrifying moment he thinks he might wet himself, out in the open, in front of his father.

Pausing at a small kitchen window, Ricky pulls up his sleeve and consults his watch. He waits for nearly a full minute, his index finger tapping out the seconds on the clock face, before he nods to himself. Reaching up, he grips the frame with one hand and pulls out a wooden stopper with the other. He pockets it, and Josh understands that his father must have been here earlier to plant it, to prevent the window from closing all the way. He thinks of this and of the metal strip his father used on the gate, and he thinks of Harriet's bedroom door closing as they left. It seems that some nights he has not been the only one awake after all.

'Help me up,' Ricky murmurs, and Josh locks his hands together for his father to step into. The boy grunts with the effort, his back straining. He hears the window frame sliding upwards, and then his father's weight disappears as he slithers inside the house. A moment later Ricky is leaning out of the window, his arm outstretched.

Josh shakes his head. 'I can't,' he whispers.

His father's face darkens. 'Take my hand.'

'I'm scared, Dad.'

'Take it now.'

'Please, I¾'

'If you don't take my hand I'll snap your fucking neck, you understand?'

Josh does as he's told, his heart racing. He is lifted up and into the house. They are in a small, cramped bathroom, pressed together between the sink and the shower cubicle. Ricky peels his son's clammy hand from his own and checks his watch again. After a moment he raises his finger to his lips and jerks his head towards the door.

They step out into a quiet, darkened hallway. Ricky does not pause, he moves across the wooden floor, past the base of the stairs and through an open doorway. As he does, he reaches into his pocket once more and produces a syringe that he removes the plastic safety cap from.

Josh follows him, the blood rushing through his ears so loud he worries that he would be unable to hear a hoard of elephants trampling towards them, never mind whoever lives in this house. His urge to piss has grown substantially, and he is struck by the absurd thought that he should have used the bathroom they just climbed into.

Creeping into the kitchen, he nearly collides with his father. Ricky has stopped just inside the doorway. Beyond him, Josh can see a kitchen not so dissimilar to their own. An island in the centre of the room, a small table set against one wall. And off to one side, a doorway to what must be the basement. He does not let his gaze linger long on that darkened opening.

Not that it is difficult. His eyes are drawn naturally to the glow of light from the open refrigerator door. A light that dies away as the door closes, where a small boy no older than nine now stands staring at them both, one hand still on the door and the other holding what looks like a chicken leg, and when Ricky leaps across the room the boy lets out a scream and Josh jumps and his bladder finally lets go and he pisses down his legs just as his father reaches the boy and plunges the syringe into his neck.

'Adam?'

A man's voice from an adjacent room. Both father and son turn at it and a moment later the speaker enters. He is tall, taller than Ricky and broader, too, wearing a white vest that shows off his wide chest and thick arms. The man barely pauses before advancing upon Ricky with a guttural growl, reaching for him, and Josh shouts 'Dad!' and is halfway across the room before he even realises he's moving, no longer able to hear the blood rushing in his ears or feel the wet sweatpants clinging to his thighs.

The man turns as Josh collides with him. He stumbles backwards. He loses his footing and slips silently through the darkened basement doorway. A moment later – a long moment later – there is the awful sound of the man crashing to a halt at the base of the stairs, and then there is nothing.

Josh stares into the darkness, panting. His hands begin to shake and Ricky takes hold of them and squeezes them tight and says, 'My boy, my boy,' over and over, and still there is no hint of movement from the basement and finally Ricky reaches over and flicks on the light and there, lying at the bottom, his neck clearly broken, lies the man that Josh has killed.

'I want to go home,' Josh says quietly. 'Please, Dad, please take me home.'

'In a minute,' Ricky says, switching off the light and closing the door. 'We'll leave in a minute.'

And he abandons his son there, sitting on the kitchen floor, his clothes sodden and stinking, next to the unconscious body of another boy whose own father lies dead not ten feet away, and from upstairs Josh can hear a woman's muffled screams and a dull *thud* that repeats, over and over, and when his father finally returns he is drenched in blood and smiling and holding up a large, empty suitcase into which he bundles the sleeping child.

'Come on, then,' Ricky says, popping out the handle and placing the case onto its wheels, 'let's go.'

Chapter Thirty-one

The boy – Adam – is Ricky's fourteenth child. Ricky sits now and watches him sleep. There is something he finds so peaceful about watching a child sleep. It cleanses him, it makes him feel like everything will be all right. That the answer is right in front of him. That all he has to do is grasp hold of it.

Ricky has decided to try something different this time. When Adam wakes, he will explain to him about his system. About the hierarchy. He will explain that if Adam had been one of his earlier children, he'd be waking up chained to the wall of a cellar in a cabin in the woods. That he'd spend a few days there until he'd proven himself. Until he'd shown Ricky that he could eat a meal without hurling it onto the floor, that he could hold a conversation without calling Ricky names. After that, he'd be upgraded. From the cellar in the cabin to the basement of the family home. Sure, it was still underground, but this was warmer, and it had better food, and regular, normal people living upstairs. And, more importantly, it gave him the potential – to be upgraded again, to move upstairs to a proper bedroom, to sit and eat at a dinner table with a proper family. To have a real, genuine life. To be safe.

But Adam is bypassing that system. He is being brought into the house directly. He is being shown responsibility and trust. He is being double-upgraded before he's even *started*.

It was clever, Ricky thought, to use that word. *Upgraded*. It stressed the importance of what the act meant. Ricky knew how it felt to be upgraded. It had happened to him one time when he was flying coach to Denver. The lady at the gate had smiled at him and told him he'd been selected for something they called *premium economy*. Ricky had gotten to sit near the front of the plane with a complimentary beer and some extra legroom. After that, he'd been an Air Wisconsin man for life.

I think we are onto something, Ricky.

Ricky thinks so too.

Josh sits on his unmade bed and wonders how he is ever going to feel normal again. He cradles the wooden train in one hand, running his thumb over the smokestack in an obsessive manner. He tries to think about anything other than this morning's events. He paces the room, he stands at his window and studies the dogwoods. He contemplates running a sharp blade across his skin. Just letting the pain push everything else to one side, even if only for a while. But the thought of piercing his flesh, of watching his own blood run down his arm, is too much.

After a while he hears Adam moving around downstairs. His father has placed the boy in the spare bedroom, which sits directly below his. Josh crouches down, then lies flat on his stomach, his ear pressed to the floor. Through the thick carpet he can make out the sound of footsteps, padding softly around the perimeter of the room. Josh imagines him trying the handle of the locked door or pulling on the bars bolted across the window. After a while, Adam stops moving around so much, and a short time later Josh hears the sound of him crying.

'You crossed a line today, son.'

That's how Ricky explained it to him. On the drive home, through the brightening streets. Josh's hands clamped together to try to stop them trembling, and in a suitcase in the trunk, Adam slept.

'But that's all right,' Ricky went on. 'I had to cross that line once too.'

'I killed him,' Josh said quietly.

'You killed in service of the Midnight King,' his father told him, and for the second time that morning he reached over and took his son's hands in his own and squeezed them tight. 'And that is a great honour.'

'But he's dead because of me. I'm . . . I'm going to go to *prison*¾'

Ricky shook his head roughly and squeezed Josh's hands tighter, so tight they made him squeal. 'You're never going to prison, son. Do you hear me? Never. I'll keep your secret. I'll keep your secret and you'll keep mine.' And then, when Josh said nothing in return, when he simply stared out the window and saw again the surprised look on the man's face as he'd tumbled backwards through the basement doorway, he added, 'We're family, Josh. We're *family.*'

He said more after that. About how Adam had come to him in a dream, about how the boy had asked for Josh – asked for him by name – and Ricky, he hadn't known why but he knew he couldn't ignore it, because the dreams were always right, they always came true, it was simply a matter of *belief.*

Now, lying on his back on his bedroom floor, holding the forgotten toy of one dead child and listening to the cries of another, Josh finds himself starting to believe.

Perhaps Adam had asked for him after all – just not for the reason Ricky thought.

Chapter Thirty-two

Josh takes his time to enact his betrayal.

He knows that's how his father will see it. Especially now, in the days after Adam's abduction. Ricky seems to consider their recent outing to the suburbs as some kind of father–son bonding session. He seems utterly unable to understand that Josh feels sick to his stomach – that he has felt sick to his stomach ever since it happened. Since before that, even. In fact, Josh cannot comprehend a time when he *didn't* feel sick, or weak, or ashamed, or scared. And seeing his father show tenderness after he has murdered a man only makes him feel worse.

So he bides his time. He leans into his father's affections. He helps out around the house: sweeping the leaves in the backyard, shampooing the trunk in the car, bringing Adam his home-cooked meals on a tray and leaving them in the middle of the room.

The boy hasn't tried to engage him in conversation, which suits Josh just fine. The less the boy speaks to him, the easier this will be. Josh doesn't wish to be Adam's friend. He doesn't want to get to know him or to make him feel welcome. He doesn't want to give the boy any indication of what he is about to do, not if there is even the slightest chance of Ricky being tipped off.

It happens on the evening of the fourth night. Ricky is keen to bring the boy to the dinner table, to have him eat with the rest of the family. Harriet – who at sixteen is aloof and uninterested in anything but herself – doesn't have an opinion on the matter. But Josh thinks it is an excellent idea.

'We could get takeout,' he tells his father. 'We've not had Chinese in ages.'

And Ricky smiles and pulls him into a hug and Josh has to swallow down the reflex to push away, he has to wrap his arms around his father even as his skin crawls and his stomach churns.

'I'll be back in half an hour,' Ricky says, and ruffles Josh's hair before he leaves, like Josh is eight years old again and Ricky is a loving father.

Josh sits in the living room and turns the television on, but he does not watch it. He tracks his father's station wagon as it pulls out of the driveway and disappears from view. He sits and waits for another ten minutes, fifteen minutes, until Harriet has finally gotten bored of reading her magazine at the kitchen table and has wandered upstairs to stare at herself in the mirror. Then he forces himself to wait another minute – just one, just to be sure that he really has the downstairs to himself.

And then, *then* he moves. First, to the small cabinet above the sink. He takes down the mug – the one on the far left, the one with *MUSIC CITY* stamped in faded text – and turns it over. The key falls into his palm.

Headlights rake the kitchen. Josh turns around to see the horrifying sight of his father's station wagon pulling into the drive. He is back early. He is back *early*.

Josh wraps his fist around the key and runs. Through the kitchen, through the living room, past the front door. Behind him he hears the mug shatter. Music City in pieces across the linoleum floor. No time to stop now, his father's shadow on the window as he passes outside. Harriet's voice from upstairs: 'Josh? What are you doing down there?'

He flings open the back door, then goes to the locked bedroom. It takes him three attempts to make the key fit. When he finally turns it and stumbles inside, he finds Adam pressed flat against the wall. For the first time Josh makes eye contact with the boy, motioning with his hands, making hissing sounds as he gestures towards the opened back door. He is unable to make words. Fright has clamped down on his throat. He can hear his father entering the house, can hear footsteps from above as Harriet comes to investigate.

'Josh? Where are you?'

Finally, Adam moves. He springs from the wall and flees from the room. Josh watches him race down the hallway and through the back door and out into the cool night. The boy has barely vanished around the side of the house when his father appears at the opposite end of the corridor. 'Forgot my wallet,' Ricky announces, laughing and shaking his head. 'Honestly, you'd think they'd let me at least *order . . .'*

His father's voice fades out as he takes in the scene. His beady eyes move from open door to open door. Finally, they settle on his son.

Josh sinks to the floor. He lets the key fall from his hand.

Ricky steps towards him slowly and¾

Chapter Thirty-three

The problem with Josh is that he doesn't understand what his father is doing. And yes, of course, Ricky must share some of the responsibility for that but why does he have to make things so goddamn *difficult* all the time? He never *listens*, he *never fucking listens*, he's too wrapped up in his own head, too much like his *mother*, too fucking sensitive, fucking *mental illness* that's what he's got. Nearly ruined it, the ungrateful shit, nearly ruined *everything*. Well maybe things will be different now. Maybe he'll finally see, maybe they'll all finally see¾

Chapter Thirty-nine

Ricky is making roast chicken for dinner. It is his mother's recipe. You put lemon zest and butter under the skin to help keep the meat moist while it cooks, then place the whole thing directly over a tray of potatoes. They soak up the chicken juice and go crispy all at the same time.

Harriet sits at the table now and watches as he carves the meat. Thick slices laid onto oven-warmed plates, next to those perfect roast potatoes and caramelised carrots.

Ricky comes for Josh later that night. Once Harriet is in bed. Once the neighbours that might overlook them have turned out their lights.

Josh is awake, of course. It is difficult to sleep when you are hungry, and he has been hungry for days now. For at least as long as he has been in this room. Still, it could be worse. There are no restraints in this room. No thin mattress on the floor. Just a lock on the door and a piece of wood bolted over the window.

When the door opens that evening, Josh doesn't realise that it's late. It's hard to keep track of the time without natural light. He cowers in the corner at the sound of the padlock. Starts to cry at the sight of his father. Ricky is panting and sweating, his face covered in a thick sheen. Josh barely notices. All he can think of is the smell of cooked chicken his father has brought with him. It makes his stomach ache. It makes his throat go slick, like a dog's.

'I think that's enough now,' Ricky says, stepping back from the doorway. 'Why don't you come and have something to eat.'

And he leads Josh through to the kitchen. A plate is made up for him on the table: slices of chicken and potatoes and the leftover vegetables (which are cold now but Josh doesn't care). The boy continues to cry quietly as he eats, but he manages to finish the plate and when Ricky asks if he would like any more he nods, wiping his nose on his sleeve.

Once he is finally done, Ricky takes his plate and stacks it neatly in the dishwasher, rinsing the little bits of food off into the garbage disposal so they don't become trapped in the machine and start to smell. Josh stands next to the table and watches him nervously. His fingers interlock and come apart, over and over.

'How was that?' Ricky asks. 'Did you enjoy everything?'

Josh nods.

'Good,' Ricky says. 'Now come with me.'

And he takes Josh out through the back door and into the garden, and over to the spot in the far corner where the fence line separates their yard from their neighbours. The same spot where Ricky has spent the last hour and a half working, working hard enough to break a sweat, and Josh remembers the thick sheen that had covered his father's face and the way he was panting, he remembers it just as he sees the hollowed-out earth his father has dug, and when his legs buckle his father is there to catch him and hold him and tell him not to worry, that everything will be okay, and Josh is so tired that he wonders if his father is right, if everything *will* be okay, and besides he just doesn't have the strength to fight any longer, and as he is pressed into the cold ground his last thought is that it has started to rain but it is Ricky who has begun to cry, great racking sobs, so powerful that they nearly drain him completely until he thinks of Marjory's self-help book, and that *nothing worthwhile is ever easy*, and how it is all right to cry, it is natural, it is healthy, it is nothing to be ashamed of.

32

ISAAC

His cell buzzed.

Isaac blinked. Looked over at it like it was some foreign object, his brain working slow.

It was properly dark outside now. He checked his watch, tried to remember what time he'd started reading. Tried to work out *what* he'd been reading. The story was disjointed; there were clearly chapters missing, and someone had torn out the whole back half of the book. And yet it made a strange sort of logic. Isaac could feel it, like a Rubik's cube in his head, slowly clicking into place.

He set the manuscript down and reached for his phone.

'There you are,' Alison said. 'I've called three times.'

Isaac rubbed his eyes. 'Must have had my phone on silent.'

'Everything all right?'

'Sure. Why? You checking up on me?'

'Just seeing how you're getting on,' Alison said. 'No need to get defensive.'

'Sorry. Been a rough day.'

'No further forward on Lucas?'

'Not really. Seems no one gives a damn if you don't have a badge.'

'What?'

'Nothing.'

'Still think it's him?'

'Yeah. I just need more time to prove it.' Isaac pinned the phone against his shoulder and pulled away from the kerb. He scratched his left arm. 'I've got one last idea for today.'

'What's that?'

'Lawrence Hughes.'

Alison sighed. 'Really, Isaac? Again?'

'I'm getting nowhere with anyone else. Hughes is soft. I can get him to talk.'

'You're going to get yourself arrested.'

'Fine with me. I need a sit-down with Copeland and Hayes anyway. There's only so much I can do on my own.'

'You're not on your own.'

Isaac scowled. He took the off-ramp, his car rattling over the lane markers. 'You know what I mean.'

'I know what you mean.'

'Listen, I'm nearly at Hughes's place now. I'll ring you later, all right?'

'All right. But Isaac, please, take it—'

'Easy, yeah, don't worry.'

He ended the call. His chest still fluttered, his guts still burned, but that was good. It meant he was getting close.

Pulling up outside the studio apartment, he slid his cell into his pocket and got out. He climbed the steps and saw lights flicker from inside. He hammered on the front door. Third time in two days.

'Hughes! Open up!'

No answer, but that wasn't much of a surprise. Isaac bent over and peered through the grimy window. Saw the messy room, the takeout cartons and the pile of clothes. Saw the glow of the small flatscreen

TV in the corner by the little kitchen table. Saw the arm dangling motionless off the edge of the armchair. Saw the gun, still hanging from one finger.

33

Isaac threw his weight against the front door. It flexed and cracked but didn't break. He swore and leaned back, grunted as he kicked it just beneath the lock. The cheap wood exploded.

He ran for the armchair. An old movie on the TV, Kurt Russell in the snow with a beard and a parka. Lawrence Hughes was slumped in front of it, his skin grey. His eyes were shut and his jaw half missing. Guy had shoved the barrel under his chin before pulling the trigger. There were teeth in the ceiling.

Isaac turned away. He didn't need to see this. The smell was bad enough; sweat and days-old chow mein. For an awful moment he thought he might add his mother's leftover fried okra to the mix. He stepped out of the living area. Left Hughes and his broken face behind. His throat was dry, he needed water. Doubted he'd find a clean glass so didn't bother looking. Turned the kitchen tap and drank straight from the faucet.

He was wiping his mouth when the apartment was flooded with lights. Cruisers spinning red and blue. A couple of cars pulled up outside with a screech.

'Shit,' Isaac murmured.

Technically he hadn't done anything wrong. But he knew how it looked. Knew all too well what local patrol officers might do, especially the ones with itchy trigger fingers responding to reports of shots fired. He glanced at the little bathroom window. Tried to work out if he could get himself through.

Footsteps moving towards the front door. Screams from the television set as tentacles burst from a shaking dog's stomach. A burning in his guts that screamed louder. He breathed out slow as the broken front door burst open.

'Easy, fellas,' Isaac said, his hands already raised, his fingers spread wide. 'I'm unarmed.'

The officers glanced over at Hughes and shouted at Isaac to turn around. He did as he was told, then two pairs of hands were on him, driving him hard against the wall.

He was taken to an interrogation room. Given a plastic cup of water and told to wait.

It was the same old game Isaac had played back in Baltimore. Didn't matter how good an interrogator you were, there wasn't a questioner that could hold a candle to a suspect's paranoid mind. You leave most folk alone in a bare room, sat at a table bolted to the floor with nothing but a cup of water and their own reflection in a one-way mirror; shit, they'd be just about ready to pop before you even got started.

He didn't stare at the glass wall. He kept his face impassive. Inside he was all knots, his stomach cramping, his heart racing. His left forearm itched like hell but he locked it all away and tried to look bored. Settled himself into the plastic chair and waited. Seemed like he was doing a lot of that lately.

After an hour or so the door swung open and Copeland walked in. The detective didn't look up. He had his head down in a file. Hayes followed two steps behind with a glare that could wilt steel.

'I thought you'd leave me waiting longer than this,' Isaac said. 'I barely had time to start sweating.'

Copeland raised his eyes and gave a thin smile. 'Think of it as a professional courtesy,' he said.

Hayes closed the door and they both took a seat opposite. Copeland closed the file and set it to one side. Isaac glanced at it briefly. Wondered if there was even anything inside. He'd tried that trick before too. Stared at blank sheets with a furrowed brow like it was the most interesting thing he'd read all week.

'All right,' Copeland said. 'You want to start by telling us what you were doing at Lawrence Hughes's residence tonight?'

Isaac gestured to the digital recorder sitting in the corner. 'Do we not bother with that in Nashville?'

'I thought we could just have a conversation.'

'Ah. More "professional courtesy"?'

'Sure. Isaac, what's going on here?'

Isaac looked away and rubbed his temples. Copeland had been straight with him before. About Chloe Xi's body washing up in the park. He'd been straight when he didn't have to be, when most cops wouldn't. That meant something to Isaac.

He sighed and leaned forward. 'Is this the kind of conversation where I spout hypotheticals and nine months later I'm listening to them being thrown back at me in court?'

Hayes snorted. 'You've been spending too much time with Eddie Morrison.'

'Guys, do I need a lawyer?'

'Relax,' Copeland said, and spread his hands out on the table. 'Just help us out here.'

Isaac took a long drink from his plastic cup and weighed his options. 'I'm still looking into Chloe's murder,' he said. 'Following up on a theory. I went to Hughes to run it past him. Guy had shot himself before I arrived.'

'Family paying you to do our jobs now?' said Hayes. 'I'm hurt.'

'Don't be. Family aren't paying me anything. Far as they're concerned, I was hired to bring her home alive and I failed. I'm doing this on my own dime.'

'How noble.'

Copeland said, 'This theory of yours. This the same one you were telling us about at lunch the other day?'

'Same one.'

'Christ,' Hayes said.

Isaac ignored him. Kept his eyes locked on to Copeland's, said, 'Fact is, without my badge most people out there aren't willing to talk to me.'

'I'm shocked,' Hayes muttered. Copeland's mouth twitched.

'Look, I need your help,' Isaac said. 'I know who took Chloe, but I need *you* to prove it.'

Hayes leaned forward. 'You have got to be—'

'Wait a minute,' Copeland said, holding up his hand. He was still watching Isaac carefully. 'Give us the name.'

'Can I have a word with you?' Hayes said to his partner.

'Lucas Cole,' Isaac said. 'Local author. Recently hanged himself in his motel room.'

'Same Lucas Cole who wrote this?' Copeland said, and pulled *The Midnight King* out of the folder in front of him.

'You boys searched my car. You have a warrant for that?'

Copeland ignored him. 'Why Cole?'

'Because he's the Music City Monster.'

Hayes was turning purple. He twisted in his seat, forcing himself into Copeland's line of sight. 'We are not listening to any more of this.'

'Speak to the medical examiner,' Isaac said. 'I guarantee you Cole's got a recent animal bite from the family dog. Run Cole's DNA against whatever they found in the dog's mouth. Hell, just dig him up and look.'

Hayes reached over and snatched up the file from the table. He flipped it open and said, 'I got three sets of witness statements from neighbours that saw you harassing Hughes. Banging on his door. Yelling.'

'You really think I'm stupid enough to make all that noise and *then* shoot him?'

'I think I don't trust one word out of your mouth. All this Music City Monster crap. It's a smokescreen, it's bullshit.'

'Now wait a minute. This bullshit? Detective, seventeen years ago Lawrence Hughes escaped a serial killer and then pointed the finger at the wrong man. I draw a straight line between him and Lucas Cole, and a day later Hughes paints his own ceiling. A *day*. That's not a coincidence, that's a cover-up.'

'Maybe it is. Maybe by you.'

'Jesus, why would I shoot him? I *need* him. He's the only victim who can positively identify Cole.'

'But Hughes wasn't interested in playing along, was he? All those visits, you must have riled him up. And I'm not saying you did it on purpose, but we all know you're an emotional man. Hughes pushed your buttons, and there wasn't anyone around to stop you this time.'

'That's your theory? I lose my temper and stage a suicide? Look at the crime scene, look at the *ballistics*—'

'Oh, I've got twenty men working that apartment right now, Mr Holloway. Whatever you did, I'll find out.'

Isaac rolled his eyes. 'Twenty men, give me a break. You're a worse cop than me, Hayes, you know that?'

'Keep up the quips, pal. Bottom line? I've got you at the scene of an attempted homicide. You're in big trouble.'

'"Attempted"? Jesus, Hughes is still *alive*?'

The interview room door swung open. All eyes jumped to the young, nervous-looking officer standing there. Hayes just about leapt for him. 'What is it?'

'Uh, sir, Mr Holloway's lawyer is here. She's asking to speak with him.'

'His lawyer?'

'Yessir. Says her name is—'

'Bennett,' came a voice from out in the hallway. 'Alison Bennett. And I sure as shit better not find my client being interrogated without legal counsel by a couple of detectives who are damn well old enough to know better.'

The officer at the door stepped back as Alison pushed her way into the room. She took in the scene. Glared at Copeland and Hayes.

'Oh my good Lord,' she said quietly. 'Please don't tell me you boys kept the recorder off too.'

'Now listen here—' Hayes started.

Alison jerked her head back. 'Excuse me? No *you* listen, Detective. This illegal interview is over. My client hasn't been arrested, and he's leaving with me. Right now.'

Isaac stood up. Neither officer made a move to stop him. Hayes looked like he wanted to flip the table. His partner was lost in thought.

Out in the corridor, Alison berated him. 'What the hell were you thinking, talking to them like that? Christ, you of all people should know better.'

'I needed their help,' Isaac said, a little defensively. 'I figured a conversation was a conversation.'

'Honey, sometimes I wonder about you.'

'You don't think I could last in prison? You forget I've been pumping iron?'

Alison looked skyward. 'Isaac, I swear to God if you use the phrase "pumping iron" one more time, I will phone the damn police on you myself.' She paused, then added, 'Did you tell them about Cole?'

'Yeah, I told them.'

'What did they think?'

He shrugged. 'I guess we'll find out.'

At the front desk, Isaac collected his belongings from the duty sergeant. Cell phone, wallet, a half-empty packet of Rolaids. He followed Alison through the main doors into the cool evening air. One final glance back and there was Copeland, standing staring at him next to those little plastic chairs, his face flooded with light and impossible to read.

34

NATHAN

Nathan spends the days after Chloe in a strange sort of stupor.

It is almost as though a line has been drawn, a division in his life. For the first time there is a before and there is an after. He is different now, he is changed. Killing Chloe has changed him.

It comes as something of a surprise to Nathan. After all, Chloe is not the first person he has killed. That honour goes to Lawrence's father, who Nathan spinelessly shoved in the back and down those basement stairs. But that was more of an accident. Chloe is the first person he has truly chosen to murder.

At first it is not a bad feeling – at first it is more like no feeling at all. His demons have gone quiet, gone truly quiet, as though they may have left him entirely. It isn't the same as when he cuts himself or holds his palms over a burning flame. Those are temporary fixes. Those are simply muting the volume, muffling out the sounds.

It is almost too much to hope for, Nathan thinks. He has lived with these urges for so long, he is unsure how to live without them. He sits in his father's armchair and eats breakfast cereal and he tastes it, for the first time he tastes it, and it is stale and soft and the milk is thin and he cries as he eats it – not because it is awful but because it is wonderful. Because when you have forgotten how food tastes, or how colour looks, or how restful sleep can be, it is difficult to imagine what you would not do to bring them back.

He cries not because a little girl's life wasn't worth it, but because he worries that maybe it was.

The first evening he spends watching the news. Footage of Mallard Point Park; police cars and yellow tape and men in white suits, and tired reporters speaking in sombre tones to respectful anchors who turn to their colleagues and say, 'Such a tragedy, Susanne,' and, 'You just can't imagine what her family must be going through,' and, 'Now don't forget that sunscreen, this weekend's going to be a scorcher.'

Nathan holds his breath whenever the detectives give a statement to the press, but it is so obvious they don't know what they're doing. They speak in platitudes, in clichés, in long pauses and empty sentences. They have no choice, he has left them nothing to say. They will find no trace of him on her body. If there was, they would have it by now, and they would not have kept quiet. They would have flashed it on every news channel in the state. They would have come for him with the type of righteous fury you only find in the God-fearing South.

And whenever he doubts that, he reminds himself that he was careful, that he followed the rules. Ricky's rules. His father's rules. And sometimes he is thankful for that and sometimes he wishes that he had made a mistake, that they would knock on his front door, that they would come for him and take him and save him.

Things change on day two.

Nathan wakes late, stretched out across the sofa where he must have fallen asleep. He is still dressed and the television is off. It is the morning of his father's funeral, and all of a sudden he is unsure how he feels about that.

He showers quickly. The water scratches him, his skin overly sensitive. A thin red line has developed on his left arm. He rubs it. Ricky Taylor had a line just like it, scar tissue from scrambling down to Marjory's body at the base of Burgess Falls.

He cooks scrambled eggs for lunch but finds they have a strange smell and so throws them into the trash. The suit he has brought with him hasn't travelled well; it is crushed in places, the fabric scored. Nathan decides it doesn't matter and besides, even if it did, he doesn't have time to fix it. Kate will be on her way over to collect him. She will be driving along the I-40 now. It is one fifteen, and their father is being buried in a little over an hour.

By the time they are in the church, Nathan feels like he is going to be sick. The building is full – so full there aren't enough seats, and some are having to stand along the sides of the room. He sits in the front row next to Kate and Bruce and behind him people make idle conversation. They make small talk in hushed whispers, in sombre tones they discuss their empty lives.

I think we should block it out.

Nathan tries. He tunes the words out until it is white noise, until it is a dull roar, like the static on a television set or the sound of water rushing over a fall. Again it makes him think of Ricky Taylor, standing alone on that cliffside, watching as his wife steps backwards and is suddenly gone for ever. A single moment with the power to change the course of so many lives. Nathan knows what that feeling is like. He closes his eyes.

Someone takes hold of his hand.

It is Kate. She squeezes it, gently, and when he looks at her she smiles at him, and it is a sad smile, her cheeks crinkling just like he remembers them doing the day he left. She was standing by the hood of their father's car, watching him board that Greyhound bus in the rain. Then, her eyes had been filled with concern, but now they are different. Now they are older, they are more tired, yet they are more hopeful, too. A naive, immature sort of hope; for a life together, perhaps, once this is all over. Once they are free from their father's presence.

'Are you all right?' she asks.

Nathan pauses, unsure how to respond. Unsure what collection of words she needs him to say.

I think we can come out of this day stronger, if we really want to.

'I think we can come out of this day stronger,' he says softly, 'if we really want to.'

Kate's smile widens, and he sees tears line the creases of those hopeful eyes. She squeezes his hand again. 'I think so, too,' she says.

Day three is the worst.

Nathan wakes late and on his bedroom floor. His head is thick and heavy, filled with syrup, and his left arm aches and his throat is dry and there is a hard ball in his stomach, a wet globule of nausea. There is a scratching coming from somewhere nearby. From under his bed, perhaps. He tries to sit up and coloured spots flash across his vision and he screws his eyes shut.

He pulls his clothes off, leaving them in a heap on the floor. He can smell something rotting and that sound is still there, that scratching sound, but when he finally opens one eye to peer under his bed the noise stops.

Moving towards the bathroom, his bare feet sink into the thick carpet. The same carpet he remembers as a child, most likely the same carpet that was there when his parents moved into the house.

He wonders how many bare feet have walked across it over the years. Each one leaving behind its own microscopic trace, shedding skin cells and bacteria, or unicellular organisms or parasitic creatures that still roam the deep folds and he quickens his pace to the bathroom and its linoleum safety.

He inspects himself under the harsh light. His skin is pockmarked with burn scars across his shoulders and down his arms. He runs his fingers over them. Each one its own story. There are more, he knows, on his back, but he does not turn to look at them now.

The red line along his left arm has worsened. It is as thick as his index finger. It is raised up over the skin and it is mottled and rough and when he touches it the flesh seems to retract.

He turns the shower on full, keeping his hand under the water as it warms. The mirror above the sink starts to fog and he sees himself, a scarred man, a tired man, fading away. For a moment he wishes he could do that for real, and he wonders if this is how his father felt at the end.

Stepping into the shower, Nathan tries to wash it all away, tries to rinse the sludge from inside his head but the water scratches him again and it is worse than before. It is razor blades against his skin, it is a thousand needles on his naked body. He turns the shower off but the water doesn't stop. It bites at him now, like a swarm of rats, and he feels something splitting the skin along his left arm. He watches as tiny claws emerge from the opening, as they widen the cavity, as something long and dark slithers out of him.

Nathan screams.

Back in his bedroom, his skin intact but rubbed raw all over. His heart is pounding. He cannot get the sensation of the shower out of his mind. Standing in the middle of the floor he pulls a shirt from his suitcase and dresses clumsily. He hasn't unpacked yet. The wardrobe is filled with his father's clothes.

He can still hear the scratching. He tells himself that it is in his head, that he is suffering from stress, from exhaustion, from anything that might explain what is happening to him.

I think we should take a deep breath, Nate.

He does. In fact he takes several, with his eyes screwed shut and his palms pressed against his ears. He breathes in slow, through his nose, and the stench of rotting flesh is so strong it makes him gag and he can still hear it, can still hear the scratching, even with his hands clamped over his ears he can still hear it and he wonders if it is the creature from the shower, if it is under the floor now, if it is following him around the house.

I think we're having a panic attack.

Nathan almost laughs out loud at the idea. If this is an attack then he is under siege because he has been panicking for *years* and that *scratching*, the scratching is deafening now, and it's coming from under the bed again and this time, this time when Nathan bends down and peers into the darkness he sees a rabbit sitting there, a white rabbit with red eyes and tall ears and the rabbit's name is Henry and he belonged to a little girl who lived three doors down, and one day when Nathan was eleven he took Henry from the wooden hutch in the girl's backyard and he played with him for nearly a week and none of his family noticed because he kept Henry in the back of a sock drawer and only brought him out when everyone else was asleep, and after he got bored he took Henry back to the hutch and left him there, just the way he had found him, propped up against some straw only somehow his neck had gotten broken and his head was twisted all the way around, much like he is right now, sitting under the bed, his body facing away and his red eyes staring back, and Nathan doesn't hesitate he springs to his suitcase and pulls out the little bag of razor blades

249

and plucks one out and rolls up his sleeve and

I think we—

drags it across his skin until the pain is all he can feel, until the filth inside him is drained, until all the noise has finally gone quiet.

35

Nathan stands at the window of the dining room and watches his friend leave. Isaac is climbing into his car, his coat pulled tight around him. A feeling begins to grow inside Nathan. A flicker of unease. A steadily growing certainty that something has just happened, something that he has missed.

Once Isaac has gone, Nathan returns to the kitchen. He looks around for anything that is out of place, but there are only the remaining beers lying out on the counter. Nathan picks them up and places them in the fridge. Standing there, still thinking, he straightens up the pile of his father's mail. His fingers run over the edge of the papers. It takes him a moment but he gets there.

The Midnight King is missing.

Isaac has taken it.

He tidies away Isaac's barely touched drink. He pours it down the sink, drops the can into the recycling. Upstairs there is that sound again, that thumping noise, and Nathan knows the dog must have chewed through its restraints and is now roaming the attic and yet it scarcely registers. His gaze is out the window. It is staring at the spot in the far corner, where the fence line separates their yard from their neighbours. The same spot where Ricky Taylor murdered his son.

And then Nathan is outside, walking across the unkempt lawn, shivering from the cold because he forgot to put on a coat. He stands over the spot where little make-believe Josh was buried and he kneels down and places his palm flat against the earth and he remembers the boy he set free all those years ago and how his father was so angry for such a long while afterwards. Angry enough to want to strangle and bury him in a shallow grave, perhaps.

He wonders how long that anger burned inside his father. Did Lucas Cole still feel it on his last morning? Did he think about his son as he sat in that hotel room, as he poured himself a whiskey and unwrapped a chocolate bar? Did he see his son's face as he slipped the noose over his head? His son as a teenage boy; did he even know what Nathan looked like now?

Kate has told him that their father regretted how things ended. Nathan doesn't know if there is any truth to that. All he knows is what his father has written down in his manuscript. A life told through the lens of another man and his pretend children. Characters divorced from reality, altered just enough to save his father from having to look too deep inside his own family.

Only he tried, didn't he? Kneeling here, with his palm pressed tight against the cold ground, Nathan thinks back over what his father wrote. Josh as a scared boy. As a bedwetter, as a reluctant participant in Ricky's madness. Josh, a boy who had never truly understood his father's compulsions. Whole chapters of *The Midnight King* are dedicated to Josh's point of view – Nathan can't help but wonder if this means something. An attempt to understand his son's life, perhaps, growing up in this house.

Which isn't to say that the man got it all right – far from it, his depiction of Josh leans too heavily into the fantastic at times – but maybe that isn't the point. Maybe it isn't about how well Lucas Cole captured Nathan's perspective. Maybe it is simply the fact that he tried.

Back in the living room. Standing over the fire. He picks up the shoebox and empties the contents into the flames. The simple items – the ribbons and the socks – they burn easily. The rest take longer. He watches the name tags flicker into nothing. He watches the wooden train smoulder. He watches until the last item is charred beyond recognition, and then he tosses in the shoebox itself.

Finally, he reaches into his pocket and pulls out the note. The list of every location his father struck. Damning evidence of Lucas Cole's transgressions. Once, he wanted to take this to Isaac. To finally give himself over. Now, however, in his new and altered form, he wonders if he wrote for a different reason. To better understand his father, perhaps. To have a power over him, something physical he could hold.

It really doesn't matter any more. Like everything else, it goes into the fire.

Perhaps the burning helps. Perhaps there is something ritualistic in the process, something cleansing. For the first time since Chloe's death, Nathan feels a calmness inside him. He reheats some lasagne – one of the many Tupperware dinners that was forced upon him by his father's adoring fans – and he eats it watching the news. The cycle has started to move on already: stories on college basketball championships and Arrington Vineyards' music festival creep into rotation.

That night, he sleeps straight through without dreaming, or if he does they are gone by morning. He showers and the water doesn't scratch. The red line on his left arm has faded. He makes breakfast and it smells fine. Like the rest of the world, he is moving on.

Nathan spends the day with Kate and Bruce. He drives to their apartment in Bellevue, their cramped home in the soiled corridor, and inside it is all still painted white, still a show home, but somehow it doesn't seem to matter any more. They have dinner together – more reheated donations, but Bruce has made a chickpea salad and sesame beans to go with it – and they do small talk and dance around their father and after a while somehow even he doesn't seem to matter any more, either.

'Do you think you'll stay in Nashville?' Bruce asks, helping himself to a second plate of chicken casserole.

'I don't know,' Nathan says.

'You're welcome to stay at Dad's place as long as you want,' Kate tells him. 'If you don't have to rush back, it might be nice to spend a little time here.'

'I might do that,' Nathan says.

It's something he's given a little thought to, of course. Coming back home after all these years away, how could he not. He has missed this life more than he realised, has missed eating dinner and drinking beers with other people. Half a life spent living alone is not really living at all. Half a life spent fighting to suppress these dreadful urges, too scared to ever open up to anyone, too afraid to release the hold on the creature that lived inside him.

But now the creature is out. And, at the cost of a young girl's life, Nathan is free from its power over him. So yes, perhaps it would be nice to spend some time here. In his home, with his family. Perhaps it would be nice to finally speak about it all with the one person who might truly understand him. Who might help him live a normal life.

'Do you remember when Dad took us to Huntsville?' he asks.

'God, that boring space museum? Of course I remember.'

Nathan smiles. 'You moaned the whole time we were there.'

'It was awful, Nate.'

'No it wasn't. What kid doesn't love rockets?'

'Have you forgotten how he made us stand in the rain and look at every single one they had? Some of them weren't even real, they were models. And that *movie* we had to watch, all those old people talking about politics.'

'I remember when he took us for burgers after—'

'—and the waiter spilled a milkshake down my back.'

Kate puts her fork down and starts to laugh. A moment later, Nathan joins in.

'The car stank of strawberry all the way home,' he says. 'Dad had to sponge clean the seats.'

They both lose it at that. Leaning forward, tears running down their faces. Even Bruce gets caught up in it.

After, when a comfortable silence has settled around the table, Kate says, 'What on earth made you think of that? Please don't tell me his car still smells of strawberry milk.'

Nathan shakes his head, smiling and wiping his eyes. 'No, nothing like that. I was just thinking that was maybe one of my happiest days, growing up.'

Kate looks at him across the empty dinner plates. She reaches over and takes his hand. 'I'm glad there's some happy memories,' she says.

'Me too.'

Bruce reads the room. He stands up and starts clearing away the dishes. 'I'll put some coffee on,' he says, beaming. 'Let you two talk a little more.'

Kate waits until they are alone before she asks it. The question Nathan has known is coming, ever since the news vans pitched up at Mallard Point Park and beamed their dreadful message all across the city.

'Did you see they found that little girl?'

Nathan nods. He cannot look her in the eye. 'Yes, I saw that.'

'I guess Daddy killed her after all,' she says. And then, when Nathan does not respond, adds, 'It's going to be all right, Nate. You're home now, you're with family.'

Nathan closes his eyes. How can he tell her what he has done? That he has taken a life so that he may finally enjoy his own? That sometimes he is thankful for it and sometimes he hates himself for it. That sometimes the guilt is so strong, it is actually worse than it was before, which just seems so cosmically unfair. Like the universe is toying with him. Like their father is toying with him. The man continuing to control his son's life from six feet beneath the warm dirt.

'Nate? Is everything¾'

'I killed her,' he says quickly. Blurting the words out in a rush so he can take himself by surprise. 'It wasn't Dad. It was me.'

The room is silent, and when Nathan finally opens his eyes he sees Kate is crying. Great, glistening tears running down both cheeks. She is looking at him and then she is rising, crossing the room in three strides to take him in her arms and hold him close. He can hear her heart racing, can feel her wet tears on his face. 'I'm so sorry,' she says, over and over, like she doesn't hate him, like she somehow understands, and of course she does, she grew up in that house alongside him, she's the only person in the world who would.

Afterwards, when Kate has sat back down and wiped her face and Nathan has wiped his own, they talk.

'Are you going to tell anyone?' he asks her.

'Of course not,' she tells him.

'Why would you help me?'

'Do you want me to tell someone? Do you want me to turn you in?'

'I don't know,' Nathan says. 'Sometimes I think I do.'

Kate sniffs and draws her legs up underneath her. The smell of coffee hangs thick in the air; Bruce has been and gone, taking one look at his wife and brother-in-law's tear-streaked faces and deciding to leave them alone. A sensitive man giving two crying siblings space after their father's funeral.

'She was in the storage unit, wasn't she?' Kate says. She leans forward and lifts her coffee. Cradles the mug between her hands. 'You already had her when I turned up.'

'Yes.'

'Where was she? In the trunk?'

Nathan cannot look her in the eyes. 'I didn't know I was going to do it,' he says quietly, his head down. 'Not until I was there. Not until I was . . .'

'Did you clean the body?'

'Yes.'

'Because that's the easiest way they'll find you if you didn't.'

'I said I did, Kate.'

'But did you do it properly? Daddy used to—'

'I know what Dad used to do. He put it in his book and I did the same, all right? I followed his instructions.'

'Why were you looking for her?'

'I don't know.'

'Did you want to save her?' Kate asks the question without any hint of irony. There is no mockery here, no judgement. She sips her coffee and waits for Nathan to answer, and when he doesn't, she adds, 'You know, Daddy would say that he *did* save her.'

'Well, Dad was a liar,' Nathan says. He has found his voice again now. 'He lied to everyone around him, including himself. He never saved anyone. Never wanted to, never tried.'

'It's more complex than that, Nate . . .'

'Please. He had a compulsion to strangle children with his bare hands and that's about as complex as it got.'

'Was she your first?'

It's a fair question. Only it has two answers, and Nathan doesn't know which one is true. He thinks of Lawrence Hughes's father; a man who died so his own father might live. Accident or not, the fact it was by his own hand seems an especially cruel twist of fate. He sometimes wonders what would have happened if the Hughes family had simply closed their basement door that night. How many further deaths might have been prevented?

'Nate? Was she your first?'

'She was my *last*, you understand? I can't . . . I can't be like this, Kate. I can't live like this, just waiting for the urge to start. It's like an itch, you know? An itch in my fucking head that grows and grows . . .'

'Do you feel it now?'

Nathan shakes his head. 'Not now, but it'll come back. It always comes back.'

'Then stay. Here, with us. I can try to help you. Bruce, he—'

'You can't help me. No one can.'

Kate sniffs and wipes at her nose. She gazes at the coffee in her hands as she speaks.

'You asked me why I stayed,' she says quietly. 'I told you it was to take care of him, but that wasn't entirely true.'

Nathan says nothing. He sips his coffee, each swallow shrinking slightly the large ball that sits in the back of his throat.

'After you set that boy free, things changed, Nate. Daddy felt betrayed. He felt like he'd lost a son, which to him was probably the worst thing in the world. And then when I came back and broke his leg . . .'

She trails off, gathers herself before continuing.

'I had to stay, Nate. He would have died without me to help him. Maybe not right away, maybe not for a long time, even. And I know, I know what you're thinking, that it might have been better if he had died and perhaps you're right, but it was my fault he was in the hospital, my fault he was in a cast for all those months. And if he'd died, well, that would have been my fault too.'

Another sip of coffee, another sniff.

'Now I look back at that time, at all the stuff that happened to me after you left . . . I broke him, Nate, you understand me? I broke him but I broke myself as well. And he made sure I stayed broken. He kept me in pieces, so much I couldn't have left even if I'd wanted to, so much that by the end of it, *he* was the one looking after *me*. And when Bruce came along . . . When Bruce came along he took me in. I was a mess and he took me in and he accepted me, and that's what I want to do for you, Nate. And I know that Daddy fucked us both up in the head and I'm sure we're never going to be quite right because of it but I *accept* you, okay? No matter what you've done, no matter who you are. You're family, and nothing is more important than that.'

Nathan sits there for a while, for a long while. He feels the lump in his throat break apart and he swallows it down in pieces, feels pressure against the backs of his eyes, feels tears spill over when he blinks. Tears for all the wasted years, for what he's done, for what he's lost. Tears for himself and tears for Kate, tears for little Chloe Xi and, yes, tears for his father, too.

When he is finally able to, he stands on unsteady feet and says, 'Can you give me a moment?'

'Of course.'

He bundles himself out of the room and into the small bathroom by the front door. He runs cold water over his face. He places a damp palm against the base of his neck. He is reaching for the hand towel when he hears it. A faint cracking sound, like the mirror above the sink is splintering but it is not, the glass is smooth to the touch. His fingers leave wet prints on the polished surface. Trace evidence of his sanity check. He wipes them away and turns off the tap, but the sound of running water continues even as the flow stops. It is a snare drum in the small, cold room. It doesn't even sound like water any more, it sounds like whispers, and Nathan bends closer, holding his breath, moving his ear to the empty faucet and he can make out words now, three words spoken in a hushed voice, repeating over and over as he feels something wet trickle down his spine and spread over his ribs, the filth pouring over him, filling the chasm inside him, drowning the empty chamber in his chest.

I think we—
I think we—
I think we—

When he returns, Bruce has joined them and is sitting next to Kate. He smiles broadly. 'At last!' he says. 'What happened, did you fall in?'

Nathan smiles and nods and says, 'Yes, I did, I had to swim back up,' and Bruce guffaws and there is a forced quality to it that makes Nathan cringe. Kate is watching him, still sitting at the table. She is not laughing at all.

'I have to go,' Nathan says. 'I'm sorry, something has come up.'

'What is it?' Kate asks.

'Can I get you a slice of pie for the road?' Bruce asks.

Nathan folds his jacket over his hands, and in the darkened folds he squeezes them together, his nails digging into his palms just about hard enough to make him flinch. His left arm is aching again and he knows if he takes off his shirt he will see the red line, just like Ricky's, thick and angry, running from his elbow to his wrist. He laughs and says, 'Just something to do with work,' and then he releases his hands and relaxes and pulls on his jacket and adds, 'But I would absolutely love a slice of that pie, Bruce.'

And he waits by the front door for Bruce to box it up and he feels Kate's eyes on him the entire time, and when Bruce finally returns he just about snatches the pie from him before leaving, back down that long corridor with the dirty smell and into the cold evening, where it has started to rain.

He drives home fast, too fast, his father's wipers old and near useless. They move the water around, never clearing it, never letting him see more than a snatch of the road ahead.

I think we need to—

Nathan bites the inside of his mouth and tastes blood. The pain clears his head for an instant before clouding over again. He needs to get home. To his suitcase, to his little bag of razors. He needs to drain the filth before he ends up strangling another rabbit, or worse.

I think—

Nathan cracks the side of his head against the window. He groans, red-tinged saliva oozing from his open mouth. He jumps a stop sign, horns blaring. The rain is heavier now, the wipers are no good. All he can see is dazzling lights – street lamps, indicator bulbs, neon signs.

Somehow he makes it home, pulling up outside with a screech of brakes, one tyre bumping up onto the sidewalk. He half falls onto the street, not bothering to *I think we* lock the car, just focusing on moving one foot in front of the other. Through the gate, along the path, up the stairs and there is a *man standing at the front door*, a man Nathan has never seen before, a man dressed in a suit and with a long, black overcoat, a man who sees him approach and raises his hand in greeting, who doesn't leave the shelter of the doorway, who reaches into his inside pocket and pulls out a black wallet.

'Mr Cole?'

Nathan nods, suddenly unable to unclench his jaw, his fingers taught, every muscle in his body taught. All he can think of is the razor blade and the sound of rushing water and the black filth.

'I'm sorry to call on you like this, I know it's late,' the man says, smiling apologetically as he flashes his ID. 'My name is Detective

Harry Copeland. I wonder if you have a few moments to talk?'

Nathan tries to speak. Tries to tell him to leave, that now isn't a good time, that he isn't exactly *himself* at the moment.

But he doesn't, because he can't. Because he's too weak, because he's *always* been too weak.

I think we should invite him in.

36

The detective shakes himself a little as he passes through the door-way, like a dog. Nathan watches droplets of rainwater land on the thick rug, rivers running off the man's shoes and onto the wooden floor.

'I appreciate this,' the man says, smiling again, his eyes roaming the large hallway. 'Is this your father's house?'

He says it like he doesn't already know but he must, he must know whose house this is. 'Yes,' Nathan answers. 'Or it was, I suppose.'

'Of course. I'm sorry for your loss.'

I think we should offer the man a drink, Nathan.

'Yes, I know.'

'What's that?'

'Would you like something to drink, Detective?'

'Oh, well, coffee if you have it. But only if it's not too much trouble.'

'No trouble at all. It's cold out there tonight. Can I take your coat?'

'I'm fine, thank you.'

Nathan turns and walks deeper into his father's house. Behind him, he hears Detective Copeland follow. He wonders if the man's gaze is still moving, still trying to take everything in. He is suddenly very glad that he decided to burn the shoebox.

In the kitchen, he fills a kettle and places it on the stove. 'Is instant all right? I'm afraid I haven't had the chance to buy anything nicer since I got here.'

'Instant is fine, Mr Cole.'

'Nathan, please. Milk and sugar?'

'Just black.'

The detective takes a seat at the breakfast bar in the middle of the room. Nathan can hear water dripping from the man's coat. It pools beneath him.

'How long have you been in Nashville, Nathan?'

'About a week.'

'Do you plan to stay on?'

'My sister was asking me the very same question earlier today.'

'Kate, isn't it?'

Nathan is opening cupboards, searching out the small bag of half-used instant coffee he knows is here. His father has tied it shut with a piece of string. He undoes it, scoops granules into mugs. His back is to the detective.

I think we need to be careful.

'Yes, that's right.' The kettle begins to whistle softly. 'You've certainly done your research.'

'Oh, it's just force of habit. Don't take it personally. I can't drop off my dry-cleaning without running a background check.'

Nathan doesn't need to turn around to know that Detective Copeland is smiling. He can hear it in the man's voice.

The kettle nudges it up an octave. He pours boiling water into both mugs. The granules melt and foam slightly.

I think we should get rid of this man. I think we should just pick up a knife and—

Nathan plunges two trembling fingers into his coffee up to the knuckles. The scalding pain cuts through him, clearing his head. He coughs, loudly, then reaches for a dishtowel and wraps it around his hand.

'Everything all right?'

'Yes. Just a little clumsy today.'

He sets both mugs on the breakfast bar. He opens the fridge to get milk, pressing his red fingers against the cool glass bottle.

'So, how can I be of help to you?' Nathan says, not meeting the detective's eyes as he pours milk into his own mug, his burnt fingers twitching, the milk spilling onto the counter.

Detective Copeland smiles again. He lifts his coffee and takes a sip, reaches into a pocket and pulls out a notebook. Starts to open it. Stops.

'Is something wrong?' Nathan asks.

'No, it's just . . .' The detective sets the book down. 'Most people? I show up on their doorstep late in the day, saying I want to come inside. First thing they do is ask me why. But not you.'

'No?'

'No. *You* invite me in, you make me a coffee – which is delicious, by the way – and *then* you ask.'

'Well, I mean, I was just being polite. It was raining out, and—'

'Oh, of course. And like I said, please don't take it personally.'

'Force of habit?'

The man laughs. 'That's right, very good.' He takes another sip of coffee before opening the notebook fully. 'I actually wanted to talk to you about your father.'

I think we—

'My father? Why? Are you a fan of his books?'

The man laughs again. He is clearly finding Nathan very funny. 'Just crossing something off my list. Tell the truth, I've never actually read his work. I'm not much of a reader. I prefer history books, if anything.'

'That's all right, I don't like his stuff much either.'

'That so?'

'Yes. Although don't tell anyone I said that.'

'Then it's our secret.' Detective Copeland smiles and takes another drink. He makes an appreciative noise. 'You sure this is instant?'

'Yes, quite sure.'

'Well, it's better than some of the fancy crap I've shelled out for, believe me. Did you know your father well, Nathan?'

I think we—

'Honestly? Not that well.'

'On the road a lot, was he? Book tours, festivals, stuff like that?'

'That's right.'

The detective consults his notebook. 'Phoenix, Bozeman, Rhode Island. He was a busy man. Did you see much of him growing up?'

'He didn't become big until after I moved away.'

'To Minnesota?'

'Yes, but—'

'And here's me thinking *this* is cold weather.' He turns a page. 'Let me see . . . I've got you in Duluth, Rochester, Sioux Falls, although I suppose that one's actually North Dakota . . .'

'South Dakota.'

'So it is.'

The detective is still smiling, only Nathan is starting to feel left out of the joke. Under the table, both his hands have started to tremble. He presses them into his thighs. 'Is there any particular reason why you're looking into *me*?'

'There's a symmetry between you and your father,' Detective Copeland says. 'You're both racing around the country, like you're chasing something. Or maybe you're running, I don't know. Do you see what I mean?'

'I'm afraid I don't.'

The detective waves his hand through the air and laughs. 'Ignore me. It's my inner history buff, that's all. I've always found this sort of stuff intriguing, these generational patterns. Sometimes it's the strangest things that run in the family.'

Nathan nods and smiles but it is a weak smile and he can feel it faltering at the edges. His mind is becoming heavy again. It is becoming harder to think. He is sliding out of himself once more.

Detective Copeland says, 'I'm actually working an attempted suicide at the moment. Man named Lawrence Hughes. I presume you're familiar with him.'

'Why would I be familiar with him?'

'Lawrence Hughes was abducted by the Music City Monster when he was a boy.'

'How awful.'

'Yes. He managed to escape, though. Said he was left alone with the back door open, if you believe that. He's something of a household name now.'

'I've not lived here for a long while, Detective.'

'No, I suppose you've not.' The police officer closes his notebook. 'Well, I've taken up enough of your time. Thank you again for the coffee.'

I think we should set him on fire and—

'Before I forget,' Copeland says, and reaches into his wet jacket. He pulls out some rolled-up papers. Unfurls them on the breakfast bar. It is a copy of *The Midnight King*. The same copy that Isaac stole. 'I wanted to ask you about this before I go.'

'That's my father's book.'

'Yes, so I gather.'

Nathan stares at the manuscript. Then he stares at Detective Copeland. The man is scratching his left arm. 'You've read it, haven't you?'

'Have you?'

'Some of it. Why? Why do you have it?'

The detective is thumbing through the pages now. 'It's actually rather interesting. Your father writes this book before he dies, about this man who murders children. And right towards the end, his son lets one of the victims go.'

Nathan doesn't say anything. He doesn't trust himself to speak. Doesn't know what the right words are. So he turns away, busying himself with tidying up. He wipes up the spilt milk and sweeps crumbs into the trash.

Copeland fills in the silence. 'And the similarities to this case ... It's uncanny, Nathan, it really is. You said you'd read it?'

'Some of it.'

'Some of it, right. What did you make of it?'

I think we—

'I didn't much care for it.'

The detective laughs again, even though Nathan definitely hasn't said anything funny this time. 'You know what? I don't much care for it either. It's dark and it's unpleasant, and whole chapters seem to be missing. But it has this weirdness about it, too. Like it burrows into my thoughts. I find myself thinking about it all the time, I can't seem to shake it. Isn't that weird?'

Nathan is ignoring him now. He makes a non-committal noise as he re-ties the string around the neck of the coffee bag.

'Did you find that?' Copeland repeats. 'When you read it?'

'Well, remember I only read—'

'You only read some of it, that's right.' Detective Copeland motions at the coffee. 'Interesting knot you've tied that with. What is it, a clove hitch?'

'A constrictor knot.'

'Uh huh. Your father teach you that?'

Nathan stops. 'What?'

'Listen to me, I'm rambling. I really will leave now.'

I think we should slice him, Nathan, slice his throat with shards of glass, stick a knife in—

'C-can I get you an umbrella, Detective? It's still raining, I think.'

'Oh, I'd appreciate that. I can drop it off tomorrow, if you're in.'

'Please, there's no need.'

Nathan makes his way over to a large cupboard, talking now, jabbering words, any words, the first words that come into his head. As he walks he can feel the filth inside him. It has filled his chest, it is in his throat. So high that if he were to bend forward he is sure it would come spilling from his mouth.

He opens the cupboard and clicks on the light. A number of umbrellas are stacked in one corner, while in the other there is a collection of bleach bottles, sponges, nylon rope and rolls of thick black garbage bags. Nathan pauses when he sees them. He has forgotten he stored them here.

When he turns around, the detective is staring at the cleaning products. Then, with a blink, he is staring at Nathan.

I think we need to do something.

Detective Copeland twists slightly on his stool as he reaches under his jacket. 'I'm going to—'

Nathan lunges forward, swinging an umbrella wildly. In one fluid motion the detective pulls his revolver and steps backwards, rising from the stool.

It is unfortunate that it is raining tonight. It is unfortunate that Detective Copeland was standing for so long in the downpour. It is unfortunate that he did not allow Nathan to take his coat. There are a great many things that are unfortunate about this evening, but at this exact moment, these are perhaps the most important three.

When Detective Copeland steps back, he moves his left heel into a small puddle of rainwater. It is the runoff from his coat that has pooled beneath him as he was sitting drinking coffee, and when he draws his revolver he shifts his weight slightly, pivoting onto his left foot. It happens quickly and it happens in near silence. The detective's left heel slides out from under him and the man falls backwards, his arms pinwheeling, his eyes going wide, and when he is roughly halfway to the floor the back of his head impacts with the metal handle of the door that leads into the living room.

It doesn't seem like a serious injury; Detective Copeland is on his feet again a few seconds later. He's dropped his gun and it's clattered across the kitchen floor, only from the vacant look on his face Nathan isn't sure the man even realises he ever *pulled* his gun, and there's blood, too, running over the detective's neck and down the front of his chest, a great volume of blood, an alarming volume, and Nathan cannot move, he cannot breathe, he cannot do anything but watch as Detective Copeland lurches from the room, towards the front door, and stumbles out into the rain.

37

ISAAC

It was the lead story on the morning news. Isaac heard snatches of it as he shaved. Only the strongest words made it through.

Eventually he strung enough of them together and emerged from the bathroom, wrapped in a towel and with half his face still lathered. The razor hung by his side. Water dripped onto the stained carpet.

Copeland had been found dead in the early hours. Slumped over his steering wheel, the car in the middle of an intersection. A zoom shot over the reporter's shoulder showed blood on the seat.

Isaac flipped between stations as he drove. Most of them didn't have anything more. A nugget on Mix 92.9 as he approached the scene: police had cordoned off a nearby property.

He made it to the end of the street before he had to ditch the car. News vans lined the sidewalk, local reporters doing their bits to camera. Behind them, yellow tape fluttered between the lampposts.

A small crowd had gathered already. Drawn by the dark energy that now infused this place. The air was charged with it. That strange, nervous excitement when death was dangled in the distance. Far enough to avoid its notice, close enough to feel the hairs rise on your arms as it brushed past.

He saw himself as Ricky Taylor. The man climbing down the scree to find a horde of onlookers huddled around his dead wife. His hand moved involuntarily to the wound on his left arm. It took him a moment to shake the image clear. To realise that his arm was fine.

A young officer spoke as Isaac neared the tape. 'Sir, I'm going to have to ask you to step back.'

Isaac glanced past him. Scanned the figures milling around Lucas Cole's house. Men in white boiler suits who knelt to examine the ground, who took photographs of the garden path, who carried boxes out the front door and loaded them into waiting vans.

A voice from the side: 'Let him through.'

They both turned to see Detective Hayes marching over. His face was twisted, his mouth churning. Isaac watched the man's nostril hairs dance as he got close.

The officer lifted the tape and Isaac stepped under. He heard whispers from the crowd. A reverence that made him sick. A sudden urge to turn around and tell them all to go home, that a man was dead, that this wasn't anything people should be witness to.

Hayes was waiting for him. Isaac approached with his head bowed. 'I'm sorry about your partner,' he said. 'Copeland was a good man.'

'I don't want to hear it,' Hayes said. 'Not today. You understand me?'

'Sure.'

'They found him three blocks from here.' Hayes jabbed a finger down the street. 'But they reckon he was dead after two.'

Isaac narrowed his eyes. In the distance he could see another crowd of people. He imagined the forensic team scouring Copeland's car.

'What do you think happened?' he asked Hayes.

The detective stepped closer and made fists and said, 'I think he came here chasing your lead and I think he got his head caved in. There's a trail of blood from the kitchen all the way to the street. I'm amazed he was able to start his car. I'm amazed he was able to *walk*.'

'What's the murder weapon?'

'No. You start answering *my* questions now. Where the fuck is Nathan Cole?'

'I don't know. He's got a sister, Kate, he might have—'

'Already tried. She's gone.'

'Ran?'

'Judging by the state of her dresser, I'd say she left in a hurry.'

Isaac tried to think it through. He could feel Hayes watching him. Could hear the detective breathing heavily. It must have burned the guy up, asking for his help.

'Can I see the house?' Isaac asked.

'Not a chance.'

'What about those boxes? Forensics have been carting them out non-stop since I got here. What's inside them?'

Hayes glared at him. 'Animals, Mr Holloway. Dead animals. Ten, at the last count.'

'Jesus.'

'Fuck Jesus. You know Nathan. *Where is he?*'

'I've barely spoken to him since I was a kid, Detective. And besides, I don't know him. I'm not sure if anyone does.'

'What does that mean?'

'It means that you need to change your approach if you want to find him.'

Hayes stepped away and started pacing. His face was red, his mouth slightly open. Isaac got the feeling the guy wanted to hit something. Maybe having a crowd of witnesses nearby wasn't such a bad thing after all.

Hayes finally stopped and rubbed his scalp. He said, 'You still think Lucas Cole is the Music City Monster?'

Isaac nodded. 'Absolutely.'

'So, what, Nathan Cole is just following in Daddy's footsteps?'

'Nathan Cole grew up with a serial killer for a father. You need to accept that if you want to get into his head.'

'Don't start telling *me*—'

'You need to get an expert involved, Hayes. A criminal psychologist, a behavioural analyst, *someone*.'

'I'm out of my depth, is that it? I should get the FBI on the phone?'

Isaac pointed at the line of forensics still streaming from the house. 'Look at those boxes. Does any of this seem normal to you?'

Hayes tried to keep his glare going, but it was already starting to fade. His shoulders were slumped, his fingers twitching. For the first time, Isaac glimpsed beyond the angry barrier and saw the core of fear that he knew lived inside every detective. Fear that something had been missed. Fear that a suspect had slipped away. Fear that a partner had died because of a mistake.

Isaac had lived with that fear every day – it was what drove him to work the streets. It was what made him beat Safia Hashim's killer half to death. It was what crushed him.

He took a step towards Hayes, half reaching for the detective. 'We can still catch him,' he said quietly. 'We can still bring Copeland and all those kids justice.'

If Hayes heard him, he didn't react. The man's gaze was drifting, unfocused. He reminded Isaac of the broken people he'd dealt with back in Baltimore. He reminded him of Chloe Xi's father.

The detective finally motioned to his neck and said, 'You're bleeding.'

Isaac touched the spot; his fingers came away red. This morning's rushed shave. He patted himself down for something to stem it and came up empty. Hayes grunted and handed him a tissue.

They were quiet for a while longer. They watched the technicians work the house.

'Copeland put in a call to the medical examiner's office last night,' Hayes said. 'Asked to put a rush on Lucas Cole's autopsy report.'

Isaac pressed the tissue against his throat and stared at him. 'When's it expected?'

'Came through this morning.' Hayes buried his hands in his pockets, started to walk away. 'Toxicology results show Lucas Cole was drugged up to his eyeballs when he died. No way he was able to hang himself.'

'He was *drugged*?'

''Fraid so.'

'What about the dog bite?'

Hayes was three steps away when he turned and answered. 'Medical examiner found no sign of a dog bite anywhere on him. Whoever took Chloe Xi, it wasn't him.'

38

Isaac sat in his car for a long while after that. Hayes's parting words kept him company.

It scared him a little, how much he'd gotten wrong. Worse, how much he'd had riding on it. How much he'd needed it to be true.

But then he'd always been like that. Always struggled to hold competing ideas in his head, to make room for doubt. It was the only way he knew how to work. Only way he knew how to live. Since moving back home to Nashville he'd started to understand how much of himself was wrapped up in being a detective. Even now, six months out of the job, it defined him still.

His cell phone rang. Alison. She must have seen the news by now. She'd be worried about him. Imagining him doing something stupid. He declined the call; he wasn't ready for her yet. For her concern, for her care. Her hand had taken his at lunch the other day and he wasn't ready to think about that, either.

Three blocks later, driving just for the sake of forward momentum. His mind running over everything. His visit to that house two days earlier. Had he put Nathan on edge? Said something to tip him off? He should never have stolen that manuscript, should never have given it to Copeland. Maybe Hayes was right, maybe he *had* sent Copeland to his death. He wondered what Nathan must have thought, opening his front door last night to find a detective standing there in the rain. He wondered how it might have happened. What Nathan might have used. He wondered about Copeland, too, running from the house, drenched in blood. Had he hoped to find safety in his car? Driving away, had his last conscious thought been one of relief?

His cell rang again. Isaac ended the call on reflex. Tossed the phone onto the passenger seat where it clattered down the side of the door. His thoughts drifted back to *The Midnight King*. Truth was they'd never really left it. He'd spent the night dreaming about Burgess Falls. Had woken to the sound of Marjory's scream.

He was crashing, he was losing it. He was Ricky Taylor sliding a plastic bag over a small boy's head, only it was Isaac who couldn't breathe.

A truck's horn brought him back. He jerked the wheel, his tyres screaming, and screeched to a halt by the side of the road. A couple walking by stared at him through his window.

He stumbled from his car, falling back against the door and taking in great lungfuls of air. With each exhalation he tried to let it all go.

Ricky Taylor.

Safia Hashim.

Ricky Taylor's hands around a child's throat.

Safia Hashim's shoe by a television set.

He was outside a cafe, one of those old houses transformed into a trendy breakfast place. This was good. His stomach would hate him but he needed a coffee, needed something to eat. Not bothering to lock the car, he went inside and ordered an Americano and a bagel and a glass of water which he drained in one go.

Finally, he was outside again. Sitting on a wooden bench, halfway through his bagel and the world starting to feel sane again. Next to him, people rocked on swinging chairs and sipped hot chocolate from chipped mugs. Across the street an elderly man mowed his lawn. This was real, this was safe. His stomach gurgled but nothing more. He was going to be all right.

Walking back to his car. Walking slow. He'd call Alison. He'd call her and meet her for lunch. He'd talk to her, be honest with her. About how she'd been right – he hadn't been ready for this case. Baltimore had left its mark on him and he wasn't yet free of it. That had to be why he was feeling like this. Why he couldn't get that damn book out of his head.

He went for his keys, then remembered he'd left his car unlocked, the keys in the cup holder. He opened the door and climbed in. He was searching for his fallen cell phone when he sensed movement from the back seat. No time to turn around before there was a sharp pain in the side of his neck. He dropped his coffee, was dimly aware of hot liquid spilling down his legs, and then everything went dark.

39

It was the smell that woke him.

His neck ached. He stretched it gingerly, wincing. He tried to reach it but couldn't move his arms.

'Oh, at last,' came a voice from somewhere nearby. 'I was starting to worry you'd never wake up.'

It was a woman. She stepped closer as Isaac's vision cleared. Blue eyes and curly blond hair.

'Kate,' he said, swallowing, his throat dry and cracked. Her name came out as a whisper.

He glanced down at himself. Thick rope bound him to a chair. It was wrapped around his arms and across his chest. It took him a moment to realise he was sitting at his parents' dining-room table.

'What's going on?' he said. His voice was stronger now. 'What are you doing here, Kate?'

She pulled out a chair and sat across from him. 'I thought it was maybe time for us to have a conversation.'

'You ever hear of a telephone?'

Kate waved her hand through the air dismissively. A glimpse of a white bandage from the edge of her sleeve. 'Some conversations you just need to have face-to-face.'

'Uh huh. Where are my parents?'

His gaze roamed. It was still morning, the light outside unchanged. He couldn't have been out for more than an hour. He wrinkled his nose. 'And what's that smell?'

'Listen to me, Isaac,' Kate said. 'Are you listening?'

'I swear if you've hurt them, Kate, I'll—'

She casually lifted a snub-nosed revolver from her lap and placed it gently onto the table. The metal made a dull clunk against the wood. 'Are you *listening*?' she repeated.

'Yes, I'm listening.'

'Good.' She leaned forward. 'Because we need your help.'

'We? Is Nathan with you?'

Kate tilted her head at the mention of her brother's name. Her blue eyes gleamed. Isaac stared at her, wondered what was going on in her mind. He tested the ropes again. The chair creaked but he barely moved.

'Kate?' he said. 'Kate, is Nathan with you?'

'Why did you come back?' she asked.

'What?'

'To Nashville. Why did you come back?'

'I really don't—'

'How come you're not a cop any more?'

'Because I beat a man so bad he drinks his dinners, you understand me?'

She shifted in her seat. He had her attention now. 'Are you a violent man, Isaac?'

He started to shake his head, then stopped. 'I didn't use to think so,' he said. 'But yeah, I guess I am.'

'That's all right,' Kate said. She stood up and wandered over to the window. 'It'll be our little secret.'

Isaac grimaced as his guts cramped angrily. Acid flared up into his chest. He pushed against his restraints with the pain. The smell was stronger now, it was harder to ignore. A bitter, pungent odour. He stared at the bottom of the door that led into the kitchen. At the faint yellow glow from the oven. Kate was cooking something.

'You want my help?' he said. 'Untie me and let my parents go. I'll do whatever you want.'

'Unfortunately, it's not going to be as simple as that,' Kate said.

'I know what's going on here. I know about your father. I know who he was.'

'Oh?' Kate seemed to be enjoying herself. 'And who was he?'

'He was the Music City Monster. And I can only imagine what growing up with him must have been like, but—'

Kate groaned. 'Let me just stop you there, Isaac. Don't bother trying to psychoanalyse me, all right? Better people than you have tried.'

'Yeah, but they didn't know what I know.'

'And what *do* you know?' She gazed out onto the street, her back to him, her voice taking on a dreamy tone. 'What could you *possibly* know?'

Isaac gritted his teeth as his stomach churned again. The stench in the house was making him gag. 'I know you took Chloe Xi, and I know you killed your father.'

Kate didn't answer straight away. When she did, it was with a toneless, mechanical laugh. 'Well. You're quite the detective, aren't you?'

'Tell me I'm wrong. Tell me that bandage on your arm isn't covering a dog bite from when you snatched Chloe at Old Hickory.'

She turned and stared at him. 'This?' And she rolled up her sleeve to reveal white gauze up to her elbow. 'I burned myself making dinner the other week. It was a nasty one.'

'Well, whatever you're cooking in there smells so bad I almost believe you. *Almost.*'

A man's voice rang out from behind him. 'Don't blame that on her, Isaac. It's my first time cooking this dish. And in someone else's kitchen, too.'

Isaac tried to turn around but he couldn't twist his head far enough.

'And besides,' the man continued, closer now, 'she's telling you the truth. She really *did* burn her arm. The dog bite, on the other hand—' He paused as he walked around to stand next to Kate. A short, balding man with a wide, rubbery smile. Kate slid her arm around him and he rested his head on her shoulder. 'I was the unlucky one there.'

He pulled up his shirt far enough to show a large white surgical dressing across the side of his ribs.

'I'm Bruce,' he said, and smoothed down the front of his shirt. 'It's a pleasure to meet you, Isaac. I know you want to see your parents, and you will, I promise you, but why don't we have a spot of lunch first? I've been wanting to try this for some time now, and the meat should be just about ready.'

40

They both disappeared into the kitchen. Isaac could hear them open-ing cupboards and murmuring to themselves in low voices. He im-agined them rifling through his parents' belongings. Imagined the snide comments as they saw the chipped plates, the odd glassware.

He strained against the ropes, his stomach gurgling unhappily. At one point he had to close his eyes with the pain. It was happening again, just as before. The same feeling of helplessness he'd felt those three days search-ing for Safia Hashim's abductor. Running off caffeine and four hours' sleep and the knowledge that he was too late, that he was always too late, that the best he could do was bring the man responsible to justice.

Only somewhere in those three days the meaning of the word had changed. Justice had moved from the courtroom to a back alley, from a judge's gavel to his own two fists. By the time he'd broken down that pervert's front door, the only justice left had been in wiping that human stain from existence. Isaac was just sorry his colleagues hadn't let him finish the job.

But now it wasn't Safia Hashim who was in danger, it was his par-ents. Now there wasn't anyone around to make him stop.

Kate finally emerged from the kitchen and went about setting the table. Knives, forks, glasses. Every so often she would fire a glance at him from the corner of her eye, her mouth twitching. She was excited.

'I need to see my parents, Kate,' he said. 'I need to know they're all right.'

'After lunch,' she said, inspecting the table. 'You'll see them after lunch.'

'I'm not eating whatever that is. It stinks. It's rotten.'

'Bruce will get angry if you don't at least try it.'

'Show me my parents and I'll try some.' She was ignoring him now. Humming tunelessly, smoothing the white tablecloth with her palm. A nervousness began to expand inside him, like an uncoiling snake. 'Kate? Show me my parents and I'll try some. Do you hear me? Show me my parents, Kate. *Kate.* Show me my fucking parents!'

He shook himself. Strained against the ropes. The wooden chair creaked. It was old, it was flimsy. He felt one of the slats shift slightly.

'There's no point trying to break free,' Kate said. 'Bruce ties the strongest knots.'

Isaac stopped struggling, panted as he stared at her. 'He's done this before?'

'Yes.'

'He's done this to you?'

The question caught Kate by surprise. 'That's a strange thing to ask.'

'Your wrist. He burned it, didn't he?'

'No.'

'Bullshit. If he's forcing you to go along with this, I can help you.'

She didn't answer him. Isaac watched her leave the room and reappear a few moments later with a jug of water.

He tried again. 'Please, help me understand.'

'Isaac—'

'So Bruce took Chloe at Old Hickory. Why? Is it the same reason as your dad? The same reason as Ricky Taylor?'

Kate's hand jerked slightly at the mention of Ricky's name. Water spilled onto the tablecloth.

'That's right,' Isaac said quickly. 'I've read it. Really worms its way inside you, doesn't it? Tell you the truth, I've not been able to stop thinking about it.'

'I'm sure Daddy would be pleased.'

'I'm right, though, aren't I? Bruce wants a kid of his own. He's following in your father's footsteps.'

'Stop.'

'Let me guess, Lucas groomed him to take over and you got passed from one abuser to another.'

'I said stop—'

'What's Bruce's problem anyway? Guy can't get it up? Only way he can have a family is to fucking snatch them—'

The kitchen door flew open and Bruce was there, striding across the room. Metal glinted as he swung the revolver.

Isaac's head spun. Blood splattered across the tablecloth, bright red. Bruce stood over him, the gun still in his hand. 'Try that again,' Bruce said quietly, 'and I'll shoot you in the head. Do you understand?'

Isaac glared at him. His guts burned. His chest burned, his arms and his legs burned. Inside he was a raging inferno.

'Sure,' he said, running his tongue around the edges of his bruised mouth. 'I understand.'

'Good.'

Bruce watched him for a moment longer, then suddenly turned towards Kate with a look of alarm.

A couple of moments later and Isaac's thudding heart faded enough to hear it too. The car door slamming, the soft *clang* of the garden gate, the sound of approaching footsteps. By the time the doorbell finally rang, Isaac knew who it was. Who it could only be.

'Isaac?' Alison called. 'Are you in there?'

41

Bruce looked over at him. 'Who is that?'

'That's Alison Bennett,' Isaac said. 'She's a friend. She's worried about me.'

Bruce checked the revolver and began moving towards the front door.

'Wait,' Isaac said. 'I can get rid of her. Just let me speak with her.'

'You'll stay in that seat and keep your mouth shut.'

The bell rang again. Alison was hammering on the door now. 'I know you're in there, Isaac,' she shouted. 'Your car's parked outside. I need to speak with you.'

'Bruce,' Isaac said quickly, 'Bruce you need to untie me. You give me thirty seconds, I'll send her on her way.'

'If we ignore her, she'll leave.'

'No, she'll come around the side of the house and look through that window' – Isaac nodded to indicate which one – 'and then you'll be in real trouble.'

Bruce waved the gun. 'So I'll shoot her.'

'It's broad daylight. Someone will hear.'

Both men turned back towards the front door. Alison had stepped to the side, her shadow filling the frosted strip of glass. Isaac imagined her trying to peer inside.

Kate took hold of her husband's arm. 'We can't afford to make a public scene. We're running late as it is. Give him thirty seconds to get rid of her.'

'Fine,' Bruce said. 'Thirty seconds. If you haven't gotten rid of her by then, I'll drag her inside and slice her stomach open in front of you. Are we clear?'

Isaac nodded.

When Isaac opened the door, Alison looked flustered. She was standing with her hands on her hips, her face red. 'Took you long enough,' she said. 'I've been calling you all morning.'

She made to step forward, into the house. Isaac didn't move aside. He'd only opened the door a crack. Enough for him to see out, enough to hide Bruce standing next to him, the barrel of the revolver pressing into his side.

'You're not letting me in?' Alison said.

'Now's not a great time.'

'What?'

'I can't talk.'

'What do you mean you can't talk?'

Bruce twisted the barrel slightly, his meaning clear.

'What are you doing here?' Isaac said.

Alison pulled her head back slightly. 'Honey, what do you think I'm doing here? I saw the news. Your detective friend.'

'Copeland?'

'Yeah, Copeland.'

'What about him?'

'What *about* him?'

Isaac knew this routine would be driving Bruce mad. He knew it was a dangerous game.

'*This* is why I've been calling all morning, Isaac. When you didn't answer I got worried. Worried you might be getting in over your head again on this one.'

'I'm fine,' Isaac said. He smiled widely, but it was a mad smile. A smile that made Alison pause and narrow her eyes.

'Are your parents in?' she asked. 'Could I maybe talk with your mom?'

'Listen to me, Alison,' he said, and he held her in place with his gaze. 'You don't need to worry about me. I've been pumping iron, remember?'

Alison blinked. 'Oh honey, do *you* remember what I said—'

'Of course I do. Now I'm really not feeling well. I'll call you in the morning, all right?'

Back in the dining room now. His hands tied behind the same chair. Bruce watched him, the revolver dangling by his side.

'Now that's all dealt with,' he said, smiling, 'how about a spot of lunch?'

Isaac shifted in his seat. Tested the ropes. Kate had tied them; they were looser than before, and she hadn't bothered with his legs. He said, 'If you think I'm eating whatever you've got cooking in there, you're mad.'

Bruce glanced over at Kate and Isaac saw her nod. Bruce said, 'You want to know what I think? I think we've heard enough from you for now.'

He picked up a napkin from the table, balled it up with one hand, and used the other to grab Isaac's jaw. Isaac tried to move his head away but Bruce was too strong. The man's long nails pressed painfully into his cheeks. 'Hold still,' Bruce hissed, and forced the napkin into Isaac's mouth.

Before Isaac could spit it out, Bruce wrapped white gauze around his face. Nearly a full roll of it, bound tight across his jaw. The napkin pressed deep into his mouth, an edge tickling the back of his throat. Isaac felt himself gag and go hot and forced a long, slow breath through his nose. If he threw up now he'd likely choke to death.

'There,' Bruce said, stepping away. 'Now you keep quiet while we serve lunch, and if you're very good I'll take that off so you can try some.' He smiled again. That long, elastic grin. 'I really think you're going to like this.'

He went back into the kitchen. Kate pulled out a chair and sat down opposite Isaac. She inspected her knife, wiping a spot with her napkin. She lifted the water jug and looked at him questioningly, and he started back at her, unblinking. She poured them both a glass.

Isaac watched her closely. He ran it all over in his mind. In his tired, run-down mind. He saw her like Lucas Cole saw her, as Ricky Taylor saw her, as Harriet. He thought about the manuscript and its missing pages, its lack of an ending.

Too late. He was always too late.

Finally the kitchen door swung open again and Bruce re-emerged. He was holding a wooden chopping board. Isaac remembered buying it with his mother. It was made of bamboo and was spiked on one side. It now held a large joint of meat. The outside was seared brown, and it was bound in string, and it glistened as it approached the table.

The aroma hit Isaac hard. He tried not to smell it, tried not to breathe it in, only that would mean not breathing at all. It made his eyes water. It made his throat go slick and his stomach flutter, and it was not because it was rancid but because it was exquisite.

Bruce was slicing the meat now. Isaac watched him; he tracked each slice as it fell away from the joint. Inside, the meat was pink and the edges were charred. The foul stench that had filled the house earlier was nearly gone but Isaac held onto it as best he could. It meant something, that smell. It meant something monstrous, something unspeakable.

'Do you know what I thought, the first time I met Kate's father?' Bruce asked suddenly, glancing over at Isaac. 'It's all right, I know you can't answer. I'm going to tell you anyway. I was in *awe* of him.'

He started transferring slices of meat to the waiting plates.

'Not because of his books,' Bruce continued, 'which I hadn't actually read at the time, but because of his ideals. His passion. Most people who feel the same urges as us, they fight against them. They try to placate it. They self-harm, they talk to therapists. They strangle *cats* for crying out loud.'

He laughed then, moving the chopping board into the centre of the table and sitting down. 'Now don't get me wrong, I've strangled my fair share of cats, but only because I was trying to fit in with society. Does that make sense? Sorry, that's another question you can't answer.'

'You'll have to excuse him,' Kate said, smiling. 'He's been waiting to taste this for so long.'

Isaac gazed at the scene before him. It was like something from that damned manuscript. The Midnight King and his stolen children, his forced family. Ever since he'd read it, Lucas Cole's words had somehow tainted the world around him. They'd wormed into his brain, they'd coated his skin. They'd filled his heart and been pumped through his veins. Something was happening to him.

Bruce picked up his knife and fork and cut into his food. He lifted a piece of meat to his mouth, then paused to stare at Isaac for a long, cold moment. Isaac stared back, unable to look away, and suddenly that stench, that putrid, cloying stink was back. It was as thick as smoke, it was all he could breathe and it was all he would ever breathe again.

Bruce popped the piece of meat into his mouth.

Isaac threw himself forward, letting out a guttural, tormented scream. The chair held.

Bruce chewed, thoughtful. 'It's not what I expected,' he said to Kate. 'And honestly, I can't say it's as nice as all those internet forums led me to believe.' He swallowed and took a drink of water. Then he picked up his plate and got to his feet. He walked around the table and set it down in front of Isaac. 'I'm going to unwrap your mouth now,' he said, 'and you're going to try some of this.'

Ricky's breath stank of it. No. *Bruce's* breath stank of it. Isaac recoiled, his eyes watering. He could feel his guts tense. He was going to be sick. Bruce leaned across the table and lifted the carving knife from the chopping board. He pressed the blade against Isaac's skin; it was still wet from the meat. With one smooth motion he sliced through the bandages. When he pulled out the napkin, a long stream of bile came with it.

Isaac retched. He drew in deep gulps of air. Bruce tossed the make-shift gag to the floor and used the carving knife to cut a sliver of pink meat from his plate. He pierced it with the tip of the blade and held it in front of Isaac's mouth.

'What is it?' Isaac said quietly.

'Open your mouth.'

'Where are my parents?'

'Eat it and I'll tell you.'

'Show them to me and I'll eat it, please—'

Bruce pressed the meat against Isaac's lips. The carving knife danced beneath it. Isaac closed his eyes as it was forced into his mouth. A sharp pain as the blade cut his lip; the hot tang of blood mixing with the meat.

As soon as the knife was clear, Isaac turned his head and spat it out. The small, bloodied piece of flesh landed on the carpet by his feet. He felt his guts contract violently and he finally threw up his morning coffee. His vomit splashed down the side of the chair. It was speckled with brown.

42

'You really need to get that checked out.'

Bruce was inspecting the vomit. Crouched over it, his balding head a half metre away. Isaac strained against the ropes. His muscles taut. Fuelled by the nightmare he'd unleash when he got free: eyeballs bursting under his thumbs, screaming mouths wrenched in two. He felt the bindings loosen further.

'I had a buddy who would puke brown crap like that,' Bruce said, shaking his head as he straightened up. 'Turned out he was bleeding in his belly. Those Rolaids will barely touch the sides, Isaac.'

'I'm going to fucking kill you . . .' Isaac said. He may have trailed off then or he may have said more, it wasn't clear. He knew his mouth was moving but all he could hear was a long, low tone. It seemed to reverberate around his chest. It fogged up his head, made it hard to

I think we—

focus, made it like he was sliding into a warm lake. His left arm throbbed but the pain in his stomach had faded out, and Bruce was saying something, walking around the dining-room table and saying something, laughing, maybe, like he'd told a joke, and it must have been a good one because

I think we—

Bruce is bent nearly double and wiping his eyes and it's funny, course it's funny, Isaac doesn't even need to hear the joke to know it's funny, and he starts to laugh and it feels good, it feels so good, like it's the first time he's laughed in a long while.

I think we need to play along for a while, Isaac.

And Isaac does. The volume knob gets turned up again and he catches the tail end of Bruce saying '. . . least we'll have plenty lefto-vers,' and Kate shakes her head and says, 'We haven't got time to cook any more,' and Isaac smiles widely because Isaac knows he needs to placate them both, just for a little while longer, just long enough to free his hands, long enough to reach that carving knife, long enough to slit both of their throats.

Bruce says, 'We have time for coffee, don't we? All good meals should finish with coffee, don't you think?' and Kate glances at her watch and gives Bruce a look that says *stop fucking around* and Bruce nods as he gets to his feet.

'I'll put a pot on,' he says, heading towards the kitchen. 'It won't take long, and then we can get started.'

Isaac knows the knife and the gun are somewhere nearby, but he does not look at them. He is smart enough to know that this will tip them off. He is smart enough to know that the longer he lets them talk, the longer he has to free his hands.

'Yes,' Isaac says, 'let's get started.'

Bruce seems pleased. He returns from the kitchen a few minutes later with a cup of coffee in one hand and the gun in the other. He sits down with the gun in front of him. The carving knife is next to the meat on the chopping board in the centre of the table. It remains just out of Isaac's reach.

The smell of the meat – if it can even be called that – still fills the room. It is Isaac's fuel now. With each breath it filters through his body, a living reminder of what Bruce and Kate have done. Of what *he* must do in return.

I think we should open them up. I think we should skin them and hang them from their insides. I think we should—

Bruce takes a slow sip of coffee and glances at Kate, who is standing watching by the window. 'Where was I?' he says, and leans forward in his chair, sliding the gun to one side so he can clasp his hands in front of him, like he is a businessman running a meeting in a boardroom and not a short, balding man at a dining-room table.

'What would you say if was to ask you—'

'Be quiet,' Isaac says.

His words cut Bruce down mid-sentence. The man is so surprised that he does as he's told. He recovers quickly enough, though, his face reddening, and he leans forward and says, 'Now listen to me—'

'I won't talk with you,' Isaac says. He shifts his gaze from one captor to the next. 'Only with her.'

It takes Kate a moment to respond. 'Why me?' she asks.

'Because you're the one in charge,' Isaac says.

The room is silent. Isaac sees what might be the flicker of a smile on Kate's face. Behind her, it is another cool, crisp afternoon. There is the glint of traffic passing the house, and the occasional rumble of a semi or the throaty growl of a sports car driving along the nearby Highway 31. It is the sound of life continuing on as normal, less than a hundred yards away.

'Now listen here—' Bruce starts.

Kate speaks over him. 'We want to know what the police have on us. On my father, on Nathan. What they pulled from my father's house this morning. We want to know what they're planning; we want to know everything they've told you.'

Bruce's voice fades out. By the time she's done, he's sitting quietly in his chair, his gaze low.

'What do I get in return?' Isaac asks.

'A quick death,' Kate says.

And so Isaac answers her, because a quick death means one of them using the gun or the knife, and a gunshot will draw needless attention so he hopes they will choose the knife, which will require them to get close in order to use it, and that is when he will strike. He tells her that the police know her father is the Music City Monster. That they'll have cross-referenced his movements with each child's disappearance. That after he killed a detective, they will suspect Nathan killed Chloe Xi as well, and that when they went to speak with Kate and Bruce this morning they found their belongings packed up and gone. 'So now they're not just hunting for Nathan,' Isaac says. 'Now they're after the whole lot of you.'

'How did the police work it out?' Kate asks.

'I told them,' Isaac says.

'How did *you* work it out?'

'Someone left me a list. I still don't know who. But it doesn't matter because your father got there first. He wrote it all down, called it *The Midnight King* like it's a story, but it's not.'

'And what is it?'

It's an incubator. It's a viral load. It's a concentrated dose of madness. *I think we all know what it is.*

'It's a confession,' Isaac says. 'One you should have burned, Kate. It would have been cleaner. Instead you left your mark all over it. Chapters missing, the whole ending removed. At first I wondered if Cole had even written one, but now I realise it was you, covering your tracks. Hiding what you did. Erasing yourself from the narrative.'

Kate smirks at that. Then she turns and leaves the room for a moment. When she returns she is holding a bundle of papers. She throws them onto the dining-room table, where they fan out enough for Isaac to recognise Lucas Cole's manuscript.

'You're right,' Kate says. 'I did take stuff out. All the ways I helped him, all the things I did. And don't worry, this is getting burned before we leave. I should have done it before, you were right about that, too.'

'He just wrote down everything you did together?' Isaac snorted. 'I've heard you should write what you know, but I guess your dad really took that to heart.'

'Yes, well. Daddy never did have much of an imagination.'

'No, but you did,' Isaac says. 'Shifting your hunting ground out of state was a smart play. I bet you couldn't believe your luck when Edward Morrison took the fall.'

'Luck is what you make, Isaac.'

'How many children did you help him kill?'

'A few.'

'He must have been so proud.'

'He was. Now tell me what the police were taking from his house.'

'Animals, Kate. Dead animals. I'm guessing Lucas killed most of them.'

'My father never hurt animals.'

'Oh that's right. He exclusively hurt children. That's why your husband liked him so much.'

'If you're trying to get a rise out of me—'

'I'm just trying to grasp the family dynamics here. See, *Bruce*, I understand.'

At the mention of his name, Bruce sits up. 'Oh?' he says, glancing briefly at his wife. 'Do tell.'

'You're the classic serial killer fanboy, Brucey-boy. You're a Lucas Cole wannabe, you're a groupie. Hanging out backstage, chugging the Kool-Aid, fluttering your eyelashes to get his attention. It's pretty tragic, to be honest.'

'That's an interesting theory.'

'Tell me I'm wrong. No, better, tell me how you *met*.'

Bruce clams up again. Kate, still smiling, steps closer. 'They met online. On an internet message board.'

Isaac crows with laughter. 'The fucking *personal ads*?' He drops his voice an octave and says, "'*Balding man seeks older male for friendship, intimacy and lessons in molesting.*'"

'Close,' Kate says, her face hardening, the smile gone. 'But my father never molested anyone.'

'You really think so? I reckoned you were smarter than that.'

'You don't know me, Isaac.'

'Bullshit I don't. I grew up here, Kate. I know you just fine. I know you lived in that house, same as Nathan. I know you must have seen things no child should ever see. Things that made your brother run away, as far and as fast as he could.' Isaac swallows, his throat dry. He studies her, the way she clasps and unclasps her hands, the way she sways slightly. 'But not you,' he adds softly. 'The things you saw? They made you want to stay.'

'All right, that's enough,' Bruce says.

'Do you even know where your brother is now?'

'I said that's *enough*, Isaac.'

Isaac holds Kate's gaze. He is challenging her.

'My brother needs his family,' she says at last, and to his great relief she moves towards him, towards the table, towards the knife. 'We're going to help him.'

Isaac studies her expression. Her face is blank. She is purposefully trying to make it unreadable. But Isaac has sat across so many tables and stared into so many similar faces. 'You're going to kill him, aren't you?' he says.

'Of course not.'

'Don't you lie to me, Kate. You're cleaning house. Lawrence Hughes knew too much so you shot him, only you did a piss-poor job of it. Poor fucker's still clinging on, even with half his face gone. Nathan's next. And as for Daddy—'

'You don't know what you're talking about.'

'I know he had dementia. What a kicker. I mean, what's the point in raping twenty-odd kids if you can't even—'

'I told you he never raped them, Isaac.' Kate's voice is ice. 'He never touched them.'

'Then why'd he scrub them so good when he was done?'

'For *respect.*'

Isaac laughs again, only this time he has to force it, like he finds all this funny as hell, like he doesn't see Bruce reaching for the gun. 'Oh, please. It's always something sexual with you freaks. Deep down you enjoy it, and your father was no different. A hundred bucks says he got hard every time he watched the life drain from their eyes.'

Kate is moving towards him again. Her body is rigid, her face crimson. 'My father didn't *enjoy* what he did to those children,' she says. 'If you've read his manuscript then you'll know that. He tried to bring those kids into our family.'

'He tried to replace you.'

'He loved us!'

'The man used to burn your brother with cigarettes. He wanted to bury him in the backyard.'

'That was different.'

'Oh, it always is, honey.'

Bruce gets to his feet now, raising the revolver. 'I think we should bring this to an end,' he says to his wife.

'Nathan told me that you two drifted apart,' Isaac says, talking fast, saying anything to hold Kate's attention. 'Does that make it easier to kill him like this? In cold blood?'

'You're not listening,' Kate snaps, and she steps towards him, into Bruce's line of fire. 'Nathan is my *brother*. I've just got him back, you understand? I'm not about to lose him again.'

And suddenly Isaac realises that she's telling the truth. That she really *doesn't* want to hurt him.

'Honey, please,' Bruce says from across the table. 'You need to move out of the way.'

I think we need more, Isaac. More more more—

Isaac looks over Kate's shoulder at her husband. 'Well if it's not you, then it's got to be him. Bruce killed your father, Kate. And I can prove it.'

'Don't listen to him,' Bruce says.

'Your father was losing his mind, spilling his secrets . . .'

Kate reaches for the carving knife, its blade making a dull rasp as it drags along the chopping board. 'Stop talking about my father.'

Isaac can feel the old chair shifting but not enough, not nearly enough. Kate is so close now, she is almost all he can see. He holds what little eye contact he can with Bruce and says, 'Did you know he was drugged before he died? What did you use to knock him out before you strung him up, Bruce? Same stuff you stuck in my neck back at the coffee shop?'

It isn't much, but it is enough. Kate pauses, turns around to look at her husband, her husband who is shaking his head and protesting only Isaac doesn't hear him, can't hear him, his focus is on Kate, is on the bindings, is on putting everything he has on wrenching his wrists apart in one last, muscle-straining effort, and just as Kate turns back he finally feels the old wooden chair give way and his hands come free as he rises, wrapping his fingers around Kate's wrist and snapping it back so hard that she howls and the knife falls away and he grasps hold of it and slashes upwards in a single, sweeping motion and Kate's throat opens up. A stream of blood arcs over the dining-room table and across the pages of *The Midnight King*.

Before Kate hits the floor Isaac is moving, throwing his weight against the table. Bruce is hit straight in the stomach and he falls back, first onto his chair and then onto the floor. The revolver spins away and Isaac climbs over the table, feral, snarling, his face and hair drenched in Kate's blood, the carving knife raised above him, and he drops onto Bruce and before Bruce can react the blade is pressed against his throat tight enough to break the skin.

'Here's how it's going to work,' Isaac murmurs. 'I'm going to kill you, but it's going to be slow. Your eyes, your ears, your tongue. Where should I start?'

'You're fucking insane—'

Isaac slides the blade into Bruce's mouth. It clatters off his teeth, it cuts his gums. Blood oozes from between his lips and runs down his cheeks.

'Tongue it is,' Isaac says. 'Now hold still or I might slice your throat.'

'You need more practice.'

The voice comes from behind him. Isaac turns. Kate is standing there, the revolver raised, his makeshift gag pressed tight against her neck. It is already sodden with her blood.

'Easy now,' Isaac says, the knife trembling in his grip.

'Let him go.'

'Don't think I can, Kate.'

She licks her lips, swaying, the barrel of the gun sweeping back and forth. 'Put the knife down and step away.'

Isaac pauses, his breathing ragged, as ragged as the man on the floor beneath him.

'Your father's not worth it,' Isaac says softly, his voice calm. 'He's not and you know it, Kate. You're better than him. Deep down you know it.'

'I don't.'

'I get it, all right? Lucas hurt you just like he hurt those children. But you can walk away right now if you put down the gun. You can be free of him, of all of this.'

'I'll never be free,' Kate says, and her voice cracks a heartbeat before she pulls the trigger.

Isaac's left shoulder buckles. The knife falls away and Bruce howls. Isaac rolls onto his back. His shoulder is on fire. He clamps a palm over the wound and nearly passes out.

He tries to sit up but Bruce is already there, pushing him down again, pressing his hand against his stomach, pressing it *into* his stomach. A strange sensation, like Bruce's fist has somehow reached inside his guts. He feels things move beneath his skin, tearing and popping. Glancing down, he watches Bruce pull the carving knife out and then slide it home again and all Isaac can think is that it doesn't hurt that much, in fact it barely hurts at all.

He hears sirens, in the distance or in his head. Kate is screaming and Bruce is spitting blood into his face, forcing his chin up. Isaac realises that he is going to slit his throat.

He thinks of his parents. He hopes it wasn't like this for them.

Then the carving knife is moving, glinting in the afternoon sun, and he is gone.

THE MIDNIGHT KING

A NOVEL BY LUCAS COLE

Chapter Fifty

Harriet stands in the wet grass of the unkempt lawn. It is early still, the sun only just starting to break the horizon. Under her coat she is wearing cut-off jeans, her bare feet sunk into a pair of old sneakers.

This is the fourth morning she has come outside. To stand here, in this spot, on the edge of her brother's grave.

It is not unusual for Harriet to be awake at this hour. In many ways, it would be more surprising if she were asleep – like the rest of her family, she too is plagued by dreams. Violent, awful dreams, in which she does violent and awful things. To herself, perhaps. To others almost certainly. Harriet cannot say for sure because she does not remember them.

It is a coping mechanism, she has decided. Her brain's way of protecting her from having to recall such dreadful imagery upon waking. Occasionally, she is able to bring something back with her: a fragment, a glimpse into another world. Lying in her bed, she tries not to see it but it is there no matter where she looks, like frames from a different movie spliced into her own.

Her solution, therefore, is to avoid sleep entirely. Instead she spends her nights hunting. Prowling the streets for someone to occupy her, to keep her awake. She drinks and takes pills, and sleeps with boys and men alike, and if she has not conquered sleep then she has at least bent it to her will, as much as such a thing is possible to do.

Which is why, four days ago, Harriet was still awake well after midnight. Why she was standing at the window watching her father dig a shallow grave in their backyard. She did not feel the need to go down and ask him why. The reason was obvious to her, after all, and a short while later, when Ricky laid her brother down in the pit and strangled him to death, her suspicions were proved correct.

But ever since that night, Harriet has felt an urge inside her. From the pit of her stomach she has felt it, a calling. And each night she has pulled on her warm coat and her tattered sneakers and crept outside to stand in the long, wet grass and gaze at her brother's resting spot.

On this, the fourth day, she is not alone: Ricky has joined her for the first time. He, too, cannot sleep, only it is guilt that keeps him awake. He stands next to his daughter and for a long while they stare at the grave in silence.

Finally, Ricky says, 'I don't know how to move past this.'

'Yes, you do,' Harriet says.

And she is right, of course. What is the cure to losing a child but to replace them?

'I'm not sure I can do it alone,' Ricky says. 'I thought Josh . . .'

He trails off, and Harriet hears his throat *click* as he swallows.

'Josh was weak,' Harriet tells him. 'He wasn't cut out for it.'

'And what about you?' Ricky glances over at his daughter. 'Are you cut out for it?'

Harriet says nothing. She can feel her father's gaze on her. A flicker in the corner of her vision; frames from her dreamworld bleeding through. Flashes of violent, awful things.

'How long has it been since you had a proper night's sleep?' Ricky asks her.

'I can't remember,' Harriet says. 'A long while.'

And for reasons she cannot quite understand, she finds herself telling her father about her dreams. She tells him that she no longer sleeps, that she no longer *needs* to sleep. Not properly, not any more. She tells him that she has conquered sleep, which is a concept he finds amusing.

'I think sleep has conquered *you*,' he says. 'But here's my solution. Help me rebuild this family. Help me find peace, enough for both of us to share. Enough to let you sleep again.'

Chapter Fifty-one

The little girl's name is Caitlin.

She is spending the day shopping with her mother, which Harriet now realises means following her mother around and carrying her bags. By lunchtime, the poor girl looks thoroughly bored. Sitting in the food court of the bustling mall, Harriet sips her Diet Coke and watches them eat. Caitlin plays with a little blue ball, bouncing it off the floor and catching it again, over and over.

Harriet and Ricky are in Fort Worth, Texas. They drove the scenic route: Alabama, Mississippi, Louisiana. It's truly incredible, Harriet has realised, how many state lines you can cross in just thirteen hours.

It had been one of her stipulations going into this. If the Midnight King wanted her help to rescue more children, then he would only get it outside Tennessee.

'There's too much activity in Nashville,' she'd told Ricky. 'After Adam's escape, you'd be a fool to try again so close to home.'

'What if I just waited?' Ricky had said. 'I could wait a long time. I've waited long times before.'

But Harriet had shaken her head firmly. 'Don't you see? They've arrested someone already. With a bit of luck, he'll take the fall for everything. You have a second chance.'

Ricky had smiled at that, and a couple of days later he'd come down to breakfast to announce that the Midnight King had given him the next child's name. It was a bit of a drive, he'd said, but they could make a holiday out of it. An All-American Road Trip. He'd even found someone local selling a motorhome at a decent price. All it needed was a bit of soundproofing.

Now, sitting in the bustling food court of a Texan mall, Harriet thinks back to her father's face as she left him this morning. His lopsided grin, his eager eyes. He is excited to be working with his daughter on this, and if Harriet is honest with herself, she's excited too. It feels nice, being this close with him. It feels right.

In any event, even if it didn't, she's not sure she would do anything different. Josh has been dead for exactly two weeks now, and Harriet has no intention of making her father dig a second grave.

At exactly 1.36, Harriet rises from her chair. She drops her half-empty can into the trash and heads for the main exit.

'Go around the outside of the building,' Ricky explained to her. 'The fire exit is just past the goods entrance, down a tight lane. Don't worry, it's not alarmed.'

Harriet reaches the door at 1.44. On the other side, she knows, are the ladies' dressing rooms for Victoria's Secret. If this shop is like all the others, Caitlin will be sitting alone as her mother tries on an outfit behind a short curtain.

'Whatever you do,' Ricky had said, 'don't open the fire exit before you're supposed to. Wait until the exact moment.'

Harriet studies her watch now. The second hand moves agonisingly slowly around the face, creeping upwards towards 1.46. She pictures Caitlin sitting on an uncomfortable plastic chair, her small feet dangling, bags piled on the seats around her.

Ten seconds.

She pictures Caitlin bouncing that blue ball off the floor. Sees her leaning forward as it flies back into her waiting hands before she bounces it again. Her mother humming a tune as she inspects herself in the mirror.

Five seconds.

She pictures Caitlin missing a catch, fumbling the ball, knocking it along the corridor. She sees it rolling across the tiled floor towards the fire exit. She sees Caitlin sliding off the plastic chair and running after it.

Time.

Harriet swings open the door. Right on cue, the ball rolls smoothly out and comes to rest at her feet. She bends down and picks it up. On the other side of the doorway, Caitlin stands still, squinting a little into the sun.

'Can I have my ball?' she asks, her voice wavering slightly.

Harriet smiles and holds it out even as she takes a step back. The sun vanishes as Ricky reverses the motorhome slowly down the narrow lane. 'Of course you can, honey,' she says sweetly. 'Here, come and get it.'

Chapter Sixty-three

I think we finally did it, Ricky.

Ricky is warming hot chocolate on the stove. It is expensive stuff – large curls of real milk chocolate that he is melting into a saucepan of milk. Usually, this is a drink that Ricky makes only on special occasions, and exclusively for the newest members of his family. To welcome them, to make them feel at home.

Twenty times he has made it now. Mainly in the cabin, standing hunched over the gas stove next to the open cellar door, listening to hear if the child downstairs is awake yet. It must be nice, Ricky has always thought, to wake up to the smell of someone making you hot chocolate.

He has made it on the road, too. In their little motorhome – while parked, of course, usually in an out-of-the-way campsite or quiet country lane, mainly because Harriet is a dreadful driver and the fear of scalding himself as the RV swerves across the road is second only to the fear of wasting such expensive chocolate.

But this is the first time, Ricky thinks, that he has ever made it for himself.

I think we've earned this.

Ricky thinks so, too. He has always felt that it is important to reward yourself for a job well done. And what job has he done better than this?

Twenty children, twenty failures, twenty baths of bleach. A lesser man might have stopped sooner, at any one of the numerous hurdles that Ricky has had to overcome. Like little Scott, the boy who started it all, refusing to join the family – that was a tough blow. Or later, much later, when Josh turned against him and set Adam free. That was tougher still.

Looking back now, it is clear to Ricky that each failure was simply a learning point, a stop along the route to success. Nothing worthwhile is ever easy, after all, and nothing has been harder nor more worthwhile than finding Vincent.

Of course, he has Harriet to thank for that. She has been transformative these past few years. She has an innate ability to draw children away from their parents without causing a scene, without resorting to violence.

She has kept him safe, too, both from law enforcement and from the rise of the 'armchair detective', infuriating busybodies who spend their days scouring dreadful online message boards and public libraries, solving crimes in their spare time, like they have nothing better to do. She has helped him cover their tracks, as simply and as effectively as fresh snow over footprints.

I think we can stop now.

Ricky thinks so, too. Because now they have Vincent. And perhaps it is ironic that Harriet found him posting on the very websites that she so despises, but where else would you expect to find a young man with the same urges as her and her father? How many people on these forums, Ricky has wondered, these people who spend their days talking about violence and murder, who share crime scene photos and theories and who love nothing more than to put themselves in the shoes of a killer, into the *mind* of a killer, how many of these people are just secretly itching to try it out for themselves?

In the living room, he can hear canned laughter coming from the television. He knows Harriet and Vincent will be curled up together on the sofa. He smiles happily as he pours the hot chocolate into two mugs and carries them out to the backyard. It is late summer, and warm still in the evenings, and Ricky breathes in the smell of the melted chocolate and the fresh air and the lemon trees that Vincent helped him plant, and he feels a peace inside him that he has not felt for a long, long time.

He settles himself down on the lawn, his legs protesting a little. He is tired, is Ricky. Tired of his dreams, tired of washing dead children in his bathtub, tired of being the Midnight King. He thinks perhaps his reign has come to an end.

Leaning forward, he places one of the mugs carefully on the edge of his son's grave. He gently *clinks* it against his own.

'Cheers,' he says, and takes a long drink. It is delicious.

Ricky spends nearly an hour there, watching the sun drift lower, the air cooling on his bare arms. It feels like an ending, this moment. It feels like a culmination. Twenty children he has taken and twenty children he has given back. His own son, he has given back. But Harriet has stayed, and she has found Vincent, and the chasm that was once open inside of him is now closed. The chamber in his chest no longer empty. If there is more to this story then it will happen without Ricky, and Ricky is fine with that.

He stays in the garden a while longer. Until the burnt sun, until the twilight sky. Through the thin curtains he can see the gentle glow of the television set, and in that moment he knows the missions will never end, he knows the dreams will never stop, and he knows who will take his place to receive them, who will take his crown and do a better job than he ever could. Her name is Harriet, and she is his little girl, his everything, his Midnight Queen.

43

NATHAN

He can hear the boy in the cubicle next to his.

The boy is humming a tune, a song Nathan has never heard before. Nathan is sweating now, despite the late hour and the cool air. His hair is matted across his forehead. His armpits are damp.

He leans against the barrier between them, pressing his palms flat against it. He feels the dried gum and the sticky patches, the scratched words and the marker pen ink. He sets his forehead against the cheap wood. The boy is still humming. The same two lines of music, over and over. The notes make Nathan's heart flutter.

He imagines pressing against the side of his cubicle until it breaks. Until it splits down the middle and he steps through, and maybe the boy is screaming but it wouldn't matter, it wouldn't be for long. He'd slide his fingers around the boy's throat and—

I think we missed our chance.

It's true. The toilet is flushing now. The boy is unlocking the cubicle, his shoes squeaking on the tiled floor. Then there is the sound of running water.

I think we need to grab him and—

Nathan digs into his back pocket and pulls out a razor. He has already removed his coat and now he pulls off his sweater and extends his arm, and he forces the tip of the blade into his skin just beneath the elbow and runs it all the way down to his wrist. The pain makes him shudder and he opens his mouth and moans as the hand dryer kicks in. Black filth pours down his arm. It runs over his hand, it coats his fingers and it spills onto the floor.

The urge fades. Not by much, but by enough. Enough to keep him inside the cubicle until the boy has left the room, until it's safe to emerge. He runs his arm under the cold water and watches as the black liquid pools in the cracked sink. It swirls around the drain like oil. He does not remember when his blood stopped being red.

After, he leaves the restroom and sits at a picnic bench under the forecourt's harsh lighting and opens a soda. He drinks thirstily. His arm is packed with paper towels and it aches in the cold, midnight air. Air thick with the smell of grease and gasoline. He sees the boy walking next to an older man, his father or brother, perhaps. They are laughing. This is an adventure for them, this nocturnal travelling. They climb into a large station wagon with a rattling exhaust and the moment they leave the forecourt they are swallowed up completely by the inky black night.

It was difficult this time, letting the boy go. His heart is still racing. He knows there are only so many times he will be able to stop himself.

Blood has started to drip onto his shoes. The paper towels are sodden. He wonders if the gas station sells bandages.

He drove for nearly four hours straight to get here. He has driven out of Tennessee and across Kentucky and now he is thirteen miles inside Indiana, where he sits in the front seat of his father's car and awkwardly wraps bandages around his bleeding arm. He has waited here too long already. Long enough to arouse suspicion. Long enough to know that Kate is not coming. Long enough to know that he is on his own again.

He called her after it happened. When the detective's blood was still fresh on his father's kitchen floor. He called her and asked her for help, and he felt like a child again, watching the rain fall as he begged her to tell him what to do.

And she told him.

She told him everything. About their father, about Bruce. It came out of her in such a flood of words that he wondered how she had ever kept it all inside. And knowing the truth, maybe it made him feel better and maybe it made him feel nothing. Sitting here, staring into the darkness, it is suddenly very hard to remember the last time he truly felt anything.

He wonders what has happened to his sister. He wonders if she lied to him on the phone. He wonders if she has changed her mind. He wonders if she has spoken with the police. He wonders if she is dead.

I think we need to leave.

He knows that going on the run like this is stupid. He knows that highway patrol will be looking for his vehicle. That they will be checking motels and gas stations on every major road out of Nashville. Maybe a traffic cop on some quiet stretch will recognise his licence plate. Maybe they will flash his photo on the nightly news and the middle-aged woman working the forecourt will tell them yes, she remembers him, she sold him bandages and a soda. They will crowd into a cramped room and watch him on CCTV following a young boy into a dirty bathroom. They will glance at each other and murmur under their breath and take notes and make phone calls and order roadblocks and extra patrol cars. They will narrow their search, and in a day or so when his cash runs out and he's forced to use his credit card, they will have him.

Nathan starts up his father's station wagon and rolls towards the edge of the forecourt. He inches the hood out, the headlamps throwing up black road that runs away from him in both directions. He sits there a while, a long while, long enough to stare down each stretch of asphalt, long enough to see what lies beyond: the vast plains, the scorched earth, the cities he's never heard of and will never visit; long enough to know that in the end it doesn't matter which road he drives because they both go the same way, you drive them long enough.

44

He has been awake for nearly twenty-four hours. Just about eight of them he has spent in this car. This old, beat-up station wagon that tracks to one side you let your hands off the wheel too much. This loud, trembling machine that makes it hard to hear the radio if you run the heating at the same time, and of course he's running the heating, it's cold now, it's the early hours still, it's 3 a.m. and the front passenger window doesn't close all the way so there's this wind, this howling gale, and Nathan doesn't just have the heating on, he has it on full blast, the little vents angled up towards his face and hands and the radio is turned up to max, the dial spun all the way to the right and it's shit the stuff he's listening to, it's southern gospel, it's Christian rock but it doesn't matter, he can barely hear it anyway, even if the heating wasn't on and the window wasn't open he would barely be able to hear it.

He's gone, Nathan. He's heading south. Coasting the edge of the bluegrass state, back into Kentucky, back into Tennessee. He passes signs for Grand Rivers City, for the Land Between the Lakes. He reads them and forgets them, he runs the cruise control, his whole life he's run the cruise control, he sees this now. Little Nathan, whose mommy died of cancer, whose daddy collected little children because his own weren't good enough, or weren't strong enough, or who the fuck knows why. Not everything has a reason. Not everyone has motivation, some people just *react*. Some people just get served shit and are told to eat it and so they eat it, they eat it every day, every goddamn day until one day they can't stomach it no more they're so full of it and so they crack, they flip the script, they do the *opposite* of what they would normally do and this isn't some big, preordained thing, this is just *reacting*, that's all, that's all Nathan has ever been, a reactor, someone who reacts, who follows a path until he doesn't.

So he killed a cop. So what. Technically the guy killed himself.

And that kid? What was he going to do, call the police? It was a gift. A *gift*. Unwanted, unasked for, sure, whatever, doesn't make it untrue. Nathan strangled that girl because he was always going to strangle that girl, because his whole *life* he'd been waiting to strangle that girl.

I think we're having a breakthrough.

Nathan thinks so too.

I think we'll be there soon. I think we're going to have a wonderful time.

Nathan nods and turns the heating down so he can hear the music a little, and he sets the cruise control to sixty and he settles back and just enjoys the ride.

45

ISAAC

Chloe Xi's funeral was on a Monday afternoon. It rained, like a movie. Everyone stood around under black umbrellas. Fifty plastic chairs and all of them empty; a groove in each seat where the water collected.

It was a decent turnout. More than just family and friends. The media had seen to that. Articles in the local press the last three days and two vans parked on the edge of the lawn now, satellite dishes cranked high. They couldn't get too close but still, they got close enough. Steadicams with optical zoom of people dabbing at their eyes, of kids gripping their parents' hands. Those were the best shots. Viewers really connected with stuff like that.

The Tennessean ran the story on page six. It might have been higher but there'd been a whole lot of murder lately. A dining-room double homicide didn't leave much room for a young girl's funeral.

Isaac read both stories from his hospital bed. He noted the important points. Not what the articles said but what they kept hush. No use of the phrase 'Music City Monster'. No mention of Edward Morrison. Maybe it meant they hadn't made the connection. Or maybe they had and they were too scared to print it. Police incompetence lets a serial killer roam the country for seventeen years while the wrong man sits on death row. Hell of a libel suit if the paper wasn't a hundred per cent.

Course Isaac knew the truth would come out. Only question was when. Personally he had all the time in the world – bed rest for the next month while his insides slowly healed. Bruce's carving knife had perforated his liver but had somehow missed any other major organs.

Only not everyone had it so good. Someone else was running out the clock: Edward Morrison was deciding his last meal, and in a little over forty-eight hours he'd be going to the electric chair.

Visiting hours in the ICU started at ten. Alison arrived at nine thirty.

'You bring my suit?' he asked her.

'Good morning to you too, honey,' she said, and hung a grey two-piece off the bed. 'Brought you a shirt and a couple ties as well, although if you want my advice you'll stick to the solid colours. I swear, Isaac, half your wardrobe looks like it came from a damn joke shop.'

Isaac scowled as he picked up the suit. 'I asked for the blue one,' he said. 'With the pinstripes.'

'I know what you asked for, only it had stains down the front. Probably from whatever nasty takeout you were eating for lunch.'

'All right, fine. Thank you.'

'You're welcome. You want a hand getting dressed?'

'Absolutely not. Why don't you get a coffee? Canteen is—'

'I know where the canteen is, Isaac. I waited in it long enough.'

She held his gaze, a faint smile. Then she turned and left him alone.

It took him longer to dress than he'd have liked. His stomach still ached, bandages across his ribs causing his skin to pull tight. When he was done he was exhausted. He sat on the edge of his bed, red-faced and sweaty, clutching a blue tie adorned with goldfish. His fingers trembled with the exertion.

Alison came back into the room. She set her coffee down wordlessly and took the tie from him. Lifting his shirt collar, she slid it around his neck. When she was done, she smoothed it down and took a step back.

'You look good,' she said.

'What about the tie?'

'Tie looks good too.'

Isaac smiled as he slid off the bed and onto his feet. He paused, his legs weak. He reached over and took hold of his crutches. Alison slid her arm around his and helped him out the room.

They travelled quietly to the elevator. Riding it up, Alison said, 'I spoke to your mom this morning.'

'Yeah, she told me.'

'She's looking forward to you getting out this afternoon.'

'Looking forward to me moving in with them even more, I think.'

Alison grinned. 'And all it took was getting stabbed a couple times.'

Isaac shivered at the memory. Bruce's face as he slid the carving knife into him. The joint of meat, with its sweet, putrid odour. Detective Hayes had come to visit him in the emergency room that same night. Had told him that his parents were still alive, that they'd been tied up in their bedroom the entire time. Turned out the lunch Bruce had been serving was elk meat. Whoever had prepared it had nicked the bladder. Isaac's mother was still trying to get rid of the smell.

The lift doors opened and they shuffled out. The ICU was busy. Nurses brushed past them holding clipboards and wheeling IV drips. A backdrop of raised voices and shrill alarms. They paused at the entrance to the ward as a porter rushed two empty beds down the long corridor.

'Your mom invited me round for dinner,' Alison said.

Isaac grunted. 'She told me that, too. Don't worry, it's not okra.'

'So long as it's not *elk*, I'll be fine.'

Outside the room, Isaac stopped. He reached up and wiped his forehead with his sleeve. Alison made a face and handed him a Kleenex.

'Before I forget,' she said, 'Hayes left his card at the nurses' station. He's looking to speak with you.'

'Well, he knows where I am.'

'I don't think the guy likes hospitals. You should call him this afternoon.'

'Maybe. You ready for this?'

'Course I am. Now listen.' She looked him square in the eyes. 'I know you and Hayes don't get along, but the guy saved your life, Isaac. Least you can do is thank him.'

Isaac shrugged and pulled himself up straight. His bandages stretched uncomfortably across his stomach. '*You* saved my life, Alison. All that guy did was shoot out my mom's dining-room window. Took her three days to get Bruce's brains out of the carpet.'

'Isaac . . .'

'All right, all right, I'll talk to him. Now come on. This is almost over.'

46

The fact that Lawrence Hughes was still alive was nothing short of a miracle. Guy had angled the revolver forward after sticking the barrel in his mouth. Missed his brain and instead blew out the top row of his teeth, most of his nose and one of his orbital sockets. A tired-looking doctor with bad breath had told Isaac there was about five degrees in it, all things considered.

Hughes had woken yesterday evening to find his swollen face wrapped in bandages and a tube running oxygen directly into his throat. By the time he did, Isaac had spent nearly a week watching daytime TV and running scenarios from his hospital bed. Hundreds of them, over and over. He placed calls. He spoke with lawyers. It was good, the nurse had said, to have something to do.

Now, he was finally about ready to wrap this case up.

Isaac and Alison shuffled slowly into the room. Hughes was sitting in bed. White gauze covered his mouth and nose. A large patch covered his left eye. His right swivelled to look at them. It was wide open and blinking rapidly. Isaac could tell the man was in pain, in pain and scared shitless. He could tell all that from his eye. From one goddamn *eye*.

'What you watching?' Isaac said, glancing at the TV. A young girl with a buzzcut was throwing a soldier across a room. 'What is that,

Stranger Things? Shit, you get Netflix in here, Lawrence? All I got downstairs is basic cable.'

Hughes didn't say anything. He couldn't, he was missing a mouth.

Isaac ambled over to the bedside and collapsed slowly into a plastic folding chair. Alison sat in an armchair by the window. Hughes's eye jumped back and forth between them. It was unsettling. He reached over and picked up a pad of paper and a pen from his lap.

What is this about, he wrote.

Isaac read it and nodded. 'Good question,' he said. 'Just gimme a moment to catch my breath.'

The room was quiet as he did. The only noise came from the television set in the corner. The place was sterile. No overnight bag on the table, no flowers in the empty vase by the window. No one had come to visit Hughes the entire time he'd been in here, Isaac realised.

He went to wipe his forehead again with his sleeve and felt Alison's stare. He dug out the tissue and used that instead.

'Okay,' he said at last. 'First thing, I'm glad to see you're still with us, Lawrence.'

Hughes scribbled something on his pad. *You found me?*

Isaac nodded. 'Yeah, I found you.'

Thank you, he wrote, his eye welling up a little.

'Don't mention it.'

What happened to you?

'I got stabbed in the belly, Lawrence. Hurts like hell, let me tell you. But, shit, we're both still here and that's what matters, right?'

He scooted his chair forward a little. The effort made him wince.

'All right, now I'm going to lay out a story for you and I just need you to listen, and when I'm done you can say if I'm talking truth or not. Okay?'

Hughes blinked at him. Isaac took that as a sign to continue.

'A little girl named Chloe Xi went missing just over two weeks ago,' he said. 'Her parents asked me to look into it for them, to see if there was anything the police had missed. And around the same time Chloe goes missing, a man named Lucas Cole is found dead in his motel room. It's a suicide, he's hanged himself from his bathroom door. Only when his toxicology report comes back it shows a high level of something called sodium oxybate in his blood. I had to look that one up, but it's medication used to treat narcolepsy. It's marketed under the brand name Xyrem. Now it's impossible, so I'm told, for someone to have the levels of Xyrem in their blood that Lucas Cole had and to still have the physical strength to hang themselves. So, Lucas Cole wasn't a suicide after all. He was murdered. And later on, when the cops find me at your apartment, they think maybe I had something to do with your shooting and so they search the place, and these guys they're meticulous, you understand me? They take notes of everything they see, photograph everything they find interesting. And inside your bathroom cabinet they find something very interesting, don't they?'

Hughes slowly wrote a single word down on his pad. He held it up. *Xyrem.*

Isaac nodded. 'Three bottles of the stuff, and made out to someone who is clearly *not* you. Now here's my theory. You were taken by the Music City Monster as a child, and you managed to escape and when the cops picked you up after you were a mess. I mean, who can blame you, Lawrence? You just escaped a fucking *serial killer*. But in this mess you were in, you gave the police bad information. And they were under a lot of pressure to make an arrest, and it ticked a bunch of boxes for them so they didn't try too hard to test your evidence, in fact they maybe just helped it along best they could. So they arrested Edward Morrison and Morrison didn't do himself many favours and long-story-short he's due to be electrocuted in a couple of days.'

Hughes reached for his notepad. Isaac held his hand up.

'Hold on, don't interrupt me, I'm nearly done. Now obviously you realised that you'd made a mistake. More than that, you started doing your own investigation. And at some point, I don't know when exactly, you discovered that Lucas Cole was the man who abducted you. That he was the Monster. I'm guessing him having his face plastered all over the back of bestselling books maybe didn't help him much. And I don't know for sure why you didn't go to the police, but I figure this was something you wanted to take care of yourself. So you made your plan, told him who you were and that you wanted to meet. Maybe you even blackmailed him a little, who knows. But you got him to that hotel room and you drugged him and you murdered him. And then . . . then you found out about Chloe Xi and you realised that you'd just killed the one person who might know where she was, and damn I don't want to imagine the level of guilt you must have felt at that moment, Lawrence, truly I don't, but I know it must have been high and I know you must have been too scared to go to the cops, so when the news reported that the family had hired a PI you figured you could help out a little, maybe push things in the right direction, so you got my name from Chloe's mom and you left your list of dead children at my hotel.'

Isaac reached for his tissue again and dabbed at his forehead. He was sweating, his stomach aching. Alison shifted in her seat and he didn't look at her. Didn't want her warning him to take it easy. Didn't want to see the concern on her face.

'Only I didn't find her,' he said, clearing his throat noisily as he spoke. 'I failed her too. And when she turned up dead you blamed yourself, and so you stuck a gun in your mouth and pulled the trigger and here we are.' He finally allowed himself to glance over at Alison. She was watching him. He looked back at Hughes. 'How did I do?'

The man in the hospital bed didn't move for a long while. His eye blurred and when he blinked he sent tears rolling down his face. The small part of it that wasn't covered in bandages, anyway. Laughter from the television echoed around the room. And all of it – Hughes, Alison, little dead Chloe, the kids laughing, fucking Lucas Cole hanging from a noose in a dirty hotel room – all of it suddenly made Isaac feel like crying too.

Instead he struggled to his feet, the pain in his belly pushing the hurt back. 'You want to help someone?' he said. 'You tell the truth about what happened the night you were taken. You tell the truth about who abducted you. There's a couple of lawyers waiting outside the room right now. You want? I'll let them in and you can tell them that it was Lucas Cole who snatched you, that Edward Morrison didn't have nothing to do with it. You do that and as far as I'm concerned, Lucas Cole drained those bottles of Xyrem all by himself with the noose already around his neck. You understand me? I've no interest in that man taking you twice.'

Hughes wept silently, his whole body rocking. He picked up the pen, wiped his eye with the back of a shaking hand and wrote a single word on his notepad, slowly, in deliberate strokes, in trembling handwriting: *yes.*

47

Isaac stood and gazed out of the window. He placed the tips of his fingers against the glass. Traced the point where Hayes's first bullet had cracked a perfect circle. It was gone now, of course, the pane replaced. But still, he could see it. The memory of it. Lying on the carpet as a madman dug a carving knife into his guts, as Kate stood and watched. A shadow crossing the room as Hayes lined up his fatal shots.

Of course he could see it. How could he not? The crack of glass, the spurt of blood. He could see it, he could hear it. He could taste it, the rotten meat. He knew he always would.

His mother asked him about it. After dinner was over. When his father was showing Alison his latest fishing gear in his workshop. When it was clear that Isaac was tired and in pain, and everyone around him had seemed to instinctively know whether to give him space or slide their arm around him and hold him close.

'I'm so happy you're home,' his mother said.

'Me too, Ma.'

'How's your stomach?'

Isaac shrugged. 'It's fine. Will take a while to heal, but nothing too bad.'

'I didn't see you take any of those horrible pills after dinner.'

'My Rolaids?' He smiled. 'Hospital gave me some new stuff. For the ulcer, I don't remember the name.'

'Didn't I tell you to get that checked out sooner?'

'Yeah, you did, Ma.'

'Maybe now you'll listen to me.'

'Maybe.'

It wasn't that late, but it was already dark out. His father had lit the firepit. Isaac watched the flames flicker in the evening breeze. Beyond it beat the steady thrum of cars, their headlights flashing through the treeline. He remembered watching them from a chair across the room. He remembered baiting Kate to bring the knife closer. He remembered the feeling of it in his hand, the power of it, the way it had twirled upwards almost like it was moving by itself. He hadn't even felt the resistance as he'd slit Kate's throat. The fact he hadn't killed her himself didn't make him feel any better; if he had, he might've avoided getting stabbed.

He'd told his mother all of this already. The mechanics of what had happened here, in her dining room. The table had a fresh chip in one side from where he'd climbed it. Isaac stared at it now. Saw himself scuttling over it covered in blood, moving like an insect, like something possessed.

So maybe he hadn't told his mother *everything*.

Like how his mind had cracked, something shifting inside him. A fog that had filled his head, a dreadful disease that he'd tried to keep locked away, that had overcome him once before – standing in a rapist's den back in Baltimore he'd felt it, driving his fists into a bloodied mess over and over he'd felt it – and maybe it had always been there, riding with him, the *possibility*, and Alison had seen it, she'd warned him about it.

Only he'd chased it down. That was the truth, no point pretending otherwise. He'd hunted it, he'd drawn it out. Maybe on some level he'd even needed it. And sure, being tied to a chair in his parents' home by

330

a couple of deranged killers might have been enough to finally drag it out of him but the cracks had started to appear before then. Had started getting worse, too, the night he'd visited Nathan.

The night he'd started reading that book.

The Midnight King.

A novel by Lucas Cole.

Isaac knew how it sounded. He knew a book couldn't have that sort of effect. A book couldn't make you mad. It couldn't carry you over the brink, not all the way, not by itself.

But what if it could nudge you? Towards it, just a little. And what if you were already at the brink to begin with? Shit, what if you'd spent the last six months living there? And what if you'd taken on a case that forced you to stay? Staring at the drop, leaning into it, breathing it in.

Well then, maybe a nudge would be enough. Maybe a nudge would be all you'd need. Like Marjory on Burgess Falls.

'Your room is all made up,' his mother said. Her voice brought him back. 'You call it a day whenever you want, all right?'

He smiled and kissed the top of her head. 'All right, Ma.'

They were still at the window when the doorbell went. Isaac's mother answered it. Detective Hayes was standing in the gloom, his large frame blocking out what little light there was. He smiled when he saw Isaac.

'Sorry to intrude,' he said. 'I left a message for you at the hospital. I was hoping to speak with you before you left.'

Isaac stepped past his mother, who shrank back a little towards the warmth of the dining room.

'I'm not sure I ever thanked you,' he said. 'Those were nice shots, Detective.'

Hayes grunted. 'Putting those two down was a pleasure. Sorry about the window.'

'Bruce and Kate are dead and the department paid for double

glazing. Everyone's a winner. What can I help you with tonight?'

'We found Nathan Cole,' Hayes said matter-of-factly. 'He's dead too.'

Isaac stared at him. 'What happened?'

'Suicide. He hanged himself in his hotel room. Like father, like son, huh?'

'Jesus. I . . . Where?'

Hayes sniffed, scratched his ear with a thick index finger. 'Some place down in Alabama. Next to the space museum. Guess he wanted to get one last look at the rockets before he went. Anyway, it's going to hit the news in the morning. I just thought you should hear it from me first.'

Isaac wasn't sure what to say. He nodded. 'Thank you, Detective. I appreciate that.'

'Sure. Oh, and he left something. It was addressed to you.'

'To me?'

Hayes reached inside his jacket and pulled out a slim envelope. 'Department's already been through it. We kept the original but I thought I owed you the courtesy of a copy.'

Isaac took the envelope.

'I'll let you get some rest,' Hayes said, turning away. 'You all have a good night.'

Isaac watched the detective make his way down the garden path and out onto the dark street. Closing the door, he retreated into the house, the envelope clutched in his hand. Alison and his parents were waiting in the dining room. Isaac could smell coffee brewing.

'What was that about?' Alison asked.

'Nathan's dead,' Isaac said. 'Hanged himself in his hotel room.'

'Oh, God.'

'He left this for me.'

Isaac set the envelope down on the table. The front was bare. He opened it and slid out a bundle of papers. The top page was a scrawl of photocopied handwriting.

Dear Isaac, it read. *I never felt like my story wrapped up the way it should have, so I've reworked my father's novel for him. Gave myself a different ending. Sitting here, in this hotel room, I finally realise that I'm more like him than I ever thought.*

Isaac's stomach tightened as he read it. His wounds itched. He moved the page aside.

'*The Midnight King*,' his mother read out loud. 'What's that?'

It's an incubator. It's a viral load. It's a concentrated dose of madness.

'It's nothing,' Isaac said. He snatched up the papers. 'No one is to read this, understand?'

I think we—

'Isaac, what—'

'*No one*,' he growled. 'In fact . . .'

He marched over to the back door and stepped outside. Almost immediately the wind picked up, the pages writhing in his hand as he crossed the yard. His stomach ached. His left arm itched. A low hiss building in his ears, like the roar of a waterfall. By the time he reached the firepit it was all he could hear.

I think we—

Isaac dropped the pages into the flames. The paper caught instantly. Behind him he could feel his parents watching; he wondered what they were thinking.

Alison appeared by his side. She slid her arm through his and together they watched the pages blacken and twist and glow and shrink. They watched as embers of Lucas Cole's poisoned words rose into the night sky, lifted by the evening breeze, and as *The Midnight King* burned into nothing, Isaac felt the itching die away and the sound of the waterfall fade into quiet.

'I think we're going to be all right,' Alison said quietly.

Isaac thought so too.

EPILOGUE TO THE MIDNIGHT KING,

BY NATHAN COLE

He spends most of the flight wondering if this is a mistake. He sits in between a large woman and a man with flaky skin and bad BO and he is served lukewarm chicken in a small plastic tray and given a cup of water with a foil lid he must peel back to drink. He did not bring a book to read or any headphones to listen to music but that is okay. He folds his hands on his lap and closes his eyes and pretends to sleep even though it is ten thirty in the morning. Beside him he can hear the man scratching his scalp and burping quietly under his breath.

When he lands he does not stop at the baggage collection hall because he has no bags to collect. He has hand luggage only, he is not staying long. He waits for a cab in a line with old people who do not understand how to use Uber or Lyft. He pays for his fare in cash and he leaves a generous tip.

His hotel is a good hour's walk from the hospital, but that suits him fine. After sitting all morning he could do with the exercise. And besides, it will be nice to see how much of Nashville has changed since he was here. Nearly two decades is a long time to be away from a place.

He is pleased to see that the city is much as he remembers. It is bigger, of course, and there is more traffic, but its heart and soul remain the same. It is still that complex, wonderful clash of old and new. He walks down Music Row towards Edgehill. He walks past major record labels and recording studios and radio stations, most of them operating out of refurbished two-storey houses. If it weren't for the signs outside advertising their artists' success, you might think it just an ordinary suburb.

By the time he reaches Twenty-first Street he has broken out in a light sweat. It is hot, it is mid-July. He stops at a Dunkin' Donuts and buys a bottle of water and drinks it standing outside, nearly in one go. He gazes across the road at the Vanderbilt University Medical Center and he checks his watch, and he realises it is past noon and that he is hungry, and so he goes back inside and orders a croissant with ham and cheese and he eats it sitting on an orange swinging chair partly made to resemble a giant doughnut. He knows that he is putting off what he has come all this way to do, and he knows it is because he is scared, but he also knows that he gets shaky if his blood sugar drops too low, and one time he even fainted in the supermarket and woke up to find a crowd of people staring at him and his carton of eggs smeared across the front of his shirt.

Eventually, however, he runs out of plausible and even semi-plausible excuses and he crosses the road to the hospital, where he follows the signs to the palliative care unit. Here, he speaks with a tired-looking lady at the front desk who nonetheless gives him a genuine smile and asks who he is here to see.

'Ricky Taylor,' he says, and when she asks whether he is a relative, he answers, 'I'm his son.'

'Oh,' she says, and her smile broadens. 'You must be Josh.'

'Yes,' he says, and finds himself smiling back. 'I suppose I must.'

Harriet is waiting for him. She is sitting in a chair in the hallway by a vending machine, and when she sees him approach she rises to her feet and rushes over and embraces him, tightly, wrapping her arms around him and pressing her face into his shoulder.

'I didn't think you'd come,' she says.

'I wasn't sure myself,' he says. 'How is he?'

She steps away from him, shrugging. 'Asleep. He's asleep nearly all the time now.'

'I'm amazed he's held on this long.'

'Oh, Josh,' she says, and she gives him this sad smile and her eyes fill with tears. 'I think he's holding on just so he can say goodbye to you.'

He nods and sits down. His lunch slithers around inside his stomach. He should have eaten a salad; processed cheese always does this to him.

'Do you hate me, Josh?'

He looks over at his sister. She is standing still, her fingers interwoven, her thumb pressed tight across her knuckles. 'Why would I hate you?' he asks her.

'Because I wasn't strong enough to get away from him,' she says quietly, sinking into the seat next to him. 'Because I wasn't as strong as you. Because I helped him, and because I enjoyed helping him.'

Josh blinks. It is the first time someone has ever called him that. *Strong.* He blinks again and this time he feels his own eyes filling with tears. 'I don't hate you,' he says, his voice hoarse.

'Do you forgive me?'

The nurse from the front desk reappears then, bending down to their level and smiling warmly at them. She sees two siblings sharing a tender moment. She sees two children mourning the impending loss of their father.

'He's awake,' the nurse tells them. 'Josh? I think he'd love to see you.'

Josh nods and gets to his feet. He glances back at his sister and thinks about her question to him. 'We'll talk after,' he says.

*

He is led further down the corridor to a small room with the blinds closed. The door is ajar, and he can see a pulsing blue light spilling onto the floor. The nurse steps away and motions for him to enter alone.

Inside, the room is dimly lit. A scattering of machines that beep and whirr, and in the middle of them all lies his father. Ricky Taylor is indeed awake. He stares at his son. In the near darkness, it is hard to see his face.

It takes Josh nearly a minute to cross the floor, even though it is only a handful of steps. As he nears, his father's face becomes clearer. The man is pale. Hopeful. He reaches out a hand, and all the weight that Josh has carried with him – all the hurt, all the pain, all the mental anguish and sleepless nights, all the skewed thinking and all the blame, all the guilt and shame and anger – all of it seems to melt away. He reaches for the words he has prepared, the words that he has been writing his entire life, waiting for this moment that he knew might never come, he reaches for them and finds they are gone, and so he reaches for his father's hand, instead, and he sits by his father's bedside and he leans forward and rests his head on his father's lap and he cries, and his father cries too and strokes his son's hair and squeezes his son's hand and tells his son that he loves him, over and over, *I love you, I love you, I love you.*

Acknowledgements

I've always been drawn to darker fiction. The stories that make you feel uncomfortable or nervous, that fill you with that lovely heavy feeling of growing dread. I remember reading *Red Dragon* as a young boy and realising that there were books out there which leaned into that darkness – and that there was a real thrill in being taken along for the ride as the reader.

But what scares us changes as we grow older, I think, and when I sat down to write *The Midnight King*, the question I had to ask myself was, 'What do I find scary?' Being a relatively new father, the answer I suppose was fairly obvious. (My wife actually went into labour the day I was due to hand in a draft of this book to my editor. Fortunately I had finished it the night before.)

When it comes to thanking the numerous people who helped me with this book, I probably have to start with my agent, Harry. This was our first collaboration, and his notes and enthusiasm for the novel really elevated the story and its characters.

Similarly, huge recognition for the incredible work of Miranda Jewess, my editor at Viper. Miranda is someone that I've wanted to work with for some time, and it was awesome to receive notes from someone who seems to love dark fiction as much as I do. When discussing whether or not a heroin addict would have the financial incentive to abduct a child, her sage advice to 'Just make him a paedophile' really cut through the chaff.

Beyond Miranda, of course, are all the other fantastic people at Viper who I must quickly mention, such as Charlotte and Emily, and all the Viper authors who have made me feel so welcome. Thanks to you all.

Thanks to Sam for your great work copy-editing the book and catching all the little stuff that had slipped past me. I promise to learn the correct spelling of 'all right' for next time.

Thanks, as always, to my podcast co-host in crime Marco, for reading an early draft and providing his invaluable thoughts.

Thanks to my wife, Lucy, for letting me forever bounce story ideas off her and for reading chunks of half-finished chapters. The book would never have got off the ground, I don't think, without your help.

And finally, thanks to my mum and dad. I realised late into writing *The Midnight King* that in all of my books so far there seems to be some dreadful parent who does horrible things to their children. I'm not sure where that's come from, because needless to say you guys have always been incredibly supportive and all-round pretty wonderful, so this book is for you.

About the Author

TK